The Great Concert of the Night

The Great Concert of the Night

JONATHAN BUCKLEY

nyrb **New York Review Books** New York

This is a New York Review Book

published by The New York Review of Books

435 Hudson Street, New York, NY 10014

www.nyrb.com

Library of Congress Cataloging-in-Publication Data
Names: Buckley, Jonathan, 1956– author.
Title: The great concert of the night / by Jonathan Buckley.
Description: New York : New York Review Books, [2020]
Identifiers: LCCN 2019022197| ISBN 9781681373959 (alk. paper) | ISBN
  9781681373966 (epub)
Classification: LCC PR6052.U2665 G74 2020 | DDC 823/.914—dc23
LC record available at https://lccn.loc.gov/2019022197

ISBN 978-1-68137-395-9
Available as an electronic book; ISBN 978-1-68137-396-6

Printed in the United States of America on acid-free paper.

1 2 3 4 5 6 7 8 9 10

For Susanne Hillen
and Bruno Buckley

January

FIVE MINUTES PAST MIDNIGHT: a call from my sister. It's not right that I should be on my own, she tells me. Nobody should be alone at New Year. She sends a picture of herself and Nicholas, glasses raised to the phone; in the background, some people I don't recognise. They've had a really nice evening; Nicholas excelled himself in the kitchen, and there's been enough champagne to float a dinghy. "Even you would have enjoyed yourself," she says. I report that I too have had a nice evening. "Doing what?" Emma demands. A film, a book, a drink. "Sounds great," she says. "Next year, you're coming to us. No excuses accepted."

I watched *Le Grand Concert de la Nuit*. Entranced again by Agamédé; entranced again by Imogen. The film transmits a presence that both consoles and torments.

•

Looking up from the book, I gaze at the chair in the corner of the room, the chair in which Imogen used to read; the lamp beside it is unlit. Gazing into the shadow, I make something like an after-image arise: turned to the side, with her legs curled up, she props the book on the arm of the chair, angled into the light. The presence is weaker than that of Agamédé. Often, when delighted or surprised by something she had read, she would read it aloud. One evening, I remember, she came upon the story of Blaise Pascal's escape from death. "Listen to this," she said. I can hear her intonation, the rise of her voice.

On the night of November 23rd, 1654, terror-struck by the storm that was then in full spate, the horses that were pulling Pascal's carriage bolted and plunged from the Pont de Neuilly. The reins snapped, leaving the vehicle perched on the lip of the road. This narrow escape, so the story goes, occasioned the revelation that Pascal recorded in the document that bears this date, a document known as the *Memorial*.

The year of grace 1654
Monday, 23 November, feast of Saint Clement, Pope and Martyr,
and of others in the Martyrology.
Eve of Saint Chrysogonus, Martyr, and others.
From about half past ten in the evening until half past midnight.

FIRE.
GOD of Abraham, GOD of Isaac, GOD of Jacob, not
of the philosophers and scholars.
Certitude. Certitude. Feeling. Joy. Peace.

So it begins. *Joy, joy, joy, tears of joy*, we read later. On Pascal's death, in August 1662, this piece of parchment was discovered by his manservant, folded inside the lining of his master's doublet. A "mystic amulet," Nicolas de Condorcet called it. Pascal had spoken to nobody about the episode that was recorded in the *Memorial*.

•

On my desk, two photos from Stourhead. The first: Imogen play-acting in front of the temple—a nymph in flight from a savage pursuer, her scarf flying as she looks back in terror; her hands are raised in a way that I have seen only in paintings by Poussin. The other: she looks directly into the lens, and her face almost fills the frame of the picture; her gaze is acute and open, offering herself to be seen as fully as any lens could allow.

•

Only twelve tickets sold today.

•

It was some time in mid-June when I first saw Imogen, in room seven. This is where people linger, because of the monsters. Casts of aborted foetuses, fearfully misshapen, occupy one section: we have examples of phocomelia, sirenomelia, acrania, anencephaly and cyclopia. There are two terrible little skeletons, each a conjoined pair: Dicephalus dibrachius diauchenos and Cephalothoracopagus monosymmetros. And above the skeletons, suspended on wires, in a posture of crucifixion, hangs the stillborn child. Its torso has been excavated to expose the major veins and arteries; the limbs have been flayed, so that the musculature may also be studied. The muscles and blood vessels gleam like varnished wax, but this is not a model. Its head is thrown back and its teeth are bared, as if in a scream; its face is directed into the light that comes from the window; it has no eyes, but it stares back with its vacant sockets. This is where I first saw Imogen.

I took note because she stayed at the hanging child for a long time. No—this is not quite true. I took note because she struck me as an attractive woman, and she was alone. Not that she was a woman who might be approached. She was on her own; few people come to the museum alone.

I was in room seven to rehang the print of Claude-Ambroise Seurat, "the human skeleton." Fussing with the spirit level, I observed her reflection in the glass that covers the print. She continued to gaze into the eyeless face. She looked steadily into it, as if in contemplation of its meaning. Frowning, she seemed to be moved to sorrow. When I left the room, she did not look up; she had not so much as glanced at me.

Some time later, I returned. She was still there, examining the pages from Vaught's *Practical Character Reader*. As if she had been waiting for an audience, she read aloud one of the captions: "The reason this man is an unreliable husband is because he is very weak in Conjugality and Parental Love and exceedingly strong in Amativeness. Young ladies, beware of such men as husbands." She laughed, and looked at me. The laugh was light and small. "Now I know," she said.

My favourite page, I said, was the one showing the woman with a white zone on the crown of her head; the white zone denotes "The Corn Faculty, or the Exact Source of Corns." I introduced myself and told her that there would be a tour at four o'clock. The tour would encompass parts of the building that were otherwise out of bounds.

Imogen thanked me. I left her to continue her perusal of the *Practical Character Reader*.

•

After the tour, Imogen returned to room seven. Certain items required further inspection, it seemed; her demeanour was pensive. When, after several minutes, she did not reappear, I moved to a spot from which I could see her, obliquely. Crouched at the Auzoux models, she peered at the dissected head, and smiled. My first thought was that I, the spy, was the cause of the smile. Then it seemed that the smile signified appreciation of the finely crafted objects. I approached.

She did not look away, even when I was standing alongside. "Hard to believe this is just paper and glue," she said.

Auzoux's papier-mâché was special, I informed her. Chopped rags and calcium carbonate and powdered cork—*poudre de Liège*—went into the recipe. That was why Auzoux's models have lasted so well, I explained. But they have become very delicate. The models had been designed to be taken apart and reassembled, but this one would no longer bear handling. I paused.

She was scrutinising the piece as closely as a detective at a crime scene. "Go on," she said.

I told her about the factory that Louis Thomas Jérôme Auzoux had founded in his home town. In the very first issue of *Nature*, Auzoux's model plants and plant organs were recommended for study. French cavalry regiments kept Auzoux models of horses' teeth for reference, I told her. This made her look up; I stopped.

"It's interesting," she said. Her smile did not suggest irony.

I confessed that I was curious. "Are you doing some sort of research?" I asked.

"In a way," she said. Her gaze invited me to take the deduction a stage further.

I told her what I had guessed: that she was an academic.

"I shall take that as a compliment," she said. Then she told me her profession and name. She was not flirtatious, and this was an enhancement of her attractiveness. "The name will mean nothing to you. And obviously the face doesn't," she observed, impersonally. "No reason why it should," she added. She had been on TV quite recently, in something called *The Harbour*. "I was the snooty wife of the mayor. I'd been having an affair with the father of the first victim, it turned out."

I apologised for not having seen *The Harbour*; in truth, I had not heard of it.

"You didn't miss much," she said, then she told me about the audition for *Devotion*. I already knew about this project: several months earlier, Marcus Colhoun had contacted me; he had visited the museum when he was a student, and had been "inspired" by it. We had exchanged emails.

The audition was a week away. I wished her good luck.

•

On the Sunday of the week in which the filming started, I met Samantha for coffee. Val was present, as was often the case at that time. She seemed to lack trust, though her victory was secure; the ostensible reason for her attendance would have been that she felt it was important for there to be no negativity between us. She was strongly opposed to negativity in all its forms, and still is.

"How are you, David?" Val enquired. She tended to employ my name at the outset; a boundary was thereby established.

"I am well," I answered.

"You look well," she said; et cetera. An exchange of niceties was all that was expected. I would have no news, she knew. In my world, every week was like every other. Val was then a student counsellor; her week, as usual, had been stressful.

I told her, not for the first time, that I could not do her job; this was sincere.

When Val excused herself and went indoors, Samantha eased back in her seat and levelled a diagnostic look at me. She stated: "Something has happened."

"Things are always happening," I said. "My life is a maelstrom."

"Come on," she said, rapping the back of my hand with a finger, as if it were an electronic device with a dodgy connection. "Something good, I mean. Tell me—quickly. We've got three minutes."

I supplied the essential information. "Good-looking, is she?" she asked.

"She's interesting," I answered.

"I'll take that as a Yes. Young?"

"Younger than me. Not young young."

Stirring the spoon in her coffee, she looked at me askance. "Is she interested in you?"

"I doubt it."

"That's the stuff—embrace defeat."

"Just answering honestly."

"You've talked to her?"

"Of course."

"And you like her."

"I do."

"And she'll soon be gone."

"Yes."

Samantha leaned forward, as if to reveal a secret. "Take the initiative, David. What's to be lost?"

Nothing was to be lost, I agreed.

"It would be good for you," she said. "An adventure."

•

We were at a café near the Pompidou. An advertisement at a bus stop, for an exhibition at the Musée des Arts et Métiers, caught Imogen's attention; it showed a close-up of a mechanism of incomprehensible complication, a thicket of golden cogs. In all the time she had been living in Paris, she had never been to the Arts et Métiers. Half an hour later, we were there. Three thousand items are on show at any time, from a collection of nearly one hundred thousand. We saw clocks, bicycles, phonographs and phones; steam engines, calculating machines, cars, aeroplanes, cameras; chronometers, gasometers, manometers, lathes and looms. Everything well displayed and informatively annotated.

The effects of the chemotherapy persisted. But the Arts et Métiers would have been fatiguing in any circumstances, she said. The scale of the Sanderson-Perceval Museum was one of the things she liked about it; the incoherence was another. Many of the items in the Sanderson-Perceval—the porcelain, the musical instruments, the crystals, the velvet mushrooms, the glass jellyfish—belonged together only because they had been collected. There was no insistence that the visitor be instructed, but instruction might proceed from pleasure and confusion. "A bit of a mess—but a nice mess," someone once wrote in the visitors' book.

•

Museums are places of contemplation; they are places of poetry; they create constellations of images in the mind. We behold a spectacular artefact or relic—an Aztec mask, the skull of an immense prehistoric carnivore, an Athenian goddess—and we marvel. Various means are employed to enhance the effect: jewellery and glass might be displayed under spotlights in a darkened room; sculpture arrayed in a white-walled hall of church-like ambience. Not every museum possesses items that are marvellous, but all objects in a museum emit some sort of charge; they have a resonant presence. Isolated for our inspection, they have an aura of significance. Having been collected, they now belong to themselves; they are untouchable.

•

Amateur dramatics at university had been the full extent of her acting experience until Antoine Vermeiren had cast her in *Les tendres plaintes*, Imogen told me, in answer to my question. Marc Vermeiren, Antoine's brother, had been a colleague of her boyfriend, at the University of Tours. In my teens, I had gone cycling in France with a friend, I told her. We had stopped overnight in Tours. Imogen and I talked about the city—the giant cedar; Fritz the stuffed elephant.

I learned the name of the boyfriend—Benoît—and that the relationship was over. Imogen's manner did not suggest that the ground was being prepared for a new relationship; or rather, I saw nothing from which to take encouragement. But Imogen would say that this conversation was the start; something about my description of the silent lightning storm, watched from the little square in front of the cathedral, with the barely remembered friend, apparently.

•

The local paper sent a reporter to talk to the director and cast of *Devotion*. He interviewed Imogen in the garden, and was duly charmed. She was unpretentious, approachable; her gestures were expansive and urgent; "vivacious" is the obvious adjective. I could see that she was telling the reporter a story. Tumbling from head to midriff, her hands conjured a costume in precise quick movements—a wide-brimmed hat; a cravat at the throat; a jacket, fastidiously buttoned; a flower in the lapel. With her fingertips she smoothed a moustache of air; her hands came together, one cupped over the other, on the handle of an imagined walking stick. She was being Mr. Dobrý, as I later learned.

Asked if she could remember when she had realised that she would become an actress, Imogen would sometimes answer that her career could be traced to a story that a schoolfriend had told her, about an elderly man from Czechoslovakia. This friend's family had moved to London when she was twelve years old, and she and her brother had soon come to know Mr. Dobrý. Near their new house there was a small park, and Mr. Dobrý could be seen there almost every afternoon, feeding the birds and the squirrels. He was an old man, but smartly dressed, always, with a white scarf around his neck on all but the warmest days, and a black three-piece suit that was never unbuttoned. In winter he wore a thick black coat that gleamed. Mr. Dobrý had a hat that made him look like a character from a black-and-white film, Imogen's friend had said. His walking stick had a lion's head for a handle, in real silver. His hair was white, and cut in an old-fashioned way; he had a lovely white moustache.

Local shopkeepers knew a few things about this refined old gentleman, but not much. He had come to England from Czechoslovakia a couple of years before the war, with a wife, who was no longer living. Mr. Dobrý's home town was a place called Karlovy Vary, where he had worked in a hotel that was owned by his family. It was an expensive hotel. His parents had remained in Karlovy Vary, but a sister was believed to have emigrated with him. It was not known what had become of her; the inference was that she, like the parents and the wife, had died. Nobody was ever seen with Mr. Dobrý. He did not seem unhappy, however, and he had money, as one could tell from his clothes. Someone had heard that Mr. Dobrý owned a hotel in London.

It was not known where Mr. Dobrý lived. "Not far from here," he told anyone who asked. He would let the children help him to feed the animals. But there was nothing creepy about Mr. Dobrý, Imogen's friend insisted. The parents all liked him. He was friendly to everyone, and he had wonderful tales about his life in Czechoslovakia. Sometimes he would show the children photographs: of hotels that looked like castles; of churches with shining domes that were onion-shaped; of ladies with parasols standing in front of colonnades and fountains. The photographs were the colour of tea. He brought coins and letters and postcards that were covered with

THE GREAT CONCERT OF THE NIGHT

unreadable handwriting. In the Dobrý family's hotel there was a piano on which Chopin had played; he explained how famous Chopin was, and showed them a picture of the piano, which stood between palm trees in a room with a glass ceiling. Mr. Dobrý would point to the faces in the photographs and recite all the names. Though he had left Czechoslovakia so many years before, his accent was strong.

Then came a month when Mr. Dobrý was missing from the park. Nobody knew where he had gone. Occasionally he had been absent for a week or two; he never gave warning of his departure, and never said where he had been when he returned. He had never been missing for a whole month. The absence continued, until one evening the friend's father announced that Mr. Dobrý had died. The story was in the newspaper.

It turned out that Mr. Dobrý had lived in a tiny flat at the end of a bus route that passed the park. A birth certificate had been found and a sister traced: her name was Edith and she had been born in Sheffield, as had Mr. Dobrý, whose name in fact was Kenneth Tate. Edith had not seen or heard from her brother for forty years; she had not known where he had been living, and knew nothing about his life. The newspaper carried an appeal for information, but nobody ever came forward to say that they had known Mr. Dobrý, under this or any other name.

How wonderful to have been Mr. Dobrý, Imogen had thought, when her friend told her the story. To have invented such a life and lived it out seemed an enterprise of genius.

•

The filming of *Devotion* began on a July evening. From the dining room I looked out onto the garden, where Julius Preston and the father of Beatrice Moore were in earnest discussion, on the bench by the sundial. Searching for the answer to the conundrum of his daughter, Mr. Moore gazed into the leaves of the beech tree that rose behind the cameraman, who stood a few yards in front of the actors, aiming the lens into their faces. Two paces to the right of the bench stood Marcus Colhoun, nodding approval. At the high point of the garden, in the crook of the wall where the irises grow, Imogen turned the pages of the script. Her skirt was a voluminous thing, with three tiers of flounces, and the pattern was a bold check, in lime green and salmon pink and violet. A paisley shawl covered her shoulders.

She was splendidly demure. Her neck and wrists were unadorned; her lips pale as paper; her hair, parted strictly down the centre, was gathered into a small tight bun. Imogen closed her eyes as a young woman applied a make-up brush to her cheeks, and when she opened them she noticed that I was at the window. She closed her eyes again and smiled into the sunlight.

Marcus took her down to the bench, talking urgently, like a coach with an athlete before the start of the race. While cameraman Joe waved a light meter around, the assistant fussed at the folds of the dress. Marcus Colhoun said a few words, then stepped back. Abruptly Imogen became Beatrice Moore. The angles of her head and neck and shoulders changed a little; it was enough for a different character to be delineated. One hand held the ends of the shawl like a clasp; the other lay on the arm of the bench, and was equally still. Not once did she look at Julius Preston; her eyes were directed past him, towards the pool at the foot of the garden. Dr. Preston's gaze never left Beatrice's face. Suddenly she stood up, distressed; she walked away, and Julius Preston followed her, up the slope of the lawn, into the sunlight. The camera stalked them and the microphone hovered above their heads, but equipment and crew seemed to be invisible to the actors. The expertise was remarkable. For some reason, this sequence was omitted from the film.

•

In Imogen's exchanges with Marcus Colhoun there was rarely much evidence of the sort of bantering camaraderie one often sees in behind-the-scenes extras. Their conversations—or the ones that I observed—were brief, almost brusque: a few gestures, a few words, as if discussing tactics. Imogen said to me: "He gets straight to the point. And we understand each other." Later, she told me that she had known immediately that Marcus Colhoun had attended a boarding school. "We're like Freemasons or ex-cons—we recognise the signs," she said. It had been like serving a novitiate. Her mother and father had endured the same childhood confinement, and therefore she'd been required to endure it too. "It makes you strong," her mother had pronounced. Imogen had felt that she was being taught how to stand guard over herself, she told me; few people were to be permitted to pass into the heart of the fortress.

•

Sometimes, she told me, it felt necessary to play the part of being an actor. "There are certain expectations," she said. For example, on occasion she had been prompted to employ the trope of the actor as compulsive observer, always taking note of gestures, idiosyncrasies of speech, behavioural tics. "It's not wholly untrue," she said. And people liked to hear about the moment at which one became aware of one's vocation. "'For my thirteenth birthday my parents took me to see *A Midsummer Night's Dream* and I was mesmerised. I knew right away that I was going to be an actor.' That kind of thing." Mr. Dobrý was a recital piece, she said; like an encore. There were days on which she could believe that Mr. Dobrý had indeed been the start of it.

•

Nothing from Samantha since the afternoon on which she gave me the news about Val's big initiative. Confidentiality is of paramount importance in the world of heavyweight commerce, so the company in question could not be named, but I was to understand that it was a top-tier organisation, and that a considerable fee was involved. Once a week, Val was to travel to the London HQ, there to conduct a two-hour "workshop" and then make herself available for individual consultations. The remit was broad. She would advise on issues relating to relaxation, diet, organisation of the workspace, et cetera, et cetera. Thus comprehensive wellness, a sense of empowerment, would be brought to the open-plan environment. The drones would be convinced of their happiness, and thereby become more effective drones. I commended Val's enterprise, in a manner that caused irritation. I used the phrase "monetising the wisdom," I believe.

"And what have you done recently?" Samantha wanted to know. "You're stagnating," she told me. It seemed that I had chosen to go down with the sinking ship. Val's "positivity" evidently offended me. Did I think that passivity was a virtue in itself? "I think you're happier living in the past," Samantha informed me.

"Aren't most of us?" I countered.

"Well, I'm not," said Samantha.

•

The museum does not allow us to reclaim the past—the past is irrecoverable. Hence the museum's pathos. The exhibits are like stars, small pieces of light from distances that cannot be bridged.

•

My first sight of Samantha—more than twenty years ago, the calendar tells me. Twenty-plus years, but I remember the scene with what seems to be great clarity. Jerome called my office—a man had collapsed in the armour room. We had to push through a group of schoolchildren who had been corralled in the adjacent room; Samantha's party, it turned out. The children were hushed, as if they had narrowly avoided a major accident. In a corner of the armour room, a large man lay on the floor; a jacket had been pushed under his head; his shirt, sky blue and too tight, was blackening with sweat. A woman held his hand as she talked to him. Her face was directly over his, and he was smiling as best he could. His grip was so strong that the woman's fingers were bunched together, and scarlet at the tips. Her calmness was remarkable; she emanated an aura of competence. Quietly, clearly, slowly, continuously she talked to the stricken man, until the ambulance crew arrived. While she talked, she looked into his eyes. *Caritas*, the greatest of the virtues. "Yes," the man said, four or five times; otherwise silent, he yielded to her assurance, to her gaze.

My love for Samantha was conceived in that moment. We might persuade ourselves that love is something that emerges over time, but in many cases, or most, it is instantaneous. What follows, the "falling in love," is but verification of what was comprehended in a second. It is a corroboration of the instinct. So many things can be seen in a moment.

•

Simone Weil: "We have to erase our faults by attention and not by will."

•

On the third or fourth day of filming, I was in the mirrored room when Imogen came in. A conversation between the newly married couple was about to be filmed there. The fabric of that day's dress was iridescent bronze, signifying perhaps the fire that had been lit in the soul of Beatrice. She stopped in front of one of her reflections, to appraise the effect of the dress. "A bold little number, isn't it? But it does impose a certain decorum," she said. Extending her arms in a parody of gracefulness, she glided across the room. In the centre she halted. She glanced over her shoulder, looking away from me. I regarded one of her images in the glass, as if studying a picture, and her image looked back at me, without expression. Then the crew arrived.

•

At the portrait of Charles Perceval and Adeline I told their story, as I always do. The behaviour of Adeline's sister, Marie, whose temper seems to have been problematic since puberty, had become unmanageably erratic. "She was frequently hysterical, the father informed the young doctor," I would have said, before pointing to the row of pessaries; the pessaries invariably provoke a reaction. Misalignment of the uterus was widely held to be the cause of afflictions such as Marie's, and physicians often fitted one of these devices to correct the irregularity. Charles Perceval refused to consider such an intervention. Hysteria was not a disorder of the womb, he believed; rather it was a disorder of the mind, or not a disorder at all. Instead, he talked to the patient; he offered, I proposed, a secular confessional. The father of Marie Hewitt was reluctant to permit such a conversation to take place in private, but the doctor eventually prevailed. So Charles Perceval talked to Marie, and she, after several consultations, became considerably less troublesome, though she later made a marriage of which they strongly disapproved, and which proved to be profoundly unsatisfactory to Marie herself. She took holy orders at the age of forty, and lived to the age of ninety-six. And her sister married Charles Perceval.

Then the fatal complication: the Catholicism of the Hewitts, and Charles Perceval's conversion. His parents, committed to the Church of England, were so dismayed by their son's betrayal that they refused to attend the wedding. But the faith of the Hewitts was to be implicated in a much graver crisis than this. It became apparent, in the later stages of Adeline's second pregnancy, that delivery of the child at full term could be extremely injurious to

Adeline's health. Furthermore, it was evident that the foetus was not developing as it should. Something could be done to mitigate the risk to the mother, but at the cost of the unborn child's life. Here I direct attention to the cranioclast, that terrible instrument. Such a step would of course have been impossible for Adeline and Charles: eternal torture would have been the punishment. The child died within hours of its birth; Adeline four days later.

The tour is always a performance. Conducting visitors around the museum, I am more voluble than my ordinary self, as I am in writing this. But on this particular day I was delivering more of a performance than usual. By the ten-minute mark, on an ordinary day, I would have finished with Charles Perceval. On the day of Imogen I was behind schedule. I had given information that I normally omitted; I had accentuated the pathos. This, I knew, was attributable to her presence. I was not making an effort to impress—not in the sense of trying to make myself attractive. I did not think that such a thing was possible. Rather, what I wanted to do was to make an impressive presentation, and I wanted to do this because of the quality of her attention. I felt compelled to sustain her engagement.

•

At the Sanderson-Perceval Museum, one spends time in a house of some splendour. This is a major part of its appeal: the visitor escapes into a fantasy of luxuriance. It offers, moreover, an experience of the genuine: in a world of proliferating fakes and simulations, the museum is a repository of the authentic. The things that it contains have an enhanced authenticity, it might be said, by virtue of their having endured.

•

I watched the tape of *La Châtelaine* on the day that I received it from Marcus. He had characterised it as "Bresson meets Borowczyk." At the time I was not sure what this meant. "It looks good," Joe had said, seeming to imply that it lacked substance. And it does look good, right from the start, where men in belted tunics and stockings appear out of the shadows and pass into the sunlight of a courtyard, a light so bright that they are obliterated by it. At the top of a tower, a crimson and gold flag hangs against a pure blue sky. At the foot of the tower, a groom is at work; the horse's flank ripples under the brush; the animal's breathing and the rasp of the bristles are the only sounds. In *La Châtelaine* there is a great quantity of silence. Conversations are observed from a distance; the actors gesture as if each movement were freighted with meaning. In the bedchamber, the lovers speak in the murmur of people under hypnosis. There are no throes of passion in the lovers' bed; they touch each other as though their bodies were hollow.

We see the Châtelaine's breasts as her lover lying beside her sees them. It was a pleasure to look at this body. The camera keeps close company with the lovers. In adoration of the Châtelaine, the lens loiters on the soft declivity between her shoulder blades; on the pulsing skin of her neck; on her lips; on her thighs. The young man is regarded closely too. Our gaze—the Châtelaine's gaze—caresses the tightening muscle of an arm, a taut buttock, a curl of hair around an ear. We glimpse a penis, tumescent, twice; and penetration, in close-up—a slow and blatant coupling, of documentary frankness.

•

"I'm useless on stage," Imogen said, as if this were an incontrovertible fact. "And applause is a problem. For me, I mean. You do your turn and you get your reward. I don't like it."

It struck me as reasonable for people to congratulate and thank the performers, I said. And wasn't applause an honest way to close the evening? The lights go up, the audience claps—the whole thing has been an illusion, and now the show is over.

She was all in favour of honesty, Imogen said, but she was not cut out to be an entertainer. "That sounds pompous, but it's how it is," she said. "You give your performance, and at the end of the evening the comfortable ones give you their approval, if they feel they've had their money's worth. And I'm speaking as a member of the comfortable community. I'm aware of the hypocrisy," she said, bowing her head to accept the implied reproach.

•

"Life consists in the sum of all the functions by which death is resisted," wrote Marie François Xavier Bichat, chief physician to the Hôtel-Dieu de Paris, in his *Recherches physiologiques sur la vie et la mort*. His book was published in 1800. Two years later he died, at the age of thirty, after falling down a flight of stairs at the Hôtel-Dieu.

•

I watched *Les tendres plaintes* last night—or skim-watched it, for the scenes in which Imogen appears. I have never cared for the actor who plays Xavier. It is hard to understand why any of these young women would tolerate this prig for more than ten minutes. And the behavioural tics are overdone: the staring eyes, the staccato speech, the peculiar gait. Everything is overdone: the unmanaged hair, the ill-fitting clothes. Xavier has no TV; such is his disdain for the modern world. He manages to rein himself in for the longest scene—with Caroline, at the concert given by his bête noire, Gaston Lasserre, a serial winner of competitions and awards, who just happens to have attended the same conservatoire as Xavier. Perhaps Imogen's self-restraint obliged him to tone it down a little. Depressed by the brilliance of Gaston, Xavier walks with Caroline to the Métro; he walks at arm's length from her, head down, like a man who has just received terrible news. "He is better than me," he complains. "He is very good," Caroline admits; she cannot lie. "I hate him," says Xavier; Gaston is handsomer and cooler than Xavier too; he drives an implausibly expensive car. It's a tough world, Caroline sympathises; it's unfair that there should be room for so few harpsichordists at the top of the tree. (*Les tendres plaintes* is a comedy, Antoine Vermeiren maintains; this is the only scene at which I smile.) "Gaston Lasserre is a showman," Xavier protests. "He is not serious." We know that Xavier is very serious. He is a scholar as well as a musician; his knowledge of the music of his chosen era is profound. Unfortunately, though, he is not a performer of Gaston Lasserre's calibre, as he knows. "He loves the applause, not the music," he moans. The whingeing continues all the way to the Métro station, where Xavier informs his girlfriend that he might as well kill himself. There is of course no possibility that Xavier could do any such thing; nevertheless, Caroline dissuades him. "The music needs you," she tells him. He kisses her on the forehead. "Tonight I have to be on my own," he says. Caroline watches him as he descends the steps and disappears. Imogen's face in these four or five seconds is the best thing in the film: we see pity, anger, affection; and her knowledge that their relationship has just been ended.

•

We were leaving my office, where I had shown Imogen some of the letters. She preceded me to the door, and as she opened it I felt compelled to tell her that Marcus Colhoun had given me a copy of *La Châtelaine*.

Registering no surprise, she glanced over her shoulder to ask: "And you've watched it?"

"I have."

"What did you think?"

My remarks were inane: I had appreciated the pace of it, and the tone; the cinematography was excellent. Blah blah.

She glanced at me again and said, without innuendo: "There are some nice images."

"Indeed," I said.

"The basket of oranges was memorable," she said, and laughed. Then she stopped at the head of the stairs to suggest that we continue this conversation some other time.

•

The final scene of *Maintenant et à l'heure de notre mort* is difficult to watch; it is difficult for anyone to watch. The woman, Marguerite, is in her bedroom, seated in front of a mirror. Motionless, the camera observes her from the far side the room; the distance implies some sort of tact. A window is open; we hear a car passing in the street; after ten seconds, a second car; a child calls out and is answered by another child. The room is bright with sunlight. Calmly, or so it seems, the woman regards the reflection of her face. We hear her exhale, then the camera is abruptly in the place of the mirror, and her face occupies most of the screen. The lens receives Marguerite's consideration. We last saw her weeping; she is not weeping now; her eyes suggest exhaustion, and vast disappointment. Then, in the space of two or three seconds, the focus of her gaze changes. The eyes widen fractionally; the exhaustion appears to dissipate. Marguerite is no longer looking at what she sees in the glass: she is looking through the glass, at us. Her gaze makes each of us feel that we are being specifically addressed. "Look at me," says her gaze. Nothing in her face undergoes any alteration; her mouth is relaxed and closed; there is no frown. She blinks, slowly, with composure; that is the only movement. She is not protesting; neither is she requesting pity. The power of her gaze is the power of absolute openness. For a full minute we are not released. Each of us must look at her; we must look into her eyes and return the gaze of this dying woman, until, in an instant, the screen becomes black. For ten seconds the screen is black, then the names scroll up in silence.

I could not say how many times I have watched this scene. My admiration is some sort of palliative.

•

She disliked the "contrived intimacy" of the theatre. "We pretend to be unaware of the audience. And I know what you're going to say," she said, raising a finger. "Film is every bit as contrived. That's true. But it's a different kind of contrivance." The camera allowed her to be natural, she said. "The camera sees everything, and I like that. There's no distance to cross. I don't have to project myself. But there's a distance too: because I'm not there for the performance. I'm on a screen, in a big dark room. People are looking at me, but I can't see them. To the audience it's enhanced reality. It's an immersion: the picture is huge, the sounds are loud. But it's just a screen— they're staring at a wall. So you're absorbed in it, but detached. That's what I like. It's more true and at the same time more false," she said.

I admitted that I had been watching from the window.

"I know," she said, making an adjustment to her hair. From an adjoining room her name was called. She curtseyed with prim dignity, in the character of Beatrice.

•

Imogen's mother had fallen a week before one of our visits. Her arm was in a sling, and we watched her as she attacked the roses with secateurs, one-armed, as if to demonstrate to an invisible assessor that the cast was a needless encumbrance. She had been thrown several times, Imogen told me. Once she had ridden home with a broken wrist and two broken ribs. This was when Imogen first spoke about the curse on the family's women. She had known nothing of her mother's diagnosis and nothing of the surgery until it was done. When she came home from school at Easter her mother told her about the operation. In her mother's mind, the cancer had been defeated: the surgeon had removed the tumour, the chemotherapy would deal with any residues, and any further invasion could be repelled by an act of will. There was barely any further discussion.

31

In the morning she spent a little longer in bed than was usual, but she was not visibly ill; she was not visibly anxious. And her mother's cancer did not return. But other women in the family had died of it, Imogen had later learned. The ordeal was inevitable, she had come to think. She talked about it as others might talk about the debilities of old age.

•

The museum enjoins us to be humble: *memento mori*, it whispers to us. Soon, very soon, your life will be reduced to fragments such as these, a ruin, a miscellany of fragments from which the past can be reconstituted only as a picture in which most of the space is blank.

•

A new message on Val's homepage: "We are living in times of great uncertainty." Politically, economically, socially, the world "is in a state of flux." It is not surprising, then, that "dangerously high levels of stress" have become "endemic" to our society. She sees the symptoms of stress everywhere. It is good to know, then, that help is at hand. Under Val's tutelage, she tells us, we can overcome anxiety, eliminate "fear and resistance," acquire "resourcefulness and resilience." We can learn to "grow and change." Her coaching is a "dynamic and self-generating process in which we work in partnership to harness and develop your skills and capabilities. I will help you to identify who you want to be, and to recognise what is preventing you from achieving self-fulfilment." She impresses upon us that her approach is not prescriptive. She has been trained in "a wide range of techniques and theories," and in addition to "mindfulness practices" often makes use of "archetypal psychology and psycho-synthesis." Solutions will differ from one individual to the next. The common denominator is that Val will always bring her full attention to bear upon the client. "My promise: to be wholly present to the person I'm working with."

February

TODAY, nobody came to the Sanderson-Perceval Museum. Not one person.

•

On our first evening, Imogen told me about the body double: "Antoine needed someone who was comfortable with the close-up," she told me. "A specialist." We had drawn the attention of the couple at the table nearest to ours. They were sixtyish, and exuded a miasma of ineradicable boredom. At the word "porn," they turned their heads in unison, abruptly, as if struck in the same instant by a waft of ammonia. The woman maintained a five-second glare.

"Likewise with the male member," Imogen continued, ignoring the scrutiny. "The erection was a guest appearance. A tricky problem for continuity, but I think it was managed well. Could you tell?"

"I could not. But I had assumed," I said.

The director had intended to use a prosthesis, Imogen explained. Instead of penetration there would have been some modest hip-thrusting; the customary decorous routine. "But the replica just didn't have the screen presence. No charisma."

At which point the woman set down her knife and fork decisively; her face took aim.

Imogen turned to face her and said, in a shopworker's tone of brisk courtesy: "Can I help you, madam?"

"Yes," replied the woman. "Could you please keep your voice down?"

"I don't believe I'm talking loudly. On the contrary. Am I talking loudly?" Imogen asked me.

"I don't think so," I answered.

"We can hear you very clearly," the woman told her.

"Then perhaps you shouldn't be trying so hard."

The husband, a man of smooth and copious jowls, now intervened. "You are causing offence," he stated. He pronounced like a magistrate.

Imogen, undaunted, surveyed the room. Nobody else was sitting within ten feet of us, and nobody was paying any attention to our corner. "I don't think so," she said.

"Yes, you are," said the woman.

"What precisely is it that has displeased you?"

"You know perfectly well."

"Was it the silicon dick? Surely not. I thought the dick was funny. But I can see that you are not amused," said Imogen, assuming an expression of some gravity.

"You are a very rude person," the woman told her.

"We cannot all be blessed with charm such as yours, I'm afraid."

From a face that had begun to pucker with disgust, the man emitted the sound of a punctured ball. His wife said: "You are spoiling our evening."

"And you seemed to be having such fun. I do apologise," Imogen replied. Turning to me, she smiled and said, brightly: "Coffee?" It was as if the complainants had vanished.

But I could not so easily disregard our neighbours; they were listening. I suggested that we call for the bill.

"Really?" she protested, exaggerating the disappointment. "I could talk to you about my family. Or you could tell me about yours. I think that would be inoffensive enough," she said, raising her voice.

Ten minutes later we were leaving. She leaned towards the woman and said to her, in a gossipy girlish whisper: "We're just getting to know each other. It's going well, I think." Then she smiled at the husband, as if he and his wife had been in our company all evening, to everyone's delight. "It's been a pleasure," she said.

•

Some time after Imogen's departure, Samantha at last remarked: "Very nice, but not really your type, was she?" The phrase would not have irked as it did, had I not heard it as an echo of Val; types and archetypes were coins of Val's currency.

My liaisons prior to our marriage were not numerous—just three of significance. No common denominators other than femaleness were immediately apparent, I might have pointed out. Instead, all I said was: "What might my type be?"

"You know what I mean," said Samantha. "She was a bit more... well..."

"Extravagant?" I suggested, attempting a tone of simple curiosity.

"Maybe."

"Posh?"

"Posher than anyone I know, certainly."

The big house had been a major element of Imogen's appeal, I confessed.

"There's no need to be so defensive."

I denied that I was being defensive; then apologised.

It was evident that I was still very fond of Imogen, Samantha observed.

We were still good friends, I said.

Samantha commended me for this. It was to my credit that I had remained on good terms both with Imogen and with herself. Val's ex-husband was more typical of the way men behave. Though he was the guilty party, he had not reacted well to Val's new relationship. It was as though his ex-wife had announced that she was carrying a disease that their son might contract.

•

We were talking about *La Châtelaine*, and Imogen said: "Tell me I was wonderful."

"You were wonderful," I confirmed.

"Do you mean it?" she said, pleadingly.

"Of course," I said.

"Oh, thank you," she sighed. "We actors are insecure people, you know. Terribly terribly insecure," she said, in the fluttering voice of an over-delicate creature.

•

A startling item in today's paper, apropos of Wellbutrin, a drug often prescribed, we are told, to treat depression caused by the loss of a loved one: "the American Psychiatric Association has ruled that to be unhappy for more than two weeks after the death of another human being can be considered a mental illness." Can this be true? Apparently so.

Another source: "The APA is proposing that anyone who can't conclude their grief and mourning within two weeks could be liable for a diagnosis." Previously, it appears, the threshold of unhealthy grief was deemed to be two months.

•

Benoît, Imogen told me, had not been entirely happy about her involvement in *Les tendres plaintes*; he was even less enthusiastic about *La Châtelaine*. Student theatricals were one thing, but this was of another order. This was not recreational make-believe. The nudity unsettled him; as did Antoine Vermeiren, whom he had disliked on first sight—"pretentious" was the word that Benoît had used. In fact, Imogen said, Benoît was perturbed by the very idea of her acting. He was disturbed that she could find it so easy to dissemble. "I had mortgaged myself"—this is what he thought, she told me. The world in which Benoît worked, the world of economics, was as far as could be imagined from the world of falsity in which she had chosen to enlist. When she and Benoît had met, she had been working as a translator; she was thus engaged in a milieu that bordered on the academic. It disappointed him that she had defected. What Benoît needed, ultimately, was someone of an intelligence that was more congruent with his—an intelligence such as that possessed by Jennifer, with whom he began a relationship within a month of his separation from Imogen. Jennifer was a brilliant anthropologist, and had the physique of a ballerina, and was English. For Benoît, English women were "sublime." They possessed a sensuality so profound that it was often invisible on the surface—though in Jennifer's case the surface was exceptionally alluring. "Creatures of the night," was how he characterised the English women of his imagination. When he had met Imogen, he had not known—as I had not known, until now—that she was not a thoroughbred English woman. "Not quite as good as the full English," Imogen mock-sighed. Benoît and Jennifer were married now. Benoît, on the cusp of forty when he and Imogen had parted, had needed to be married, she told me; I understood from this that Imogen did not need to be married.

•

We were in the Luxembourg gardens, on a bench at the Medici fountain, when Imogen told me that she was beginning to think that she would have to come back to England for the end. It was late afternoon; the air was warm in the shade of the plane trees; the reflection of the leaves put a pale green glaze on the water; a picturesque enclave of stage-managed nature. She had developed a craving for the fields of the homeland, said Imogen, as if confessing that her politics had undergone a rightward shift. "I've come over all pastoral," she said. We had been walking for a couple of hours, and she was tired; she lay on the bench, with her bag as a pillow, against my leg. "I could see you more often," she said. Every week, on the phone, her mother had asked her—almost ordered her, on occasion—to come back. Her mother was fully aware, of course, that palliative care of the highest quality was available in Paris, but it was available

39

in England too, and she would ensure that Imogen received it. Leaving aside all medical considerations, returning to the family home was simply the right thing to do: it would be an acceptance of the correct and natural order of things. (The years of boarding school, it seemed, had been but a negligible interlude in the family narrative.) Imogen would not want it to be thought that she had undergone a deathbed conversion, but recently, she confessed, she had experienced something like a craving for the view from the window of the room that had been hers. The excitement of the city had become something she appreciated primarily in the abstract; the traffic had become a drone, like tinnitus. She wanted to open her window and hear the silence of the garden.

•

Within an hour of meeting me, Imogen's brother told me that London didn't suit her. London was a terrible place, thought Jonathan. All big cities were terrible places. "Factory farms," he called them. Imogen was a country girl at heart, but for some reason she was forever trying to prove the contrary. "She's always been a tremendously argumentative girl," he said. "Sometimes just for the sake of it." That had not been my experience, I answered. "Just wait," he said. When Imogen was at Oxford, he told me, he and his parents had driven up to see her in *Measure for Measure*, and he had been terrifically impressed. The scene at the end, when the Duke proposes marriage and Imogen's character says nothing—it was incredibly powerful. "Imo did this extraordinary bit of acting. It was all in the face. So many different things going on in her mind, you could tell. Amazing. Unforgettable." Much of the play had gone over his head, he admitted, but Imogen had been so well suited to the character she had played, because she was a clever and feisty girl too. "I was just saying that you're much smarter than me," he said, as Imogen came into the room. Later, he said, he would show me the skirting board into which, when Imo was twelve years old, she had scratched some words in an alphabet that she had invented, which had letters that produced sounds that did not exist in English or in French. She had devised new names for birds and trees and all sorts of things that they would see on the long walks—the "forced marches"—that she and Jonathan would undertake on Sundays in summer. Young Imo was a prodigy of invention, Jonathan told me. It was a waste of her brain to be spouting other people's words, however talented she might be as an actress. He admired what she had achieved, but she should be a writer instead of an actor, and she should not be living in London. He wondered if I might be recruited into his campaign to bring his sister back to the good air and greenery of the native soil. "It will require great patience and perseverance, but we must prevail," he declared, overacting the soldierly resolve, for Imogen's entertainment.

•

"I won't make five years," she said to me, after the first operation, as if she had been told this as a fact, and were already reconciled to it. But she called me again, later that day, in panic.

•

Sold yesterday at auction in London, to an anonymous private buyer, for a modest sum: *The Consultation*, c. 1690, the work of an anonymous pupil of Jan van Mieris, eldest son of the celebrated Frans van Mieris the Elder of Leiden. Removed from the public gaze, the painting has been diminished; it has become a possession again. Also sold: the glass jellyfish—a fine example of the work of Leopold and Rudolph Blaschka; our copy of William Hunter's *Anatomia uteri humani gravidi*; and René Laennec's *Traité de l'auscultation mediate*, in which the stethoscope, Laennec's invention, was first described.

Though many curators have admitted to considering such sales in recent months, the Museum Association deems our deaccessions to be unethical, and accordingly has barred the council's museum service from MA membership. But the roof might now be repaired.

•

Seven or eight people presented themselves for the tour: Imogen the youngest by three decades at least. We would have started at *The Consultation*. Had it been displayed in a major gallery, *The Consultation* would not have been conspicuous, but it was the most accomplished painting in the Sanderson-Perceval collection. The gleam of the knives was expertly simulated, and differentiated from the gleam of the pewter jug; likewise the various textures of the maidservant's dimpled hand, the waxen face of the worried young man, his leather gloves, the dead skin of the chicken on the table, the fabrics. Skill was evident in the glow of the candlelit water, wine and urine. The picture was almost certainly painted in Rome, where Jan van Mieris spent his final years. He died in 1690, at the age of twenty-nine, having been in poor health for much of his life; he might be the patient in this picture, I told the group. Imogen took a step closer, to peer at the pallid young patient.

The Consultation was acquired in 1840 by John Perceval, I would have continued. His ancestor, Richard Perceval, the founder of the Perceval dynasty of physicians, was renowned for the uncommon speed with which he removed kidney stones. The museum has no image of the expeditious Dr. Perceval, but it does have an illustration of the procedure as it would have been conducted at the time. I indicated the print that shows a supine man, with legs splayed and feet hoisted by two burly men, stoically accepting the insertion of the rod.

•

Walking through town, one day before the end of shooting, Imogen apologised for talking too much. "But you're a top-class listener," she said. "You'd have made a good doctor, in the eighteenth century." And she reminded me that, in the course of the tour, I had explained that a physician at that time would have been a listener above all: the patient would relate the story of his or her illness, and on the basis of this story the doctor would pronounce his judgement. Diagnosis by letter was not unusual, I had told the group, pointing out the letter written to Cornelius Perceval by a grateful patient whom Perceval had never actually met. "See—I was paying attention," said Imogen; then the kiss.

•

I have not a single line of Imogen's handwriting. Any day, at the

43

museum, I can examine the letters of Adeline Hewitt and Charles Perceval; I can enjoy that residue of their intimacy. Every handwritten word is intimate: the ink is an immediate trace of the thinking mind, and of the writer's body. Before long, pens will be employed solely for signatures, if at all.

•

My grandfather's pen. "Moss-Agate" the gorgeous mottled green and brown is called, and the material is celluloid, a lovely liquid word, so pleasing to pronounce, I thought as a child. It was from my grandfather that I first heard it, I believe. The beautiful instrument was the first plastic pen to be made by the Waterman company; the plastic feels and looks like a valuable substance. The Waterman name, cut into the barrel, has been blurred by my grandfather's fingers. I remember seeing the pen in the room in which my grandfather had died. The pillows were still on the bed; the upper one was shaped like a bowl, as if cradling the head of his ghost. The marks of his teeth were on the mouthpiece of the pipe that lay on the dressing table.

•

An incident, after work. For a few seconds I did not recognise the man who crossed the street from North Parade, calling my name. The beard, profuse and ungroomed, was a disguise; then the features of William's face became discernible. He ran through traffic to reach me, maintaining the smile throughout, as if this encounter were an extraordinary stroke of good luck.

"Great to see you again," he said. The handshake was forceful.

"How are you?" I asked. I would estimate that he was around thirty pounds heavier than when I'd last seen him; an encouraging sign. And his sweatshirt, though not new, was clean, as were the jeans.

"I'm back," said William, taking a step back and raising his hands like a man accepting applause. "Older. Wiser. Hairier."

"So where have you been?" I asked.

"Where haven't I been?" said William. The full answer lasted for ten minutes, with no pause long enough to permit anything other than an expression of continued interest. With the van-owning friend he had travelled slowly along the south coast as far as Hastings, where they'd stayed for a while, renting a couple of rooms for as long as the work held out, then they'd cut up through East Anglia, which was a dead loss, before heading west into the Midlands, where the companions had fallen out irretrievably, after many disagreements. William had stayed in Birmingham for a year, fitting tyres mostly, then moved northwards, through Sheffield and Leeds and across to Manchester and Liverpool, then back to Leeds and up as far as Newcastle. He'd been a removals man, a labourer, a warehouseman, a courier, a house painter, a street sweeper and God knows what else. He'd worked in recycling centres and in some of the nation's nastiest fast-food outlets. "Nothing you'd want to make a career out of," as he said. At one point he'd had the idea that some sort of reconciliation with his mother might be possible. He lasted less than a fortnight in the spare room. Talking to his stepfather was like standing in front of a freezer with its door open.

Later, when he'd been shovelling asphalt with a lad whose father had recently died, he'd thought he might attempt to make contact with his real father. He had found him without too much difficulty.

That too was a disaster. No details given. "A self-pitying slob," was William's verdict. Things went "downhill a bit" after William had walked out of the shambles that his father called home. He'd ended up on the streets. Standing on Hungerford Bridge at two in the morning, he had considered whether drowning might be the answer. Instead he asked himself: "Where have I been happiest?" And the answer was that he had been happiest here, he told me. "So here I am," he said, "and here you are." Then he added, perhaps observing a reaction: "Don't worry, I'm not going to camp on your doorstep." He asked me for the time; he had to meet someone who might need a hand with some house-clearing. Patting me on the arm, as if in encouragement, he apologised for having to leave. "See you around," he said, and away he hurried.

•

The first encounter with William; or what I can reconstruct of it. We were sitting outside, near the abbey; Imogen had come down for the weekend. She glanced over my shoulder several times: a young man, twentyish, was standing a few yards behind me, importuning the people at the adjacent table; it appeared that none of them had offered him any money; he was asking them to reconsider, to no effect. Though the hair was a mess, he was not the most plausible of desperate cases: he looked more like an odd-job man than someone who was sleeping rough. "OK," I heard him say, conceding failure. "You all have a nice afternoon."

As he approached us, Imogen seemed to be thinking what I had been thinking—that this person might not be genuine. But she said to him: "Would you like a coffee?"

A sticking plaster was attached to his brow, touching the hairline; he pressed a thumb onto it, as if to focus his thinking.

"Sit down," Imogen said, indicating the seat next to mine.

He gave me a permission-seeking half-smile. I pulled the chair out for him.

"Are you hungry?" Imogen asked, sliding the menu card across the table.

His expression was that of a man who suspects he does not fully understand the situation in which he finds himself. "No cash," he said, pressing the plaster again. When he lifted his finger, the disc of blood in the centre of the plaster had widened.

"Have what you like," Imogen told him.

He would just have a coffee, he said.

"If you're hungry, choose something," said Imogen. "Are you hungry?"

He glanced at me, for guidance. "I recommend the chocolate cake," I said, pointing to my plate.

A waitress had arrived; her gaze registered the unkempt young man, then she smiled at Imogen; her smile was like a puppet's. Imogen ordered another coffee for herself, and directed the waitress to our guest, who ordered a cake as well.

"Very nice of you," he said. The finger went back onto the plaster, pressing hard.

"Let's have a look," said Imogen. Obediently he lifted an edge, revealing a cluster of sutures. She offered a tissue, which he took with a trembling hand. "You need to change that dressing," she told him.

"This'll be fine," he said, tapping his fingers on the tissue.

There was a pharmacy in the row of shops on the opposite side of the street. "I'll be back in a minute," said Imogen.

He watched her cross the road; a man beguiled. In her absence, it was agreed that she was a very kind person. That was more or less the substance of our conversation. His coffee and slice of cake were deposited by the waitress. The cake was consumed in a matter of seconds, before Imogen returned.

"How did it happen?" she asked, applying a new dressing.

He murmured his reply, as though responding to a question from a nurse in A&E. There had been a bit of bother at the place where he'd been living.

"Where's that?" she asked, in nurse-like mode, removing some specks of dried blood with the tissue.

He named a street. It was a squat; a defunct office building.

"And what's your name?"

"William," he answered.

"Imogen, and David," she said, giving him a hand to shake; he wiped his hand on his chest first. "Would you like anything else?" she asked.

"No, thank you," said William. He took a sip from his empty cup; he was worried that in return for this charity he would have to submit to questioning.

"You sure?" she asked.

"Sure, thank you," he answered, nodding too much.

"OK," she said; from her smile he understood that there would be no interrogation; he could leave.

"That was very nice, thank you," said William.

"Our pleasure," she said, and she handed him the pack of sticking plasters.

"Really?" he asked, as though this generosity were extreme. On leaving us, he bowed to her, with a hand over his heart.

•

Watched *Jumièges* last night. I remember speaking to Imogen about it; Franck Boudet had called her, to talk about the script. One of the crew on *Maintenant* had told Franck a story about his family, a story that was now becoming Franck's screenplay. The man's sister was the model for the character that Franck was hoping Imogen would play. Every week she visited their father with their mother; she was much closer to both parents than was the teller of the story. The father's health was poor: his mind was falling apart; a stroke—the most severe of a series—had rendered his speech incoherent and indistinct. He was confused, and often perplexed as to where he was and how he had come to be there. But one afternoon he seemed to wish to communicate something. His daughter was showing him again, on a map, the location of the village where her husband had been born. Her father's gaze slid around the map, apparently seeing nothing but a web of coloured lines, but then his eyes became focused, as though he had suddenly seen something that made sense to him. He became agitated, and more agitated with the effort of making himself understood. His finger quivered above the map, pointing to Jumièges; eventually it was established that he wanted to go there. Jumièges was located more than a hundred kilometres from where he had been born and had always lived. When his wife asked him why he wanted to visit it, she received no intelligible answer. Before the next visit he would have forgotten all about Jumièges, she was sure.

But he did not forget. He was like a child demanding a treat that had been promised to him. They went to Jumièges. The expedition was difficult; it was also unwise, his carers argued. But the old man would not relinquish the idea, and it was unlikely that he would live

49

much longer. This might be his last request. So arrangements were made; a nurse travelled with the family. At Jumièges, the dying man managed to make it known that it was the river, not the great abbey, that he wished to see. They came to Rue du Perrey, and there he became calm. His daughter turned the wheelchair to face the direction her father seemed to be indicating. Some small cliffs, some trees, the ferry, the green-brown meander of the Seine—it was not a memorable vista. But at the sight of this scene the old man started to smile. In recent years, he had rarely smiled. The smile dwindled; then he was crying. "When were you here?" his daughter asked. There was no answer. When she asked again he became angry. He wanted everyone to be quiet. He did not appear to notice that his wife was upset. Her own memory was becoming insecure, but she knew for a fact that she had never been to Jumièges with her husband. She would never know what memory was being revived at that place, by that ordinary view.

The actress playing the daughter is adequate, but Imogen would have been better. The long look that this actress gives the father, at the river, is simply sad; Imogen's gaze, as I imagine it, would have made us understand that she is not only seeing what her father has become—she is seeing the man that he once was, and the woman that she used to be.

●

After Imogen's departure, whenever I encountered William I did not linger; there was pressing business elsewhere, I would pretend. Finally he remarked that he had not seen her for a while. "She's in Paris," I answered.

"When's she coming back?" asked William.

"I don't know," I replied, neutrally. Imogen had grown tired of London, I told him; she wanted to live in Paris for a while. I told him about her family's connection to Paris, of which he had known nothing.

Looking down the street, he said, gravely: "That's a blow." It was as if this development might necessitate some revision of his plans.

"It's OK," I said. "We're friends. We talk."

"That's good," said William, still considering.

Imogen was about to start work on a new film, I told him. "*My Friend Claire*. She's Claire. Top billing."

"Of course," said William. Then he looked at me, his companion in loss, and said: "She was lovely." The stress was strangely on the second word, I remember.

"Indeed."

It had been like having a part-time sister, he said; a bigger and more sensible sister. More words were exchanged in Imogen's praise. When I gave him money, it felt as though I were honouring the terms of a contract.

•

From the adjoining room I heard Marcus, giving instructions. The physician's murmuring was followed by a brief response from Beatrice. Again the physician spoke; though I stood by the door, I could not discern the words. Then silence. A minute later, a high gasp. A physician-assisted paroxysm had been enacted. Charles Perceval was known to have administered this treatment to some of his patients. The inference was confirmed by Imogen's glance when she emerged from the room—a mock-sly smile, with startled eyes, as if she had been caught up in some mischief, not unwillingly.

•

In the first draft of *Devotion*, Beatrice's sister, an ostentatiously devout young woman, was the hysterical patient whom Julius had been asked to attend, thereby bringing about his meeting with Beatrice. Considerations of cost had brought about the merging of the two characters, but this revision had improved the film, Marcus told me. It had brought the film's central concerns—"obsession, madness, reason and faith"—more sharply into focus. The lard-coloured doll lay in his lap, swaddled in a towel, its single eye turned towards me. He offered to donate it to the museum, for room seven, but it was not in good condition by the time they had finished with it.

•

Though she had found the story "a bit silly," Samantha assured me that she had enjoyed *Devotion*, especially Imogen's performance. "She really has something," Samantha said, congratulating me on my good fortune. Val concurred. Imogen was "the best thing about it," Val told me. But Imogen had deserved a better film, she thought. Aspects of *Devotion* had troubled Val. The scene in which we are shown Beatrice after the wedding, preparing for bed, for example. Why, she wondered, was it necessary for us to see her naked, even if only for a second or two? Why do we not see her husband undressed? Why always the woman? Some observations were made on the topic of objectification.

Perhaps, I suggested, this had been what *Devotion* had been about, to some extent.

"Of course, of course," said Val. But she was inclined to think that the good intentions were something of an alibi. Not that she was accusing Imogen of any such thing; the fault was the director's. "It annoys me," she said, in case I had not noticed. We were at the customary café, which had a rack of newspapers and magazines for the customers' use. Taking a magazine, Val searched for evidence. It was easily found. "This sort of thing," she said, displaying pictures of a woman on a yacht. She too was an actress, and not one whose reputation was dependent upon the excellence of her body, as far as I knew, but here she presented herself in a bikini, in scenes of ersatz spontaneity: sipping a drink through a straw; shielding her eyes from the sun to gaze out to sea; laughing with a male companion. One picture was honestly posed—a coy topless shot, from the back, revealing nothing more than the undercurve of a breast. "This is what gets me," said Val. "The collusion. It gets me down."

•

First impression of Val: the lack of embarrassment was remarkable. We had met to "clear the air," on neutral territory—the café that became our favoured venue. Val's eyes compelled attention, and her posture was exemplary. Much work had gone into the maintenance of the hair's lush dishevelment; the same was true, I felt, of the air of well-being. Sauntering stride, beneficent smile, slow-blinking eyes—it all advertised the deep inner harmony that she had managed to achieve. I found the performance too studied. But for Samantha the attraction had been powerful and immediate: the conduct of

Val's son's had become disruptive; she was called to the school to discuss the situation; and in the course of the third or fourth discussion a moment of ignition occurred. I could not understand it.

•

Crossing the park this evening, I heard a harmonica. The sequence of sounds was simple and not unpleasant, if not quite a tune; the improvisation of someone who could not really play. It was William. "Another skill I picked up on my travels," he told me. "Hear how sad I am," he said, and produced a mournful fading slide of notes. He was wearing exactly the same clothes as when I saw him before; they had not been washed in the interim. The house-clearing job was for one day only; since then, nothing. I asked him if he were staying at the Melville Street hostel. The notion appalled him. "You get some desperate characters there," he said, "and I'm not desperate." For now, he's at a friend's place. It'll do for a day or two, but there's not a good atmosphere, because the friend has some dodgy mates. One of them is a dealer; a "cold-eyed bastard," said William. He had a lot to say about the cold-eyed bastard.

It was not so much a conversation as an attended monologue. I could not speak to William as easily as Imogen could. This was what I was thinking when he asked abruptly: "And what about Imogen? You still in touch with her?"

I told him what had happened.

William looked at me as though at a picture that had suddenly gone out of focus, and said nothing. He turned away and stared into the ground. "That's terrible," he whispered. Grimacing, he scrubbed at his face as if to ease an exasperating itch.

We talked about Imogen, briefly.

"It's unbelievable," he murmured. "I really liked her."

"So did I," I said.

Still gazing into the ground, he put a hand on my arm, gingerly, like a blind man ascertaining the location of a rail.

•

"Why have you been hiding her from us?" asked Emma, slighted, after Francesca had reported that my attachment to the actress was somewhat stronger than had been supposed, and that she was a charming and unpretentious person. Imogen was in the midst of preparations for *Le Grand Concert de la Nuit*, which gave some plausibility to my excuse—that her schedule made it difficult to make plans. The explanation was accepted, provisionally. Emma believed that she knew the reason for my evasiveness. She had not seen *La Châtelaine* or *Devotion*, but from what she had found out she could understand why I might not feel comfortable with the idea of introducing Imogen. But Emma wanted me to know that she was rather more broad-minded than she imagined I imagined her to be—no less broad-minded, in fact, than her daughter. "She's intrigued," Francesca told me.

The date of the visit was agreed many weeks in advance; when the day came, Imogen's mood was beginning to darken, but she was well enough, she assured me. On another day, she would have answered more expansively the questions that Emma and Nicholas had for her. They had many questions about the business of film-making; they talked to her as if she were some sort of explorer. That evening, Imogen's manner was polite, patient, modest, self-deprecating. They had expected someone more voluble, I am sure; more vivid; perhaps more glamorous. Nobody looking at pictures of the group around the table would have guessed her profession, said Emma, when she phoned the following day. This was by way of praise. The reticence had been something of a surprise, Emma confessed, but she understood why I would be attracted to her. Some people, without really doing anything, manage to transmit a certain charge, Emma said. "Charismatic, isn't she?" she said. She talked about "still waters," and surmised that Imogen might be easily bored. "I think we bored her, a bit," she said, not as a complaint. That was not so, I assured her, though there were times when Imogen was bored by herself. But there was never to be another visit.

●

Walking home, I am startled by a laugh from a young woman. The sound is exactly the delighted laugh that Imogen produced for the scene in which Julius does the sleight-of-hand trick, seeming to make his fiancée's handkerchief disappear. A dozen takes were required, because the handkerchief would not fly as Marcus Colhoun wanted it to. At each take Imogen's laugh was a perfect expression of spontaneous delight. Afterwards, Marcus remarked that it was easier to fake an orgasm than to do what Imogen had done. To make herself laugh, she told Marcus, she brought to mind an incident from her childhood: her brother being chased by a demented duck. The mirth of Beatrice is indistinguishable from genuine mirth. And her laugh is not at all like the sinister laughter of Agamédé, or the soft laughter of the elegant Claire, or the laughter of young Caroline, all of which were quite different from Imogen's.

•

Imogen started to rub her brow. After two or three slow strokes she began to rub quickly, scowling, as if trying to remove an ink-stain from her skin. Then she lowered her hand and looked right at me, fearfully. "I can't remember anything," she said. "I can't think."

"But that's not true," I said. "You're talking to me. So you are thinking."

"Words are coming out," she corrected me.

"Words are coming out in order, in sentences."

Her mind, she told me, speaking very quietly, was like a lake of black water. For most of the time the water was calm, but every now and then a breeze would rush over it and some foam would appear on the surface. That's what her thoughts were—foam on black water.

On the worst days, her mind was swarming with "pieces of sentences." From these fragments, sometimes, an item of sense, or half-sense, would materialise. These moments, she said, were like "birds flying out of fog."

•

Agamédé and the guileless Nicolas Guignon, in a chamber to which she has led him, examine a painting in which a roguish-looking man, in pink satin breeches, is playing a guitar for an audience of richly attired young adults, who recline on the grass of a romantic garden, amid roses, urns and statuary. After some discussion of the picture, Nicolas Guignon confesses to Agamédé that he has lost his heart to Delphine, his pupil, the youngest daughter of the Count. He needs to speak of the accomplishment and beauty of Delphine; Agamédé

57

allows him to. He has much to say about his philosophy of love. Sitting beside him, Agamédé listens. Then she takes his hand, as a mother would. Her demeanour becomes grave. Transfixing him with her gaze, Agamédé says to him: "But I have found that love, Nicolas, is too often a thing of the imagination. A man imagines the woman he thinks he sees, and imagines that he loves her." So few people can bear to be alone, she tells him. "This weakness is the cause of what they take to be love." Belying their meaning, the words are spoken in tones of great tenderness. The young man is weakened by the scrutiny of Agamédé, by her voice, by her bewitching hauteur, the delicious glaze of her skin, the penumbra of candlelight in her hair. He pretends to be considering what she has said, but already he is losing his heart for a second time, or so he believes.

•

"Nothing really dies," William states. We are sitting in the park; he clamps his hands on his knees and sweeps his gaze over the town. It makes no sense to talk about death because every human being is a field of energy, and every thought is an electrical event, he explains. Energy can never be destroyed. So it follows that we can never disappear. Radio waves play some part in the argument, as do sunlight and cosmic radiation. "We are information," he says. "That's what we are." The monologue is punctuated by variants of this idea. "Information can never be lost. That's a basic law," he tells me. He tells me about black holes. "You think black holes are these whirlpools in space, right? Cosmic plugholes," he proposes. Eventually everything will be sucked into them and lost forever—that's what we think. But this isn't right, says William. Scientists have a new idea about what will happen. Information will stream towards the black holes and be held there, on the edge, instead of plummeting into the abyss. In time, all the black holes will come together. And you could say that the result will be God. "All the information that there has ever been—that's God. And we will be part of it. We will become part of God," he explains, with every appearance of rationality. His manner is that of a physicist rather than an evangelist. "I know you're not sure about this," he says. "These things are difficult to understand."

•

In London, at night, we saw a couple admiring the spectacle of luxury that had been staged in the window of a furniture shop: tables that cost as much as cars; carpets created by picturesque craftspeople in picturesque villages. In the next doorway a hand was held out. The gaze of the window-shoppers slid over the human object; the act of semi-blindness might have been determined by shame, or embarrassment, or a belief that the beggar is there by choice, or is not truly destitute. Reasons can always be found. Not a rare occurrence; we have all done it. "I am not seen, therefore I do not exist," Imogen remarked, on Oxford Street.

March

ONLINE, a Q&A session with Antoine Vermeiren, recorded in Paris after the release of *Le Grand Concert de la Nuit*; intermittently subtitled. The attire is smart, and slightly dandyish: sugar-white shirt; a black suit of self-evidently expensive fabric; similarly fine footwear. The one exception to the monochrome scheme is the hosiery: violet socks. The other extravagance is the hair: a thick sweep of striated grey, just short of collar-length. For every question he has several hundred words; the voice is drowsily low-decibel; as he speaks, his left hand describes curlicues in the air, mimicking the turns of his thinking; it holds a cigarette, which is deployed with easy technique, like a miniature baton. The right hand is for raking the hair. Before each answer, the hair is raked or a cigarette sipped.

Inevitably, a questioner remarks that the subject of sex is prominent in Vermeiren's oeuvre; the director is invited to share his thoughts on the subject. Another cigarette is lit at this point; Vermeiren considers the lights in the ceiling. "Sex is not that important," he pronounces. "Sex is of less importance than work," he goes on, squinting into the light. Work, productive work, is what makes us human; the separation of sex and work is the basis of civilisation. "And I work very hard," he says. The cigarette is halted in mid-air, in anticipation of a downbeat. "But sex is also of great importance," he resumes. Some of the things he says are things that Imogen said to me; the same phrases are used. But he goes further: sanctity and transgression, he maintains, are inseparable. Nobody could deny, he proposes, that the libertine is closer to the saint than is the man who has no desire. His work is "profoundly spiritual," Vermeiren asserts, because "the things of the body *are* the things of the spirit." A strong emphasis on *sont*—as if the syllable were a hammer with which, at a single blow, he shatters the carapace of hypocrisy.

The characters in *Le Grand Concert de la Nuit*—indeed, in all of Vermeiren's films—are loquacious, extremely so, a member of the audience observes. "They deliver speeches," she says, at which Antoine Vermeiren smiles and nods; he encourages her to continue; she is pretty. The question has something to do with rhetoric. The eighteenth century was the golden age of rhetoric, Vermeiren states. That is why he likes that period so much. That is why he loves the music of the eighteenth century. "It is reasonable music, but it has passion," he says. He suggests that the questioner has identified a paradox that lies at the heart of *Le Grand Concert*: "These people talk about their wildness, but how can wildness have a language?" He wants it to be understood that *Le Grand Concert de la Nuit* is not merely set in the Baroque era—it is Baroque *in spirit*, because Baroque art is concerned with "the representation of what cannot be represented," and is imbued with the "melancholy of failure." There is something of the Baroque in Vermeiren's answers; the logic is hard to discern, but the performance is enjoyable, like an opera with fine music and an unfathomable libretto.

He must be *absolutely* clear: he is no apologist for violence. This is something that he deplores in American culture: its appetite for violence without consequence, its use of violence as entertainment. Within a minute he has declared himself to be a vegetarian. This is connected to his ideas on Christianity. Contempt for animals is intrinsic to Christian morality: "The beasts are beneath morality, and therefore *disgusting*," he explains. "I do not share this disgust," he says. *"Deus est anima brutorum.* God is the soul of beasts." The cigarette performs an intricate loop.

His next film, he announces, will be based on the life—the *outrageous* life—of Georges Bataille. A script has been written. He has much to say about Georges Bataille, about the "reversal of values," the "profound affinity between erotic pleasure and religious exaltation," et cetera. The accusations that were made against Vermeiren, a few months later, no doubt played some part in the annulment of that particular project.

•

Pierre/Vermeiren walks down the main street of Vézelay, so self-consciously that he appears to be suffering the after-effects of cramp; his hands hang like lumps of chicken meat. And the ghastly smile that he does: intended to suggest a deep and dark and illusion-free mind, but more suggestive of toothache. Vermeiren believes, I suspect, that his creativity transcends any considerations of mere technical competence. He can no more act than I can.

•

Francesca tells me that I should pack a copy of Lucretius for my Roman holiday. I will like him, she promises. How could one not admire a man who, writing in the century that preceded the arrival of Christianity, argued that the gods neither created us nor have any interest in what we're up to? Why would any deity create a species as vulnerable as humans and then confine them to this inhospitable lump of rock and water? Why bother? Do the gods crave amusement? No—they reside in a place of infinite tranquillity, and have nothing to do with the world in which we live. They do not punish us and they do not reward us. Nature is the ruling force of our world.

•

As did many of his coevals in the medical profession, Samuel Vickery believed that one could read in the contours of the skull the character of the mind within. The head-bones of criminals were not of the same form as those of the law-abiding, he maintained, and in proof of this theorem he displayed in his consulting room three skulls that he had acquired. They were of Italian origin, and were said to have been removed from the skeletons of a swindler, a violent drunkard and a matricide. All three came into the possession of John Perceval, and are now in room seven. The trio of criminal skulls are placed on a shelf at median adult head-height, so that they may meet the viewer on more or less equal terms.

I showed Imogen the skull of the belligerent drinker; the bumps of the cranium were indicative, supposedly, of a propensity to Combativeness. Having bought this item, John Perceval had shown it to a colleague who, like Samuel Vickery, was an adherent of the pseudo-science of phrenology. The skull, John Perceval explained, was the brain-case of a *commedia dell'arte* actor from Cremona. From the irregularities of the dome, he proposed, it was clear that this individual had been an exemplar of Wit and Mirthfulness. The colleague, after careful examination of the specimen, concurred with his analysis.

Looking through her reflection at the matricide's skull, Imogen said: "An upholstered skull. That's what a face is." She glanced at me, with a rueful smile. Years later, in her room, she would look at her wasted arm as it lay on the sheet, and say: "The bones are just about ready to come out."

•

Walking down Union Street I catch sight of Samantha amid the shoppers and strollers, fifty yards off, heading towards me; two seconds later, as if she has sensed that she is under observation, she glances up the road, hitting me immediately, in the instant in which—feigning a sudden distraction—I detach my gaze from her. Having briefly simulated an interest in a display of jackets, I look in her direction, thinking she might have taken the opportunity for evasion. But Samantha would not be party to such pretence; she is approaching; she has prepared herself. So I smile; the smile is intended to let her know that I had seen her immediately, and was simply waiting for her. Her smile tells me that the deception has not been successful.

"Seen something you like?" she asks.

I indicate a tweed jacket, the most conservative item on show. "What do you think?"

"A bit too horse and hounds?" she suggests.

She has a point. "How are you?" I enquire.

Her headmaster has announced that he'll be leaving in the summer; he's off to rescue an underachieving school in Liverpool. The topic sustains a one-minute conversation.

"And what about you?" Samantha asks.

"I'm OK," I answer.

"That's good."

In parting, I send my best wishes to Val. This is accepted wryly, with no words. Anyone passing within earshot would have mistaken us for ex-colleagues, at best.

•

Wherever he goes, William tells me, a CCTV camera is pointing at him. It's like being an animal in a zoo. It's worse than that, because the cameras make him feel bad about being himself, whereas a monkey cannot feel bad about being a monkey. It is like being accused all the time, says William. He has done nothing wrong, but the cameras make him feel that he has. In every corner of the town he is being judged and found guilty.

•

A woman of my age, emerging from room seven with the expression of someone who has just been grievously insulted, tells me that the warning notice should be more strongly worded. "There are some horrible things in there," she says: the dissected baby, for instance; the syphilitic head. Children could be given nightmares, she tells me. Later in the afternoon, shrieks of delighted disgust from a boy and girl in room seven; aged ten and twelve, I estimate. "Is that football thing real?" the boy asks me. He points to the twenty-five pound ovarian cyst. "It's real," I answer. "What about that?" asks the girl, indicating the placenta in which repose the fractured bones of a foetus that was killed by its sibling in the womb.

"That too," I tell her. "Sick," says the boy, and they go back for another close look.

•

I remember when Samantha first used the word "narrative" in talking about herself. It was a word for which Val had developed a penchant. Val's mission was to help people to "take ownership" of their "personal narratives." And now Samantha had come to understand her own story with a new clarity. While sorting through some boxes that she had brought away from her mother's house, she had come upon a wallet of photographs. The photographs were miscellaneous in subject and in age. One made her linger: a picture of herself, at fourteen, with friends in what appeared to be a park. In the middle was Barbara, the beautiful one; to Barbara's left, madcap Janet; to Barbara's right, Gillian, the high-flyer, who eventually went to Oxford to study law, and forsook her old friends entirely; and beside Gillian, Samantha. She had forgotten how she had once felt about Gillian; looking at the photo, at the smile and the sidelong glance, it was so obvious, said Samantha. And before Gillian, she now remembered, there had been someone else, a delicate but regal girl, two years above her, whose elegant walk—as though she were following an invisible and extremely narrow path—Samantha had tried to emulate.

Imogen, at the age of fourteen, had been enthralled by an older girl called Hulda, a glorious blonde Amazon who threw the javelin as if intending to kill. Such adorations are commonplace, as Imogen said. Remembering Hulda, she felt no embarrassment at the infatuation; she felt nothing, because the smitten Imogen existed only as a source of memories. But for Samantha, there was a lesson to be learned from the past. She saw that she had allowed herself to be diverted from the right road. The manifold forces of conventionality—overt and covert—had prevailed over her, and consequently she had become someone who was not truly herself. Gillian had been directing her towards a road that she had not taken, and the years of marriage had been a diversion. Not that she regretted those years, I was to understand. But thanks to Val, Samantha's narrative had at last come to make sense.

The former husband's story, on the other hand, has yet to achieve a satisfactory form. No sense of a through-road there, as yet.

•

In her correspondence with Charles, Adeline played the part that was expected of a woman in her position. Again and again she praised her fiancé's intelligence and denigrated her own. Her husband-to-be was "the quintessence of sympathy," she wrote, quoting the words of her sister, who similarly revered him. In an episode of self-doubt— an episode that to me seems inauthentic, as if she had felt under an obligation to admit to a transient loss of confidence on the brink of matrimony—Adeline wondered if her "inferior" mind and lack of education might not in time prove burdensome to him.

The letters provide ample evidence that Adeline's mind was far from inferior. I removed from its file the five-page letter of October 5th, 1854. As Imogen started to read it, I told her what she would find there. I can recite much of this letter from memory. Protestantism is anti-scientific, Adeline proposed, because it places unqualified reliance on the word of the Bible. But the Bible is a book composed by men, and is imperfect for that reason. And the Protestant preacher compounds the error in ruling his flock by means of words. He interprets the words of the Bible on their behalf, immersing them in a "cloud of speech." The Godhead is "beyond all language," Adeline proposed. The figure of Christ is the mystery of the divine made visible, and the display of the Host is a truer communication than any sermon. The contemplation of the Cross is "a consideration of evidence." And is not the practice of the medical sciences a consideration of evidence too?

Furthermore, in its attitude towards sin, in its emphasis on confession and forgiveness, the Catholic Church, Adeline argued, is true to the reality of our lives, and in this respect its doctrines are aligned with the medical sciences, which adhere to "the facts of what we are." The Mass is a bond of love, and so is the doctor's mission. She cited the rule of Saint Benedict: "before all things and above all things special care must be taken of the sick or infirm so that they may be served as if they were Christ in person; for He himself had said 'I was sick and you visited me,' and 'what you have done for the least of mine, you have done for me.'" Thus Charles's father was mistaken in talking of the "mere superstitions" of Catholicism. The Roman church is the church of life, Adeline maintained. It is a living thing, a tree; the Protestant sects are "dead branches, grown too far from the nourishment of the roots."

Imogen was looking at me. "An obvious question, but I'm going to ask it," she said. "I take it that you and Adeline are of the same persuasion?"

"Far from it," I answered.

"Really?"

"Really. Of no persuasion at all."

She narrowed her eyes at me, as if I had presented a puzzle.

•

The museum: an assemblage of objects removed from the flow of time, protected from the depredations of utility. A nest of objects; a nest is a place in which things are born.

•

We had been talking about *La Châtelaine*. Imogen asked: "If I'd told you that there had been no stand-in, what would you have thought?"

All I could say was: "I'm not sure."

"Perhaps you would have liked me less." She added: "This is not an accusation."

"I don't know," I said. "I don't think so."

We had reached the hotel. "Let's go on for a bit longer," she said. We were walking a pace apart. With the smile of a friend, she looked at me and said: "But it would have made a difference, wouldn't it?"

"In some way, I suppose so."

"The thing is," she said, looking ahead, "I might have done it without a stand-in. It was discussed."

A reaction was required of me. "In the interests of realism?" I proposed.

"If you like, yes."

A woman with a terrier was coming towards us; we stopped to let her pass. When she had gone, we were the only people on the street. We were standing outside a large tall-windowed house; in the living room, a woman was watching TV; upstairs, a man sat at a table, looking into a laptop. The scene is as clear as my first sight of Imogen. As we stood in front of the house, she said that she had read a wonderful line somewhere: anyone observing a "distinguished woman" making love would think that she was either ill or mad. As the woman in the living room reached for the remote control, Imogen moved away, and with a single finger hooked my elbow. "The Greeks got it right," she said. For them, the body was an "instrument of joy." With Christianity, sex became a shameful business, with procreation as its only excuse; the body—or rather, the woman's body—became a form of property. "It's a long downhill road from Athens to Adeline," she said.

We were back at her hotel. "Have I surprised you?" she asked, but not, it seemed, in the hope that she had; it was an enquiry as to the nature of my reaction. "Disappointed you?"

"Neither of the above," I said.

She smiled and gave me a studying look. "I have never cheated on anybody," she said.

At home, I watched *La Châtelaine* again. Watching Imogen, I found myself experiencing something like jealousy, so soon.

•

In 1198, before assuming the papacy as Innocent III, Lotario dei Segni wrote in his *De contemptu mundi*: "Man has been conceived in the desire of the flesh, in the heat of sensual lust . . . Accordingly, he is destined to become the fuel of the everlasting, eternally painful hellfire." Even when perpetrated by man and wife, sexual intercourse, Lotario wrote, is infected with "the desire of the flesh, with the heat of lust and with the foul stench of wantonness." *De contemptu mundi* gives evidence of its author's "deep piety and knowledge of men," the Catholic Encyclopedia informs us.

•

When she was eight years old, Imogen told me, there was a party at her house. The word "party" was perhaps too festive in its connotations. It was a gathering of many adults, on a summer afternoon, with quantities of champagne. The reason for this gathering could no longer be remembered. What she could remember was an incident that she witnessed, towards the end of the afternoon.

The sun was setting; she was playing on the lawn. Among the children was a local girl of whom Imogen was not fond: an aggressive and clumsy child, and a whiner too. Neither was Imogen fond of the girl's parents: they were as humourless as their daughter. The father's hair was silver, though his face was not old, and the mother had legs that were as thin as a stork's. They appeared to dislike each other—to find either of them, said Imogen, all one had to do was go to the corner of the garden that was farthest from where the other was standing.

The game had become boring, and the whining child was getting on Imogen's nerves. She decided to go indoors. The whiner's father was ahead of her, on the terrace steps. At the threshold of the house he missed his footing and stumbled; this, Imogen would later understand, was the first time she had seen a severely inebriated man. She followed. In the hall he turned left, towards the dining room, but before Imogen had entered the house she saw him come out of the dining room and cross the hall to the library. She saw him smile, as if an opportunity for mischief had presented itself. The situation was intriguing. On tip-toe she advanced to the centre of the hall, and from there she could see the silver-haired man creeping across the carpet in the direction of the big window that overlooked the garden; he was creeping in the same way that Imogen was. She moved to the doorway and peered in. At the big window stood her mother, looking out at the gathering; she was holding a cigarette in her left hand, at a distance from her face, as though passing it to someone else. It was very strange, Imogen thought, that her mother did not seem to be aware that she was no longer alone; the intruder was almost within touching distance. Then the amazing thing happened. It all happened in the space of two seconds.

Imogen's mother was wearing a beautiful dress; it was the colour of young cherries, and reached the back of her knees. The girl saw the man crouch down, take hold of the hem of the dress and quickly lift it, as if whisking a dust sheet from a chair to see what was underneath. He raised it so high that Imogen could see her mother's knickers. The knickers were pink and startlingly large. Only for an instant were they visible. At the touch of the air on her thighs, her mother swivelled and smacked the man across his face. It was not a lady-like slap. It was a full-force whack with a rigid hand and a long swing of the arm, as if she were smashing a tennis ball back. The noise was tremendous. The man staggered; he put a hand to his jaw as if he feared that something had been broken. That was when he saw Imogen at the doorway. Her mother saw her too, but turned back to the window, and calmly brought the cigarette to her lips. The man pushed past the child, glaring at the floor; one side of his face was now a different colour from the other.

In all the years that followed, her mother never mentioned this outrage. The man and his wife were never seen at the house again.

But one evening, near the end, Imogen fell asleep in the afternoon and when she woke up her mother was there, sitting in the window, turning the pages of a book of wildlife photos. As Imogen looked across the room, at her mother, a question spontaneously came out of her mouth: she asked about the incident with the silver-haired man. Her mother could not remember it; she could not even remember the man in question, she said. Imogen described him in as much detail as was available; she described the scrawny wife and blundering daughter. Her mother now thought she could dimly picture the girl, and her parents, but of an encounter with the father she professed to have no recollection. Episodes that seem important to a child often have no importance for their parents, she explained. Imogen did not believe that she had forgotten it, and knew that her mother knew that she was not believed. It was almost certain, Imogen thought, that the encounter had been what it had seemed to be: the stupid prank of a man who was drunk. Her mother wished it to be forgotten simply because it had been unseemly, and had involved a loss of temper. There was, however, at least one other possibility, the improbability of which did nothing to diminish its persistence. On the contrary: it was so unlikely that the thought of it was impossible to dismiss, like a malicious and uncorrected rumour. But nothing more was said about it.

•

In another of her letters, Adeline tells Charles that his father misunderstands the function of images. "He mistakes signs for idols," she writes. "We pray through them, not to them," she says. In *Devotion*, Beatrice makes the same comparison; the line was a late addition, made after I had shown Imogen this letter. Catholics are polytheists, John Perceval countered, and their saints are "subaltern gods."

•

For the past couple of days William has been washing cars. You can get away with paying people so little nowadays, he informs me, that a hand-wash is cheaper than a drive-through car wash. He's making more than he's been managing to get on the streets recently, but only a bit more. There are better jobs around, he knows. "Better, but still rubbish." There's a vacancy he knows about, in the kitchen of a care home. He could do the work, but they want someone with experience, and a proper address. "And you've got to be confident, friendly and enthusiastic," he says. "I could do friendly. At a push." He's sleeping on a different sofa this week, in Shaws Way, in the flat of a friend of the friend whose sofa he was using last week. This lad's girlfriend works as a cleaner, and she suggested to William that he should check out the company's website, because they were always looking for new people. "So I checked it out," he tells me, and he starts to laugh. " 'We are seeking enthusiastic and reliable candidates. You will need to be able to demonstrate how you have delivered great customer service and how you meet our excellent standards,' " he recites. "They always want enthusiasm. For fuck's sake—enthusiasm. Has anyone in the entire history of the universe ever been enthusiastic about shoving a mop around? And references, on headed paper. Where am I supposed to get references from?"

I commiserate, and give him money. I could afford to give him more, of course; much more. But I allow myself to accede to arguments opposed to generosity. William would squander it. Thus I excuse myself.

•

In Adeline's letter of September 15th, the one in which she wrote "I love you" for the first time, she informs her beloved that her father wonders if Charles's willingness to abandon the Church of England might not be an expression of his love for Adeline rather than of a newly awakened acceptance of the doctrines of Rome. He holds Charles Perceval's intelligence in the highest esteem, but is of the opinion that knowledge does not "form the mind"—it only "occupies" it. "Apprehension of the unseen is our foundation," her father maintained, as I quoted, while Imogen scanned the letter. The Church of England, he argued, was a church of no doctrine; it was a ministry of the state, and its theology was an accident of history. For his part, Charles's father was for some time of the view that his son had been bewitched by this young woman; how else could one explain his sudden conversion to the "bogus mysteries" and "perfumed ceremonials" of the Roman church?

•

Following Francesca's lead, I come upon the story of Gian Francesco Poggio Bracciolini. Though he served as secretary to no fewer than seven popes, Bracciolini seems to have had a highly developed taste for earthly pleasures. In the spring of 1416 he visited the spa at Baden, and was much taken by what he found there. In a letter from Baden, he wrote of his delight at having discovered a place where men and women bathed together, in a state of undress. A "school of Epicureans" had been established there, he wrote. "I think this must be the place where the first man was created." In January of the following year, at an unspecified German monastery, Gian Francesco Poggio Bracciolini made an even more significant discovery: a manuscript of Lucretius's *De rerum natura*, a work of the highest reputation, but lost for centuries. In a monastery; the only known copy.

•

Full-price visitors to the Sanderson-Perceval Museum today: seventeen. Revenue: £85. Reduction of visitor numbers since the introduction of the £5 charge: sixty percent.

•

First evening in Rome. In the park of the Villa Borghese for the approach of dusk. Air warm and motionless; the pine trees standing in shadow, but their branches full of light; grass turned briefly to the colour of coral. To accompany this scene of urban pastoral, the soft drone of traffic, with now and then the call of a horn. A large and handsome dog, such as a shepherd might have employed. A good-looking young woman and a good-looking young man pause at a statue. The climate, the light, the shadows, the trees, the beautiful lovers, arm in arm—from these elements arises a melancholic well-being, a nostalgia with no object, a mood of all-accepting surrender that is nothing but a mood, but sufficient.

•

In Santa Maria Maggiore. Looking up from my guidebook, I noticed a man who was sitting in a chair against one of the columns on the opposite side of the nave—fiftyish, well dressed. He was leaning forward, with his forearms on his thighs and his hands joined, not praying, it seemed, but in thought. His eyes were open and trained on his hands. Tourists passed close to him, incessantly chattering, but he was not distracted. His demeanour was that of someone in contemplation of a problem to which no solution was apparent; there was a heaviness in his gaze, suggestive of guilt; from time to time, the fingers of his right hand closed on his wedding ring and turned it. An obvious deduction. For five minutes or more he sat there, gazing at his hands. When a woman came out of the confessional box he stood up, straightened his tie, and entered. I continued to read the account of Santa Maria Maggiore. It's an old guidebook; ten pages are devoted to the church. I had time to read all of it before the well-dressed man emerged. Evidently his sins were weighty. At last the curtain was drawn back and he stepped out. He did not look like a man who had been relieved of a burden; he was still unhappy. But he appeared to be a little clearer of mind; there was the possibility of a solution, perhaps. Standing by the chair in which he had been sitting, he adjusted his cuffs, as though in readiness for an important meeting. He walked down the nave to a pew that was free of tourists; there he sat down and bowed his head.

•

The wreckage of the forum. Over there, the remains of a building

77

that was raised five centuries before Christ; and there, another remnant of the ancient city, built a thousand years later. Columns, steps, walls, stones. The chaos is harmonious; the dusk applies its tone to every stone and brick; nothing dominates; the eye moves through the scene unhindered. The inscriptions, incomprehensible to most of us, are now little more than decorative embellishments. Stopping at one of the arches, I admired the beautiful lettering. Imogen had imagined a performance: hundreds of people deployed around the forum, reading aloud from Virgil, Julius Caesar, Pliny, Plutarch, Catullus, Seneca, et cetera; a cacophony of speeches, letters, memoirs, poems, epitaphs. We, the living, would become the intruders in the city of the dead.

•

An unexpected diversion in the church of San Crisogono—the shrine of the Blessed Anna Maria Taigi, died 1837, beatified 1920. Until today, unknown to me. Having renounced the frivolity of her youth, for almost fifty years Anna Maria was favoured with visions of a "kind of sun" that was crowned with thorns, and through the agency of this sun-like object she was able to see into the future and "the secret of hearts." She experienced ecstasies, of course, usually while receiving Holy Communion, but also at less exalted moments of the day, such as when doing the laundry. (She was married and had children. "First and foremost, she was a wife, mother and daughter.") Anna Maria witnessed shipwrecks in distant seas and shared from afar in the sufferings of missionaries in China and Arabia. She observed "the eternal lot of the dead." Furthermore, "the grace of healing was bestowed upon this humble woman." Sometimes she healed the sick with the touch of her hand, but often she effected her cures by means of an image of Our Lady, or a relic, or oil from a votive lamp that she kept burning on the altar at which she worshipped at home. An example: a "lady of the princely house of the Albani" was dying of cancer of the womb until Anna prescribed a drop of oil from her lamp; the afflicted lady applied the oil to her skin, and the following night the tumour disappeared. The Blessed Anna Maria Taigi died on June 9th, 1837, and the procession of pilgrims commenced almost immediately, despite the outbreak of cholera that had struck Rome. We are told that the Lord had promised her that the cholera would not strike before her death. As soon as she expired, "the scourge broke out."

Her body was brought to San Crisogono in 1865, and three years later, when the coffin was opened, the corpse was found to be incorrupt. Now she lies in a glass case, clad in a gown like a nightdress. She wears a white bonnet, fringed with lace, from which some curls of golden hair protrude. Her face—pale and softly wrinkled—has a smile of great serenity. A rosary is entwined in the fingers of her left hand. It is something of a shock to see this pretty old lady, lying in her glass box, as if in deep and untroubled sleep. But the skin of the pretty face is wax, not flesh, as is the skin of the shapely hands. The body of the Blessed Anna Maria Taigi is a doll with an armature of true bones. As I was examining the effigy-corpse, a young couple came up and stood beside me. Said the man, in the tone of someone who has chosen his words carefully before speaking: "That is utterly disgusting." I smiled my agreement.

The floor of the church, on the other hand, is a thing of beauty: thirteenth-century, an intricate patterning of porphyry, serpentine, white marble, grey marble. Whorls and discs and arcs and squares of coloured stone—quasi-Islamic geometries, a work of perfect abstraction, transcending the mortal, the merely figurative. It was created, we would like to believe, by craftsmen who subsumed themselves gladly to their repetitious and difficult work, to the glory of God, the supreme creator. We have no names for the artisans who made this wonderful floor. But one man has left his signature. Having paid for its restoration in 1623, a Borghese cardinal felt compelled to leave his mark: his family's heraldic emblems, a crowned eagle and dragon, in clumsy mosaic.

•

Entering Sant'Agostino, I saw by the entrance a woman on her knees, weeping, at a sculpture of the Madonna. Her hands wrestled each other in front of her face. As I turned away I saw that I had mis-seen: these were tears of gratitude. Before leaving, she pinned a rosette of pink fabric to the wall beside the statue, in the Madonna's line of sight. Many other rosettes, in pink and blue, were already attached there, with a number of padded fabric hearts, also pink and blue. This Madonna is credited with the power to effect miracles in conception and childbirth. Her stone foot has been so eroded by kisses that a silver replacement has had to be fitted. Sant'Agostino was popular with Rome's pre-eminent courtesans, I read; they frequented the church in their bouts of penitence. Fiammetta Michaelis, the beautiful mistress of Cardinal Giacomo Ammannati Piccolomini and of Cesare Borgia, is buried in this church, as are other celebrated women of the same profession. They have no tombstones.

In the Vatican, two days ago, I inspected the votive offerings from the Etruscan temples of Caere. The little terracotta heads, limbs and organs would have been left at the shrines by the thankful and the desperate. They are perhaps of the same family: the Etruscan miniatures; the pink and blue padded hearts of Sant'Agostino; the trephines, saws, files, bone brushes, perforators and calipers acquired by Benjamin Sanderson. In 1905, at University College Hospital, a tumour was removed from the brain of Benjamin Sanderson by Victor Horsley, inventor of Horsley's Wax and co-inventor of the Horsley-Clarke apparatus, of which the museum owns an example. When Benjamin Sanderson amassed his collection, and acquired the property of the Percevals, was the motive not, at least in part, that of the person who makes a votive offering?

•

A long walk along the river, at dusk, to look at Monte Testaccio, the hill of broken pottery. A detour for the pyramid of Cestius, then back to Monte Testaccio, where I had taken note of an enticing restaurant. No table was available at that hour—or not for a solo male tourist. Returning to the river, I passed another trattoria, uncharismatic in appearance, with an exterior of smooth new brick and matching brown awnings. As I hesitated, on the opposite side of the road, three women appeared, moving towards the trattoria with purpose. One of the three, walking a little in front of the other two and apparently the designated leader, turned back to say something, and I heard an American voice. The leader seemed to know what she was doing; she had the air of someone who was confident that her companions would enjoy the experience that she was about to give them. So I followed, at a tactful distance, and was shown to a table adjacent to the women's. The place was no more than one-third full; it appeared that we were the only foreigners present.

The menu was not wholly comprehensible to me. As I was reaching for the phrasebook, the leader looked over, and smiled, and said: "Would you like a recommendation?"

She was in her mid-forties, I guessed, and the youngest of the trio by a decade or so. She was slight and perfectly groomed, with a short crisp bob of dark hair and photoshoot-quality make-up. The capacious white shirt, a man's shirt, suited her very well. A recommendation would be appreciated, I told her.

"Go for the *cacio e pepe*. Spaghetti with pecorino and black pepper. Home-made spaghetti. It's fabulous."

I thanked her. The decision had been made for me. Moving on to the main courses, I opened the phrasebook.

"If you need any help," she said; the tone was of sincere courtesy; she might have been an employee of the restaurant.

"You've been here before?" I asked.

"Many times," she answered. She came to Italy every year; this place was one of her favourites. "Genuine *cucina povera*," she said. The use of the vernacular was not for show; to my ears, the pronunciation was indistinguishable from the native. This area used to be the poor part of town, she explained, as her companions discussed their choices; the city's slaughterhouse was here, and the kitchens of the neighbourhood made use of all the inexpensive stuff—tongue, liver, tail. "*Quinto quarto*, the fifth quarter," they call it.

"Rachel," said one of her companions, touching her arm. "We need some assistance here."

A conference ensued, much of which I overheard. Rachel advised on the food and the wine, and her friends accepted her suggestions, as would customarily be the case, I felt. The forceful clarity of her speech was lawyer-like; the finish and bearing were suggestive of high income. The waiter came, and she spoke to him in Italian, on behalf of the group; he found her attractive too.

Having placed my order, I took the book from my pocket.

One of Rachel's friends whispered to her neighbour. "Sure," said the other. Rachel leaned over to me. "Join us," she suggested. "If you'd like to." I took a seat next to her.

The whisperer introduced herself: April. A robust and genial woman, twice the girth of petite Rachel; she looked around the restaurant as if every inch of it proclaimed delightful authenticity. The third of the group, Audrey, wore a floral dress in which a vehement red was the dominant note; she was silent for much of the time; she seemed at heart unhappy. They were from Long Island, and were on a food tour, beginning in Turin and ending in Naples. Each had a phone, on which the stations of their journey had been recorded. April invited me to scroll through her snaps. The three women smiled at tables in Venice, Bologna, Florence, Perugia; there were many photographs of dishes and jovial kitchen staff. In a Chianti farmhouse they had taken a two-day course in the region's cuisine; April and Audrey were to be seen slicing vegetables at an outdoor table; Rachel stirred a pot, closely supervised by the portly boss; in another shot, the boss, laughing, had an arm around the shoulders of Rachel. At many restaurants, men had felt compelled to take hold of her in this way. April and Audrey went unmolested, it would seem.

"I detect a theme," I commented, displaying a picture of Rachel smiling thinly next to a bearded giant, whose left hand was on her hip, while the right flourished a cleaver.

"Everywhere we go," said April, rolling her eyes. "Even if the wife is there, they've got to have a Rachel hug."

"It's kind of irritating," said Rachel. "There's this assumption that you're going to want to get hugged."

"If you're cute," said Audrey.

"Or small," April mock-lamented. "But I've heard they like them big down south. I'm hoping. I take your point—it's kind of irritating. OK. But once in a while. A hug. A little hug. I could live with that."

April's divorce had been finalised last month, Audrey informed me.

"A younger woman," explained April. "Slimmer, younger, dumber. His secretary."

"Original," Audrey commented sympathetically.

"No, but it's love," sighed April. "It has nothing to do with her tits. Except he paid for them. But it's OK. I've got the house. And my friends. And my freedom. Free at last, Lord. So we're celebrating," sang April, with a chink of glasses. "And what about you?" she asked. "I mean, what brings you here? What's your line of work?"

I told them.

Rachel wanted information. She had many questions, and with every question I became more convinced that she was a lawyer. At one point, I winced at my own voice; it seemed that I was flirting.

"This place must be heaven for you," April ventured. She had to admit, though, that she didn't get much of a buzz out of the museums. "Too much stuff. And too many people like me," she explained. "And it's like you're under pressure to be amazed. That just doesn't work for me. I can't just turn it on." They had been to the Vatican. With hundreds of other people, like a crowd for a ball game, they had trudged down that never-ending corridor, for their appointment with Michelangelo. By the time they reached the chapel, she was not in a receptive frame of mind. "Yes, I can see that this is really something," was April's reaction. "It's totally spectacular. I can see that. I appreciate that it's incredible. But I'm just not feeling it."

Audrey concurred: the Vatican had exhausted her. Audrey was often exhausted, I sensed.

"But I'm not an artistic person," April confessed. The people and the atmosphere were what she loved about Italy. "And the food, of course. I do love my food. I love my food so much. I'll diet when I'm dead." On invitation, she removed a forkload of pasta from Rachel's plate. "Rachel's the cultured one," she confided loudly. "Her partner's an architect. They have a wonderful house." Rachel was instructed to show me some pictures of the wonderful house.

After a little persuasion, Rachel produced her phone. A reel of images was called up. The house was modern, a single-storey building with huge windows and a lot of raw stone on show.

"Show him the kitchen," urged April. "It's amazing," she assured me.

The kitchen could have accommodated half a dozen cars. In the sink and cooker areas it looked like some sort of operating theatre, and the fridge was a hi-tech monolith. At the seventh or eighth photo, a woman who was not Rachel appeared, stirring the contents of a bright copper pan. In another, she raised a glass in the direction of the photographer. She had the look of someone who was at home.

•

Having seen a man apparently beseeching the image of a saint, Imogen remarked that this was perhaps not an irrational action: all the evidence suggests that God is arbitrary in the distribution of his favours, so why should he not, once in a while, accede to a request from a random member of the public? The image was the comely figure of half-naked Saint Sebastian, reclining like an odalisque, his limbs adorned with three golden arrows. This is not Saint Sebastian dead. He survived the arrows, and on his recovery took it upon himself to berate the emperor Diocletian for his persecution of the Christians. Taking exception at being upbraided in this way, and by a person who by rights should have been dead, Diocletian had the young man beaten to death with cudgels, a scene that is rarely depicted. In the chapel on the other side of the church from Sebastian's tomb are displayed one of the near-fatal arrows and a segment of the column to which the archers tied the saint. Also on show are a piece of the Crown of Thorns, a tooth and some bones of Saint Peter, an arm of Saint Andrew, a tooth of Saint Paul, an arm of Saint Roch, relics of Saint Fabian, the skulls of the canonised popes Callixtus I and Stephen I, fragments of the skulls of the martyred saints Nereus, Achilleus, Avenistus, Valentine and Lucina, and a stone indented with what one is asked to believe are the footprints of Christ.

•

In the church dedicated to Saint Stephen, the first Christian martyr: dozens of inspiring deaths, unflinchingly depicted. Saints boiled and skewered, flayed with spiked brushes, roasted, dismembered with blades, stretched, sawn in half (vertically, through the brain), pulled apart by horses, crushed, decapitated, and so forth. Hands and tongues and breasts are chopped off. Every mutilation is suffered with good grace, as if submitting to a haircut. There are no grimaces or howls of pain; screams would only have flattered the pagan butchers. Sacred hardcore.

•

Strange scene on the tram. In front of me, facing each other from opposite seats, sat a large soft woman and her male companion, perhaps forty years of age to her fifty, and considerably smaller, in all dimensions. He appeared to be a man of fretful disposition, raised to a greater anxiety by current circumstances. Their relationship, I felt, was in its early stages; he was on probation; it seemed likely that they had become acquainted online. The man sat straight-backed, knees and feet together, with a small backpack on his lap; a sheet of paper rested on a guidebook, on the backpack—a list of sights, with what appeared to be times for arrival and departure, plus entrance charges. A lot depended on the outcome of this trip, I felt. No sense of pleasure was transmitted by the woman's gaze; her eyes seemed to acknowledge, rather, that the city had not let her down, so far. One intuited that she had often been let down. Several times the man leaned forward to lightly seize her arm. "Sweetheart, sweetheart," he whispered, every time, pointing at a building, then at the corresponding photo in his guidebook; he might add a comment, at which she would concede a small smile, as if he had to be humoured. Again and again: "Sweetheart, sweetheart," urgently, always repeating the endearment. Her smile was always the same. It did not appear that they had argued; there was no annoyance in her demeanour, just an affectionate condescension. He must have said "Sweetheart, sweetheart" ten times in as many minutes. Only once did she speak. He made some reference to their plans for the afternoon, I think, at which she responded, sharply, with something that began with: "We are doing it because…" He acquiesced immediately; sitting straight, looking directly ahead, he did not say another word. At the stop before mine she rose and moved to the door, as if alone; the little lover followed. On the pavement, she took the timetable from him, checked it, then strode off. As they entered a side street she turned, smiled, and brought her lips down onto his mouth, quickly, for a semi-second, as if stamping his face with a mark of her approval.

•

Ludovica Albertoni was sixty years old when she died of a fever, but the Ludovica Albertoni sculpted by Bernini, marvellously, is youthful in her fevered ecstasy. She is beautiful; the stone is etherealised. Her face is Imogen's face, her hands are Imogen's hands, her dying eyes are Imogen's. Which is not to say, as Charles de Brosses quipped, speaking of Bernini's *Saint Teresa*: "If this is divine love, I know it very well."

•

Before the airport, time for one last sight: Sant'Andrea della Valle. In the dome, high above the floor of the church, above the golden walls, a welter of clouds and bodies; amid the celestial turbulence, the Virgin is being taken into the light of Heaven, which is signified by the circle of light in the lantern of the dome. I discern a large figure, clad in red and Virginal blue; a kneeling man, wearing black; a nude male, seated; cherubs; cloaks. Without the use of a lens, the scene is not legible from where we stand. We comprehend the action, but cannot properly see it. A painting created to be imperfectly visible.

•

Tonight, on BBC 1, part one of *June 6, 11pm*. An adulterous businessman is involved in a hit-and-run accident, and "finds himself lost in a labyrinth of lies." The businessman is played by Richard Hatton—the Richard Hatton with whom Imogen was once involved. More of his hair has gone, and his face has lost some definition, but I recognised him immediately from the small photo in the paper. I remember the evening: we came out of the cinema near Hyde Park Corner and he must have registered Imogen's voice, because he turned round with some purpose, as if his name had been called. As soon as he saw her he moved in, arms wide; his delight was immense. Visually he was interesting: sharp facial bones, strong jaw, very tall, lean. Though several years short of forty, he had a receding hairline, but the profile was photogenic in a Mahler-like way. The combination of tweed jacket, white T-shirt and well-worn jeans was artful. "An old friend of mine," was how Imogen introduced him. His quick smirk clarified the meaning for my benefit. He gave me a handshake of potent masculinity. When he suggested a drink, she looked at me, in the hope, I felt, that I could improvise an excuse. He saw the glance, I am sure, but it did not deter him.

He bought the drinks; in return, Imogen asked the opening question: "So how are you?"

Richard was very well; Richard was busy. He was about to start work on a TV three-parter—he was going to be an outwardly respectable man whose mind was a seething pit of violent fantasies.

A "ticking bomb," was the phrase he used. The role had entailed a great deal of research. Some of the things he'd been reading had really messed with his head; he told us a horrible story about an outwardly respectable rapist-murderer.

"And what about you?" he finally asked Imogen, after ten minutes. The eye contact was powerful; his self-belief was impregnable.

He did not enquire as to how we had met, or what I might do for a living. While Imogen was talking, he glanced at me a few times, thinking, obviously: "What does she see in this one?" A reasonable question; I have often asked it myself. But what troubled me more, at that moment, was that Imogen had been in a relationship with this tedious and self-absorbed character.

When we parted he kissed her and said that he would call, which he did, the following week, to suggest, with little preamble, that they might meet one afternoon and go to bed. One of the things that Richard most admired about himself was that he always went straight to the heart of the matter. Within two days of meeting Imogen, she told me, he had informed her that they were attracted to each other; the statement was made plainly, as if he were merely observing that her hair was the same colour as his. And she was indeed attracted to him. He was an intelligent actor, and his bluntness was disarming. Before long, however, it became apparent that the intelligence of Richard Hatton was a somewhat cosmetic quality. He was intrigued by the paradoxical phenomenon of himself: it was strange that he had become an actor despite the fact that he was, essentially, a "deeply introspective" person. Some people, he knew, disliked him for what they took to be his tactlessness. Honesty was not the easy way to make friends, he knew. He submitted himself to regular sessions of self-inquest, he told Imogen, making it sound like a regimen of quasi-monastic spiritual discipline. But in fact, she said, Richard studied himself "as if reading the Sunday papers"; he skim-read himself, to divert himself, and perhaps learn a little. And by the following day he had forgotten everything he'd read the day before.

Imogen was not the same person now as the one she had been when Richard Hatton had been her lover. The relationship had been brief, and was no sooner commenced than regretted. "But he is very good at his job," she said. I watched part one of *June 6, 11pm*. Richard Hatton was not very good, I thought. Too much staring into the carpet as if into the pit of damnation; too much stroking of the brow. Too much acting.

•

Lucretius on love: "This is the only case in which the more we have, the more the heart burns with terrible desire. Food and drink, when taken into the body, enter their appointed places easily, and thus our desire for water and bread is satisfied. But from a lovely face or blooming complexion nothing comes into the body for us to enjoy other than images, flimsy images, and vain hopes." *De rerum natura*, Book Four. Saint Jerome maintains that Lucretius became insane after taking a love potion, and composed *De rerum natura* in his lucid intervals, prior to committing suicide.

April

GRAND PARADE: William on a bench, with his head resting against the stone balustrade. At first I thought he was asleep, but then a group of students walked past him and he sat up to speak to them. One of the students, acting as spokesman, turned a pocket of his jeans inside out. William smiled and put a finger to an eyebrow by way of salute. He wiped his face with his palms and leaned back.

Only when I sat down did he open his eyes. "Well, hello there," he said, in an approximately American accent. A clot of ketchup hung in his beard. He closed his eyes; he was worn out, not drunk. And he had lost a tooth. "You're looking well," he said, and laughed.

At this point, although he was in a bad way, I had no intention other than to give him a modest amount of cash, as usual.

"What happened to the tooth?" I asked.

"Came loose, pulled it out," he answered. "Saved myself a fortune."

People were walking past us all the time. "It's good to see you," he said, "but I'll have ask you to move on in a minute. No offence. But if they see me talking to you, they think I've got some sort of social life. Got to be on your own to maximise the sympathy. Or have a nice dog." He turned to look at me. "Maybe I should invest in something fluffy. What do you think?"

I asked him where he'd been sleeping. He'd been in another

squat, he told me, but a developer had sent some heavies round, and now the place was boarded up. "So where will you be tonight?" I asked.

"Give us a hundred quid and I'll try the Holiday Inn," he answered.

As though it were of no consequence, William said he was thinking of doing something that would get him put away. "Just for a few months," he said. "Decent accommodation, edible food. Companions not always top-drawer, but beggars can't be choosers, can they?" It would be easy enough to do, he assured me. "Walk into a corner shop, put a hand in the till. Piss on a policeman. The possibilities are endless."

I am content with my life. I have no need of company. But I found myself saying to William, as if speaking a line that had been prompted by another voice: "You could stay at my place."

Slowly he turned his head to look at me; the look was almost a glare. "Yeah, right," he said.

"There's a spare room."

He studied my face, as if reading a text that was written in a foreign language, of which a few words seemed similar to English. "You serious?" he said.

I assured him that I was.

"Really?"

"Really."

"I don't get it."

"There's nothing to get."

William considered the pavement for some time. "A bed for the night—that's a tempting offer," he said.

Detached from myself, hearing something like "*In this scene, I play a charitable man,*" I said to him: "A bed for as long as you need."

"I can't afford it," he said.

"You don't have to pay," I told him.

"I mean, I can't afford anything. Rent, food—"

I repeated: "You don't have to pay." I would give him a room for as long as it took him to find work and a place to live.

"That could take some time," he pointed out.

"I appreciate that," I said.

William scrutinised my face. "You can trust me," he said. "I'm a straight bloke."

We shook hands, and then we walked across town together, discussing the house rules.

•

I was destined to my profession, Emma has often said. My brain is like a museum; images occupy my memory as exhibits occupy their display cases, she thinks. But ten minutes ago, summoned by no stimulus of which I was aware, a scene re-presented itself to me: the Bristol shot tower, its concrete bleached in the sunlight, against a blackening sky. Imogen smiled as I explained the shot-making process. I cannot see her face, though I know that she smiled, and made a joke about the deluge of information. Rain was soon falling, heavily. And this, it seems, is all that remains of that afternoon; everything else is lost. Perhaps at some point in the future another fragment of that day will appear, of its own accord, and I will not recognise the source.

•

Portions of fabric that had been in contact with the remains of saints were deemed to have absorbed something of their holy aura. These scraps, known as *brandea*, were venerated as relics. Pilgrims could manufacture their own *brandea* by rubbing a piece of cloth against a saint's tomb, or by various other modes of transfer. A flask of holy water, filled at a shrine, was credited with healing properties. Likewise dust brought back from the Holy Land. Saint Aidan, I have read, took his least breath while leaning against a buttress in the church of Lindisfarne. Splinters from this buttress, by virtue of its contact with the saint, became healing relics, as did scraps from the stake on which the severed head of the Christian king Oswald had been displayed. These splinters could be dipped in water to make a medicine; a sort of sanctified tea.

(A connection here: the piece of clothing worn by the loved one, and kept by the lover for many years, in her absence; not for the sake of any specific memory, but because something of her presence inheres in it. This scarf, for instance. Its colour, blue-grey, is one of Imogen's attributes.)

•

There was a colour that Imogen had particularly liked since she was a small girl, she told me; or rather, a particular embodiment of that colour—a deep reddish brown, with a certain kind of metallic lustre. Whenever she saw it, which happened infrequently, she had a moment of happiness, no matter what her mood before that instant. She recalled asking herself one day, having just seen a car of that colour: "Why does it make me happy?" Was it connected with some incident that she had forgotten? Over and over again she asked herself: "Why does that colour make me so happy?" And then, she said, she had found herself in a "labyrinth." She could remember this moment precisely: she was fourteen, it was spring, and she was looking out of the dorm window. She had suddenly realised that she was repeating the question mechanically; her mind was functioning "like a questioning machine." Then it occurred to her that her mind was not like a questioning machine—a questioning machine was in fact what it was. The question about the colour and her happiness had been caused by a spark inside her head. And this realisation— that the question was a product of that spark, and that the spark had nothing to do with herself—was in turn the product of a spark, as was this thought, and this one, and so on and so on and so on. "Imogen sometimes seems to be less than wholeheartedly among us," her headmistress once remarked.

•

When she was a child, she had wondered what it meant to "make love"; as a young woman, she had come to realise that people very often "make love," in the sense that love, or what people take to be love, is frequently nothing more than a by-product of sex. And we do not achieve spiritual union through the act of love, even when the other person is someone with whom we are in love, she understood. On the contrary: at the supposed moment of fusion each individual is more alone than ever. I think of what I saw at the *maison de maître*: the clashing bodies; everyone engulfed in their own pleasure.

•

For a long time Marguerite has wanted to visit New York with her husband, and now at last, after several postponements, they are in that thrilling city together. It is everything that they expected it to be. They have seen the sights that they had wanted so much to see—the Met, Ellis Island, Central Park, the Whitney, et cetera, et cetera. They have eaten at some excellent restaurants. The weather—it is early autumn—could not be better. It is unlikely that they will return to New York; a year from now, Marguerite may no longer be alive. So they must make the most of every hour. But the demand is self-defeating: this experience is too burdened with significance to be enjoyable. They stand at the window of their hotel bedroom, looking towards the river. Philippe stands behind Marguerite, with his arms around her; she places her hands on his; they love each other, still, after so many years. The situation is ridiculous, she remarks. They must not allow themselves to be tyrannised by circumstance. New York is New York, after all. "And besides, everyone is always dying," says Marguerite. Her husband kisses her hair. Below them, the traffic flows down the avenue; the red lights flow like bright lava. When Philippe goes to the bathroom to take a shower, Marguerite stays at the window. With a finger she traces the scar, which is Imogen's.

•

At Samantha's school, a colleague had been sacked after the discovery of his affair with a pupil. Everybody had been surprised, Samantha told me, because the teacher in question was an unassuming and rather buttoned-up sort of character. On the other hand, he was in his late forties, and divorced, and the girl was attractive.

"Speaking as a buttoned-up sort—," I began.

"That's not what I meant," Samantha interrupted. "And Imogen was not seventeen."

"She was not," I conceded.

She gave me a long look, then asked: "So how is she?"

For a moment I thought I would lie. But I answered: "Not good. Not good at all." I told her what was happening.

Samantha cried, and put a hand on mine. For an hour we talked; for that hour we were almost remarried.

•

Imogen's mother phoned on the Thursday night, to tell me that Saturday would be the end. When I arrived, Imogen was asleep; the rain on the glass was even louder than her breathing. Her face was the colour of bone; her head lay on the thin web of her hair. She stirred, and her mother whispered: "David is here." With a movement only of her eyes, she looked at me. A smile formed slowly. "Hello," she said. She turned a hand towards me; it felt as fragile as a fern. Clenching her eyelids, she said: "This is horrible, isn't it?" The rain became quieter, but did not stop. She slept again. The dawn light began to seep into the room, insipid and ghastly. When Imogen awoke, she moved her head, slightly, to see the lightening sky. She spoke my name; it came out of her mouth as a sigh. She looked at me, through the death-mask of her face. It was a long look, and strong, as if, after great hardships, the end of an expedition had been achieved, and we were seeing together the fabled ruins; the effort had cost us everything, but we had succeeded, just the two of us. "I love you," I said. "Versa," she answered. I held her hand. Her eyelids convulsed and her mouth opened, in astonishment at the pain. Then she said, quietly: "That's enough. Close the door." Her mother and Jonathan were at the window, looking out, side by side. At that phrase—"Close the door"—her mother turned, as if this were the signal to commence the procedure. She moved to my side and put her hand under my elbow to remove me, with the greatest gentleness. She walked to the door with me, and stepped out. Facing me, she clenched her jaw to stop the trembling, and drew a breath, and embraced me, quickly, sharply. She said nothing, and went back to her daughter. She closed the door softly, as one would close the door of a sleeping infant's room.

•

Five cigarettes a day was Imogen's mother's allowance to herself; on the basis of something she alleged that Christiaan Barnard had once said, she had decided that this number was well below the threshold of safety. "I have a very strong heart. And it's my only vice," she informed me, after the meal. Dissuasion was futile. Having recovered once from cancer, she now regarded herself as indestructible, Imogen said. We were in bed, in the room that had been prepared for me; Imogen's male companions were always given a room at three or four doors' remove from hers. Her mother had received me graciously, but I had no matrimonial potential: I was her daughter's latest whim—not uninteresting, but certainly of no durability. When Imogen was talking about *Devotion* her mother's gaze, at times, suggested that what she was hearing was an account of an extended holiday, rather than of her daughter's professional life; she was waiting for her real life to begin.

•

Once, I now remember, I was with Samantha and Val when a young man approached us. The day was mild, but he was wearing a heavy jacket and a pullover; the jacket, once pale blue, was black with grease, as were his jeans; his hair was a rank fur. He cupped a hand and held it towards Val and Samantha; as I recall, he said nothing; he had given his speech to half a dozen tables, and it had made no difference. Val dug into her bag and fiddled in it. She dropped the coin into the grimy hand like a pill into water. I was no better: my donation was larger but not large, and I passed it over with a cringing smile of compassion, eyes averted.

"Poor boy," said Val, when he had gone. We issued a collective sigh. "But what can you do?" she asked the air. We agreed that there was nothing to be done.

He crossed to the other side of the road, where a young woman was waiting for him. Lard-coloured flesh showed through holes in her jeans; her dreadlocks were like lengths of rusted wire wool. She was tiny, and was shivering.

This must have some bearing on the offer to William.

•

It is utter insanity to take in this person as a lodger, Emma tells me. I know virtually nothing about him. "He could be a thief. He could be dangerous. For all you know, he has mental problems." Most of the people who are sleeping rough have serious mental problems, she states. I don't think William is dangerous, I answer; but just to be on the safe side I could ask him. "He's upstairs at the moment," I tell her. "Probably helping himself to my socks." Emma snaps: "Don't try to be funny, David." She instructs me to tell him that he can stay for a specific period of time and not a day longer; I should draw up a contract, right away. Not once does she use William's name. "For an intelligent man, you can really be an idiot," she concludes.

•

While helping with the preparation for the meal—if there's one thing he's learned over the past few years, he says, it's how to peel vegetables quickly—William asks if any of Imogen's films are in my collection. I take out *Les tendres plaintes* and *Mon amie Claire*, the only ones I could watch in company. We manage ten minutes of *Les tendres plaintes*—"This guy is a total arsehole," William pronounces —before fast-forwarding to the scenes in which Imogen appears. There's too much talking, and the sound of the harpsichord is a horrible noise. "What's the point of playing it?" William wonders; it's like using candles instead of lightbulbs, or writing with a goose quill instead of using a laptop. With *Mon amie Claire* he has a little more patience, principally because there is considerably more of Imogen in it. He watches her episodes closely, as if learning from a classroom video. "She's brilliant," he tells me. Once Claire has left the film, we abandon it.

THE GREAT CONCERT OF THE NIGHT

•

On first viewing, *Mon amie Claire* did not greatly engage me either, and I have watched the film from beginning to end only once since then. But I have watched one scene many times. Danielle has taken Claire to the best restaurant in town. The decor is counterfeit Belle Époque, with huge mirrors and lots of gilt-effect mouldings and mahogany-coloured woodwork and scarlet plush. The menus are bound in thick leather, like precious manuscripts. Before sitting down, Claire notices the threadbare fabric of her seat. Almost fifteen years have passed since Danielle spent a summer month with Claire's family in London. For Danielle, the reunion is going well, though life has dealt her friend a considerably better hand than the one she herself has been given to play with. By the time the two women reach the restaurant, we know about the success of Claire's business. We have seen pictures of the photogenic kids and husband, and the enviable house. Danielle has been less lucky. She believes that life is chiefly a matter of luck; we understand that Claire has already diagnosed this as one of Danielle's limitations. Promotions that should have been Danielle's have been awarded to less deserving candidates. Her daughters are uncontrollable. Her health is less than excellent. (We have observed that the exercise machine in the garage has done little service.) Her husband, Michel, a decent man, has become dull. In the bedroom nothing much is happening any more, as Danielle confided within an hour of her friend's arrival. But Michel is a reliable man, she says, unaware, of course, that Michel has taken an immediate fancy to the svelte and successful Claire. While studying the menu, Danielle relates Michel's latest setback at the workplace. The waiter arrives; at Danielle's request, he explicates some of the menu's more ambitious dishes. While Danielle interrogates him about the wines, Claire looks out of the window. Night is falling on the charmless street. A woman walks slowly past, with a fat dog on a sequinned lead. Claire's reflection is sketched lightly on the glass. This is the moment—the ten seconds in which Claire gazes out of the window of this mediocre restaurant. We see that she is bored, and wishes that she were elsewhere; we see her guilt at finding Danielle so tiresome; we see compassion for hopeless Danielle, and an instant of self-questioning; and we know that she will not abandon her erstwhile friend—she will do something for her; she will rescue her from her grubby little husband. "Let's have the Savennières," Claire interrupts, having—we realise—heard every word of Danielle's conversation with the waiter, despite seeming to be lost in thought.

•

Life is always preferable to the only alternative that's on offer, Imogen's brother stated, and his wife concurred. Helen told Imogen about something she had read, somewhere. A journalist had interviewed people who had jumped from a height, intending to die, but had survived the fall. They all said the same thing: that at the moment of letting go they had known that they had made a terrible mistake, a mistake that they would never be able to correct. Death had seemed so enticing, but now they were overwhelmed by the horror of it; for those few seconds, they were in hell; life was everything, they suddenly understood. This was true of every one of them. They were all so grateful to have survived, Helen told her sister-in-law, taking hold of her hand. But the situation was not quite the same as that of Helen's reprieved suicides, Imogen explained: she was already on the brink of the pit. It was more than possible that her experience might prove to be the opposite: the last few minutes might be the most wonderful of her life.

•

"I don't lie," Imogen once said to me, in the course of an argument in which Vermeiren featured. Not as a boast but as a statement of a principle, just as one might say: "I don't eat meat."

•

Our last visit to the Louvre—a cool day; the air lightly grained with mist. Finding it cold, Imogen wore the black coat and the red cashmere scarf that I had bought for her. She was tired before we arrived; before deciding to go in, we sat in the gardens for a while. Never again would we do this, we knew. We did not go far into the museum. I remember looking at a bronze mirror, Etruscan; the Judgement of Paris was incised on the back of it. The mirror was barely more reflective than the floor. Even when new, it could have given only a shadowy image, one would think; it must have removed all colour from what was shown to it. In the world from which the bronze mirror had come, most people would have had no clear image of themselves, as Imogen remarked. No wonder Narcissus had been so bewitched by what he saw in the pool. A world without reflections would suit her quite well, Imogen said. Some days, when confronting her face in the mirror, she had the feeling that she was looking out

through a stranger's skin, or through a face on which a make-up
artist had worked for hours.

•

On last night's shift, William reports, he was paired with a Polish
girl called Magda. The first sight of her gave him a bit of a turn,
because for a moment he thought she was someone he had seen
before, when he was in London, working as a labourer. Almost every
morning, for the best part of a month, he would see this woman as
he walked to the building site. She used to sit in the window of a café
that he went past. She was well dressed and slim and nice-looking:
trouser suit; long straight dark hair, pale skin, straight nose, small
mouth. But what had really struck him about her was the way she
often stared into her coffee, as if it were a crystal ball. He sensed her
character. "Sad but hopeful, and clever," he says. He would have liked
to talk to her, but that was never going to happen. Once, however,
he passed her in the street at the end of the day, and they exchanged
a glance, a glance that was "like a message." It amazed him that she
had been aware of his existence, though on a few occasions she had
been looking out onto the street when he walked by. Then one
morning, in the middle of the week, she was not there; the next day,
too, she was absent; she never came back. But he had come to think
that he would see her again one day, or that the glance had been
telling him that something significant would soon happen, something in which she would be in some way involved. And when
he first saw the pale and slim and black-haired Magda, a young
woman who might have been the London woman's sister or cousin,

THE GREAT CONCERT OF THE NIGHT

he wondered, for an instant, if this meeting might be a fulfilment of that meaningful glance. Was this the destined moment? The idea was dead within a few minutes. Magda had no interest in any conversation. Making the toilets as clean as new dinner plates was all she was interested in—that, and getting a better-paid lousy job as soon as possible.

•

In their configurations, certain scenes in *Chambre 32* are the same as some scenes at the *maison de maître*: the man and woman, coupling; the witness. The woman, Roberte, is Imogen; she returns the gaze of the witness, her husband, who loves her, and whom she loves; the gaze has duration, and complexity. The gaze that Roberte directs at the camera, her husband's proxy, in the bedroom of the Hôtel Saint-Étienne, is similar to the gaze that I received at the *maison de maître*. But it is not the same. Roberte is a huntress, a destroyer. At the climax she is still Roberte, the triumphant Roberte.

•

Roberte on the bed, naked, supine, looks to the side; the point of view changes—suddenly the camera is looking her in the eye. From the quality of her gaze—complicit, affectionate—we understand that its recipient is Pierre, her husband, the owner of the Hôtel Saint-Étienne. Auguste, the favoured guest, enters the frame; also naked, erect, he kneels beside Roberte. He places a hand on a breast; the hand slides over her skin, and as it descends, the viewpoint moves again; we see Roberte's face in profile, smiling. Her mouth opens, in a silent gasp; she closes her eyes. When her eyes open again, with a surge of excitement, we see what she sees: the small aperture below the painting; the eye. Pierre observes the splendid Roberte in abandonment; perhaps his gratification is enhanced by the pretence that his spying is unobserved, and that a betrayal is happening. The lens moves in on the body of Roberte; its movement signifies arousal. I can watch this scene now, but it is distressing, even if the anguish is less than I felt when the film was new. It has been occluded by a greater anguish. But when I watch *Chambre 32* the lesser pain is reawakened; again our relationship fails.

•

Nothing had inspired her to become an actress, Imogen told me, in the garden of the museum. She was not even sure that it would be true to say that she had ever decided to become an actress—it was something that had happened. "My mother will tell you that I've always liked showing off," she said. "But it's nothing to do with showing off," she assured me. "I enjoy being different people—that's what it is. 'You must change your life.' You know that line? Well, I change my life on a regular basis. It's exciting," she said, with a shrug.

•

Thirty-one visitors today.

•

La Châtelaine: the moment when, in ecstasy, Imogen turns her eyes

107

to the camera, and the candlelight gleams in her tears. Ovid: *Adspicies oculos tremulo fulgore micantes / Ut sol saepe refulgent aqua*—her eyes glittering with tremulous brightness, as the sun glitters on clear water.

I can find few reviews of *La Châtelaine* in English. One critic, reporting from a film festival, professes to have enjoyed the film, though he found it self-conscious, and not quite the serious work of art that the director evidently believes he has created. Another writes that some people were claiming that they found the sex scenes boring. "All I can say is that nobody was looking bored at the time," he writes.

•

On occasion, in good weather, William slept in a cemetery, he tells me. His favoured berth was a slab that had cracked along its length, down the centre, and had subsided a little, to form a sort of hammock. A mat of ivy covered the marble, making a mattress. Below the stone lay the remains of someone called Amos Deering, born 1823, died 1884, and his wife, Emily, "who rejoined him" in 1897. It was comfortable, William assured me, and he liked the names of the occupants, though not as much as the names of the nearby Cornelius Febland and his wife Tabitha, née Villin. The names created a nice atmosphere, says William; he felt comforted by them; he would recite them like poems. Cemeteries are special places, he says, because of the energy that flows through them. "It's all about lines of force," he explains. Burial sites, churches, ancient settlements and monuments—all sorts of significant localities lie along these lines of force. If one were to take a map and draw lines between them, the pattern would be obvious. William has seen such a map, and it was amazing. It was like an X-ray of the land. People have it the wrong way round: they think graveyards grew alongside churches, but in fact the dead were there first. Before there were any churches, villages grew where the lines of force intersect, and that's where the dead were buried. Obviously the villagers weren't aware that this was what they were doing. It's the same with magnetic fields: we can't feel them, but they have an effect. Stonehenge, Glastonbury, the pyramids—they are all connected. The ancient structures are like transformers for the energies of the earth, says William, spreading his arms as if to receive the rays. In the cemetery where he used to sleep there were some graves that had an obelisk instead of a cross. "Those people knew what they were doing," he informs me. By raising an obelisk, the creators of those memorials were aligning themselves with the pharaohs, not with Jesus. The Egyptians knew all about energy, says William.

•

Shortly after the death of his mother, Arthur Perceval was entrusted to the care of one of his father's cousins, in distant Durham. He was three years old, and he would never again see the house in which he had been born. It is possible that he never saw his father again either. We can only speculate as to why Charles Perceval might have thought that a conclusive severance would have been in the best interests of the boy. In Charles Perceval's journal there is not a single reference to his son. The archive has no letters in which Arthur is mentioned, other than the one dated November 9th, 1882, sent from Durham, informing his father of Arthur's death. Having trained as an architect, at the age of twenty-four Arthur Perceval had gone to Rome to study; ten months later, in Ravenna, he shot himself, in circumstances of which we know nothing. Perhaps in killing himself he was also killing the father who had rejected him, Imogen proposed; the father who was to outlive him by almost thirty years.

•

On hearing more about John Perceval, the father of Charles, Marcus Colhoun gave some thought to the idea of introducing the figure of Julius Preston's father, or rather the memory of him, and of his work. It was remarkable that, in an age in which puerperal fever was a common cause of death immediately after childbirth, no woman under the care of John Perceval ever died of it. Indeed, it was remarkable that John Perceval should have made this branch of medicine a speciality: obstetricians were not generally held in high regard at that time, and the Royal College of Physicians regarded the delivering of babies as ungentlemanly work. The secret of Perceval's success was simple, I explained to Marcus: he was in the habit of washing his hands before and after contact with his patients. I told him about the eminent surgeon of that period who worked in a gown that was brown with the blood of his previous operations. And just one year after Queen Victoria had been anaesthetised with chloroform during the birth of Prince Leopold, John Perceval was using chloroform to reduce the ordeal of labour. The pathos of the death of Beatrice would be heightened were the father of her husband to be given the attributes of John Perceval. A terrible irony that she should die in childbirth—but a cheap irony, Marcus Colhoun decided.

•

"You should tell my mother about the hand-washing," said Imogen. "A hygiene-based horror story would be right up her street." It was not the pain that had made childbirth so traumatic for her. The pain was not inconsiderable, especially with Imogen. ("Difficult right from the start, she told me," Imogen said.) But she could cope with the pain. Pain was in the mind and could be disregarded, or almost. But she was revolted by the mess of childbirth. It offended her, the filth that her body expelled along with the baby. Imogen wondered sometimes if her mother regarded all sexual contact as an unhygienic mêlée of bacteria and viruses.

•

In London, on the streets, William came to know someone who had been in prison for fifteen years, for killing a man in a fight. He had become a model prisoner, trusted by prisoners and staff alike. He was a "listener"—someone in whom the others could confide. The person he had killed had once been involved with his sister; he was a pimp; he'd done time for GBH as well. Within a few months the relationship was over. The young woman came home to her brother one evening with a black eye and a cracked tooth. There was a confrontation outside a club, a brawl that was started by the pimp, as the court accepted; it ended with the stabbing. The killer pleaded guilty; he was contrite. But, he told William, he really couldn't say that he was sorry that this person was dead. Although he had expressed remorse, remorse was not what he felt. He accepted that he had done wrong in putting an end to this individual, however murderable his victim might have been. For society to function, punishment was necessary; this he understood. So when he had said that he was sorry, what he had meant was that he accepted his sentence. And the next time he found himself in a situation that was getting out of hand, he wouldn't pull out a knife, probably. But that was not because his moral compass had been realigned during his time in prison—it was because he had left his former self behind, which was not quite the same thing. Having been removed from the streets for a few years, he had become somebody who was unlikely ever to do what the earlier version of himself had done.

And William wants me to know that already, having had a roof over his head for less than a month, he has come to feel that he has moved on, as a person. In the past couple of years he'd been a bit close to the edge at times, he admits. For instance, in London one night he'd just snapped when someone in a big car had almost knocked him down at a crossing, when the lights were on red; the driver said something to him, something "uncomplimentary to the homeless community," so William took a coin out of his pocket and scraped it across the doors, then ran like hell. "I don't think I'd do that now," he says, as if assuring his probation officer that he is making good progress. "Can't say I regret doing it, though," he adds.

•

For a short-term fix in times of glumness, Val suggests that one might consider acting. Pending a more enduring solution, we can brighten the soul a little by addressing the symptoms of our woe rather than the cause. "Make yourself smile for thirty seconds," the life-coach urges, "and just see what happens to your mood." By means of this simple ruse, obstacles can be surmounted, positivity achieved. A virtuous circle is established. Give, and you will receive. Smile, and the whole world smiles with you. "Sometimes your joy is the source of your smile, but sometimes your smile can be the source of your joy." Sound science underpins her advice, Val informs us, imparting news from the neurological frontline. When one smiles, benign chemicals are released: pain-inhibiting endorphins; dopamine, so important to the brain's pleasure and reward centres; and, best of all, serotonin, the depression-lifting neurotransmitter. Any smile can do the trick, says Val, but for maximum efficacy she recommends going the whole hog, with the Duchenne smile. Taking its name from the physician Guillaume Duchenne, this is the *ne plus ultra* of smiles, making use not merely of the zygomaticus major, the muscle that bends the mouth upwards, but also the orbicularis oculi, by which the eyelids are operated. The truly joyful smile is dependent upon the orbicularis oculi. It used to be thought, Val tells us, that whereas the zygomaticus major is subject to voluntary control, the orbicularis oculi is not. This is why fake smiles are "mouth-only smiles." However, researchers have demonstrated that people can, after all, volitionally activate the orbicularis oculi and thereby "put on a Duchenne smile." We are directed to an academic paper, titled "The Deliberate Duchenne Smile: Individual Differences in Expressive Control." It is not clear to me why this research was thought to be necessary. Cinema has hundreds of examples of perfectly simulated Duchenne smiles. At 27:15 in *Devotion*, for example, or 1:09:19 in *Les tendres plaintes*.

•

For a year or more, when she was at school, Imogen would daydream about her island. The image of her island, she told me, came from a book in the school library, in which aerial photographs of the Indian Ocean showed little islands crammed with lush vegetation, set within water as blue as copper sulphate. She imagined living alone in such a place. The trees would bear fruit perpetually; fish would teem in every pool and river; the sun would shine from dawn to dusk. With nobody to speak to, she would soon lose all sense of herself as Imogen. If there were nobody to look at her, she would lose all sense of herself as anybody. No boundary would separate her from the world. She would live in nature as happily as a monkey, she told herself.

•

William asleep when I get home. At seven he appears. While I cook, he makes sandwiches for himself. Thus a semblance of independence is maintained. He buys his own food and makes a cash contribution, but the money he is paid by the agency would support nobody. Some nights, his labour is not needed; tonight, however, he is required to present himself. He likes to work at night. He enjoys the peacefulness of it, being alone in a brightly lit office, with the city in darkness outside. Sometimes, it's like being at sea. Even when it's boring, it's better than most of the jobs he has done over the past few years. For one thing, it's not doing damage to his health.

He's reading a book about the search for alien life, a subject that has been on his mind a lot recently, he tells me. In the small hours of the morning, when he stops for a quick bite, he gazes out at the sky and wonders which of the two possibilities is true: we are alone in the universe; or we are not. He is inclined to think that the conditions that were necessary for life to have developed on earth are so improbable that it's likelier that we're alone. Even if this is not the case, he has learned from his book, we might as well be alone, because there's virtually no chance that we could ever detect any life that might exist in the far depths of space. There's virtually no chance that any living beings, in any star system, could ever make contact with any other. Scientists have argued that all civilisations have a limited time span of a few thousand years. Ours will be destroyed by climate change; others would expire for other reasons. If that's the case, there's no way that contact could be made across distances of millions and millions of light years. Worlds would bloom and die in total isolation. "And with that cheery thought," says William, "I'll leave you to your evening."

He goes back upstairs with a plate of sandwiches and a beer. I read in the living room; he reads in the room above. At eleven-thirty he goes to work. In the morning, as I am leaving, we might meet on the street, but sometimes he stops at a café or takes a walk through the park before returning to his room. The walk helps him to sleep. Most days, it is evident that he has not even opened the living-room door during my absence. He is drinking much less than he used to, as he had promised he would. William is the ideal tenant. But his life is in suspension. And I am his gaoler, albeit a well-meaning one. My charity is oppressive.

May

BENOÎT HAD WANTED to be present on the set of *La Châtelaine*; he was uneasy about what the film seemed to be becoming. Imogen conveyed the request to Antoine Vermeiren. "The idea is ridiculous," he said. "Would Benoît allow me to look over his shoulder while he's doing his work? No. It would absurd." But in Paris, talking about *Chambre 32*, Imogen said to me, as we were walking over the Pont de la Tournelle: "I would have been happy for you to be there." It became a long walk. "This could be the end of a beautiful friendship," she said, before telling me about the *maison de maître*. At the conclusion she kissed me. It was not a kiss to restart an affair; it was more a kiss of alliance.

•

"It's not about happiness," she said, of the *maison de maître*. "I don't go there to be made happy."

•

Last night, a documentary about life in Cornwall's fishing ports: decline, hardship, resilience; resentment of fishing quotas and bureaucrats and second-homers; all as one would expect. One surprising episode: a young man from the West Midlands, whose sole experience of life at sea has been a return trip on the Dover to Calais ferry, is taken on as a crew member, for a two-day trial. He discloses to the camera that he's really a singer-songwriter, but hasn't been getting the breaks. "That's how desperate we are," says the captain. The boat is barely out of sight of the harbour when the new recruit begins to turn green. By the time the nets are being dropped, he's curled up on his mattress with a bucket. Having half-recovered, he takes his place at the gutting trough. The slurry of fish guts provokes another fit of vomiting. "He's absolutely bloody useless," William heckles. "I'd give it more of a go than that twazzock." At a gorgeous shot of the sunrise—rich orange light seeping over the sea, under a lid of graphite-coloured cloud—William expresses an interest. In the course of the next hour, the notion gathers power. They don't need a CV or qualifications, William points out. He is stagnating here; the sea and the wild terrain of Cornwall could be exactly what he needs. It stands to reason, given the shape of the country, that there should be a concentration of energies in the southwestern peninsula. The stone circles of Dartmoor are proof. We talk about the places in Cornwall that I saw with Imogen. By midnight, a decision has been reached. As if disinterested, I urge caution.

•

Visitors to the Sanderson-Perceval today: nineteen. But two weddings next month, and a magazine photoshoot. All possibilities for revenue generation are being explored.

•

"The sun is the eye of god," says the Count to Nicolas Guignon, who will be dead, at the hands of the Count's myrmidon, before the sun rises. Midnight has already struck. The concert of the night is in its third hour. Torches burn along the length of the path on which the Count and the young man are walking. "The judging eye of the sun cannot see us," says the Count, smiling pleasantly. Guignon imagines that the Count is alluding to his relationship with Agamédé, who is known to be the Count's mistress. We hear a Boccherini quintet. The musicians are playing in the belvedere that now comes into sight. It is a large and elegant structure, with ten white columns supporting a tent-like roof of patinated copper. Black muslin has been hung between the columns. The candles that have been set around the music stands are visible from outside as patches of dark gold on the black fabric. We see Agamédé now: she stands beside a stone cornucopia, alone, listening to the music. She closes her eyes at the sweetness of it. The light of a flame gilds her face and throat; it shimmers on the grey-blue satin of her dress. Agamédé is as lovely as a woman in a Watteau *fête galante*. In the shadows of a bower, Guignon admires her as she listens. Her beautiful solitude fascinates him.

•

The Count, seated with Agamédé in an alcove of the garden, within sight of the belvedere, closes his eyes and takes her hand, overcome by the voluptuous melancholy of the music. He envies these servants of Euterpe, he tells her, taking her hand. He has composed some simple pieces, but his talent is negligible. "I would give everything to be another Couperin," he tells her. "Everything," he sighs. His hand trembles. He has just recovered from a fever, from which, at its zenith, it had seemed that he might die. At times he had felt that his body was losing its substance in the furnace of the illness, he tells Agaméde. The boundary between his body and the material of his surroundings had been dissolved; his flesh had become indistinguishable from the air that flowed into and out of his body—indeed, from everything. He hopes that the hour of his death will be even more exquisitely pleasurable. "The highest bliss at the ultimate moment. Our final reward," he murmurs. "Until then, we have music," he says, putting a gallant kiss on Agaméde's hand.

•

Nicolas Guignon opens his eyes and sees painted beams above him; he has been brought to the music room; we see that he knows where he is. Hearing footsteps, he tries to turn his head, but the muscles of his neck have lost all strength. Now the face of the Count, his patron, appears in front of the ceiling, smiling. But the Count does not speak, and Guignon cannot; his tongue barely stirs in his mouth; it is like an anemone in a tiny pool. His face is greasy and as pale as the candles that have been placed around him. The Count smiles; he wipes a finger across the young man's brow, firmly, as if removing a mark from the veneer of a table. With distaste, he inspects the fingertip. Guignon's eyes strain to ask a question that the Count does not answer. "My physician will attend to you," says the Count. "Do not be afraid," he says; his voice is strangely muffled; it seems to be issuing from behind a mask. We hear footsteps: hard heels on wood. A bag is set down on the floor, close to the couch on which Guignon is lying; we hear a jangle of metal instruments. Were he able to move, just to angle his face an inch or two to the side, he would recognise the black-cloaked man who is kneeling at the feet of the Count, opening the bag: he is the gardener. The knife that the gardener takes from the bag is like a little sword, with a flat and gleaming blade, sharpened along both edges. From beneath the couch, he pulls out a porcelain bowl. Guignon's hand, taken gently by the false physician, offers no more resistance than a slab of fat. Thick fingers, stained grey by the soil in which they have worked for many years, stroke the inner surface of Guignon's forearm. The blade is placed athwart the excited vein. The incision will remove the poison, the Count tells the stricken young man. Brick-coloured blood begins to flow down the bright white curve of the bowl. The blood deepens quickly. We hear the shuddering of Guignon's breath. The Count takes his victim's other hand, as if to comfort him. From the musicians' balcony, Agamédé observes the murder. Her face has the composure of death, yet tears are streaking from her eyes; she is a weeping statue. For fully ten seconds the camera presents Imogen's face, impassive, weeping from unblinking eyes.

•

There has never been an audit of the Sanderson-Perceval collection. Only I know exactly what is in the storerooms. I could sell a dozen items, and the loss would not be detected. A walnut box contains miscellaneous coins of various dates and nations, none in mint condition, none rare. Another box holds an array of magic lantern slides, showing scenes from Puss in Boots and Cinderella; some scenes are missing, and many of the slides are cracked. Under a dust sheet lies a broken longcase clock. There are faulty microscopes, globes of various types of marble, some chipped porcelain, mould-damaged books, tarnished surgical equipment, knick-knacks garnered from various corners of Europe. For as long as we retain these objects, nobody is going to see them.

For anything of any age, however, there is always a collector. It would be easy to find a buyer for *A Padstow Schooner*. Showing a flat little ship lying on a sea like a ruffled carpet, the picture was displayed as a painting by Alfred Wallis until a connoisseur of Wallis's untutored art informed us that we were in possession of a fake. The picture is faux-naïf, not naïf. Irrespective of its authorship, someone would buy it. Fake Wallises have sold at auction, albeit for a fraction of what a genuine article would fetch. Perhaps one day our fake would resurface, in Wallis's name, adorned with bogus provenance. Such things have happened.

Sometimes, after a glass or two, I have pictured myself dropping a cash-stuffed envelope into the letterbox of the Melville Street hostel, under cover of darkness. The self-satisfaction of charitable action, anonymously executed.

•

The false Wallis was acquired by Manfred Sanderson, the last of the line, the man who bequeathed the house and its contents to the city. Manfred's brothers, Frederick and Albert, were both gassed at St. Julien. This is where the guided tour always ends: at a photograph taken in the Royal Crescent in June 1914, with Benjamin Sanderson at the wheel of his Star Torpedo tourer; Manfred occupies the seat beside him; behind them sit Frederick and Albert, who would be dead within the year. It is difficult to see this picture for what it was—a simple snapshot of an afternoon's outing. Knowing the denouement, one imposes a shadow of death, of fate.

•

Did Antoine Vermeiren, I pretended to wonder, give himself the role of Pierre as a cost-cutting measure? Or was it that he regarded himself as a competent actor, despite all the evidence to the contrary? Vermeiren/Pierre is the most natural person in the film and therefore, in this context, the most false; in some scenes, it as if he has wandered out of a documentary and into a film of a quite different kind. At times, Vermeiren/Pierre seems to be suffering from a constriction of the throat. The proximity of the camera appears to embarrass him; he blinks like a pale-eyed man in strong sunlight. Sometimes he seems to be listening to a prompt, through an earpiece. There was no earpiece, Imogen told me, and money had not been a factor. It had been a risk, to cast himself in the role, but she thought that the risk had paid off—or so she said. There were moments at which one might suspect that this was not a professional actor, she conceded, but these did not detract from the film. In fact, she asked me to believe, Vermeiren's lack of professionalism was a positive quality. His awkwardness augmented the strangeness of the film; there was something uncanny about certain scenes, as if Pierre were in the midst of a lucid dream. And it had not been Antoine's intention that we should surrender to the drama of the film, Imogen argued; we should think of him as a puppet-master who has made sure that his hands can be seen. This argument was ingenious, but weak; I accused her of not believing what she was saying. An idea had fastened itself to me: that Antoine Vermeiren had been her lover. We argued, and I left. We would have one more night together.

•

"I detest pornography," proclaimed Antoine Vermeiren. Pornography is anti-erotic; it is a manifestation of the "despair of the impotent," a symptom of "our diseased social structures." Actors in hardcore films have reduced themselves to the role of components in the money-manufacturing machine, he stated, though he was at pains to point out that he would never condemn those women who, having been brutalised by lovers or husbands or poverty, decide to submit to this degradation. In such contexts, one must take care in using the concept of assent, he pronounced.

It was alleged that Vermeiren had promised roles to two young actresses in return for sexual favours. He did not deny that certain sex acts had been proposed, but contended that the young women had misunderstood or misrepresented his auditioning process. The acts that they had been encouraged to perform would have been crucial to certain scenes in his film. It would have been remiss of him, he maintained, not to determine beforehand whether or not these aspiring young artists possessed the requisite boldness of character.

Vermeiren often praised Imogen's boldness; her courage. She was courageous in *Le Grand Concert de la Nuit* and even more courageous in *Chambre 32*. When the first allegations against Vermeiren became public, she and I argued. There were reasons to doubt the word of the actresses, Imogen told me. And for some people, Antoine's "persona" was a little too combative, a little too "pungent," she conceded. Coercion, however, was anathema to him. Film is always a collaborative art form, said Imogen, and Antoine Vermeiren's films were more collaborative than most; "mutual respect and trust" were fundamental to his way of working.

•

A Saturday evening, mild; Imogen had met me at the station, and we had decided to walk to Soho, to eat there. The conversation became difficult as we reached Portman Square. We were waiting for a gap in the traffic when she said: "Antoine phoned this morning." Her voice was like that of a doctor, preparing her patient for ambiguous test results. What Vermeiren had in mind was something that had developed out of the Bataille project. Slipping a hand around my elbow, she told me what he was proposing: the sex would not be faked. It would, however, only be a performance, she assured me. She asked: "How would it be if you didn't know me? What would you think of the actress then?" My mind at that moment lacked the equilibrium necessary for the consideration of this hypothetical situation. "But I do know you," was all I could answer. "It would be an act, that's all," she repeated. "Do you doubt that I love you?" she asked. We chose a noisy restaurant in Chinatown, perhaps because it would not be possible to have a conversation there. "It'll probably never happen," she said. If it did, I eventually told her, I would try to accept it. I would fail to accept it, I knew.

•

"You have to find the character within yourself," Imogen had once said, in an interview. It was merely one of those things that actors say, she told me—as a writer might say that everything she writes is fundamentally autobiographical. She had become Roberte—the cold and manipulative Roberte—so easily, it seemed; she had discovered her—uncovered her—not created her. When the hapless Auguste, on his last night in Vézelay, implores her to read the confession that he has written for her, I recognised the immovable composure, the light but decisive pressure of the lips, the slow fall and rise of the eyelids. The abrupt withdrawal that was signified by Roberte's eyes—I had seen it before, when we had argued. In the memory of those arguments I seemed to be observing Roberte, or a version of Roberte that was not yet fully achieved. The way Roberte narrowed her eyes and turned away, without speaking— that was Imogen. The controlled evenness of Roberte's voice, when her anger was at its highest pitch—in our last argument, Imogen's voice had taken on that tone, that timbre. It was like remembering a rehearsal. I hated Roberte in part because she had changed Imogen, or changed the Imogen that I saw.

•

When I recall our final evening, I remember a person who is myself, but not quite in character. I talked to Imogen as if I were her father. I remember using words such as "prurient" and "meretricious." I delivered a judgement: "You are making a mistake." Then her laugh, like the incredulous laughter of Roberte. Now, if I watch Roberte, the art of Imogen's performance is more apparent than it was. But I hardly ever watch Roberte. I will never find any merit in *Chambre 32*.

THE GREAT CONCERT OF THE NIGHT

•

An American psychologist has identified no fewer than six subtypes of a psychological condition known to believers as Histrionic Personality Disorder. The "theatrical" subtype is said to be "mannered" and "affected," and to "simulate desirable or dramatic poses." Moreover, the character of the "theatrical" HPD subtype is often "synthesized," I read. There is a caveat: "Any individual histrionic may exhibit none or any of the following traits." This is what it says—*may exhibit none or any*. Furthermore: "Because the criteria are subjective, some people may be wrongly diagnosed." It comes as no surprise to read that HPD is also known as "hysterical personality" and that "this personality is seen more often in women than in men."

•

Edmond and Jules de Goncourt, in their *Journals*, referring to Blaise Pascal: "There's another showman of the abyss!"

•

In *The Book of Margery Kempe*, which has a claim to be the earliest English autobiography, the author records her visions of Christ and the words he spoke to her. He gave her several orders; one such order was a command to take the Eucharist every Sunday. This she did. It seems that her extravagant piety was regarded with some suspicion by the townspeople of Bishop's Lynn, as were her outbursts of devotional wailing and writhing. For most people in England at this time, communion was an annual devotion, undertaken at Easter. At other times, the Host was something to be seen, not consumed. The monstrance, the instrument of display, was of paramount importance to the cult of Eucharistic piety; spiritual communion was achieved by means of sight.

•

A year after becoming a Carmelite novice, Maria Maddalena de' Pazzi (1566–1607) was struck by an illness that almost killed her. On her recovery, she began to experience visions, which often took the form of dialogues with Christ, or the Word, as she often denoted Him. During these raptures she disgorged words at such a rate that the nuns had to work in relays to transcribe them. For six years these visions were daily occurrences; the record of them filled five volumes. The self-mortification that Maria Maddalena practised was extreme. At times she wore a crown of thorns, and a corset to which nails had been attached. She would walk barefoot through snow, and burn her skin with molten wax, and put her mouth to the wounds of lepers. Always in poor health, she was bedridden for the last four years of her life. At the end, all her teeth had gone and her body was covered with sores. When her sisters offered to move her she told them to desist, for fear that contact with her flesh might awaken their sexual desires.

•

Adeline wrote: "I reject a faith that demands continual reference to one's self. We should not luxuriate in feeling. Love must look outward."

•

William can't believe how easy it was to get work. All it took was a few hours, asking around the harbour. "They'll take anyone with a full set of arms and legs," he reports. He's already done one shift, and it was amazing. Calm sea, thick mist. "Nothing visible beyond the boat." Then he saw something that spooked him: far out from the shore, they passed a submerged rock, on which a huge clump of seaweed was rising and falling. "Like a sea-monster's hair," says William. "It totally did my head in."

•

Auguste has come to Vézelay to study the abbey—specifically, the sculpture of the tympanum. The details of the book on which he is working are vague, but it has something to do with the representation of the Crusades in medieval art. The tympanum of the abbey at Vézelay is of particular interest, he tells Roberte, having directed her attention to the lintel, where the ungodly peoples of the world are depicted. The camera moves over the procession of grotesques: the dwarfish, the misshapen, the swinish, the elephantine. These images are a political statement, Auguste explains. Just fifteen years after the tympanum was carved, Bernard of Clairvaux came to this place to preach for a second Crusade. Later in the same century, Richard I of England and Philip II of France met in Vézelay before embarking on the Third Crusade. While Auguste delivers his lecture, the camera observes the face of Roberte, as she studies the sculpture. Thanks to Auguste, as she tells him, she is seeing the building more clearly than ever before.

The coupling of Auguste and Roberte had been nothing but sexual pleasure, albeit sexual pleasure of quite a different order from anything that Auguste had hitherto enjoyed; now, at the abbey, he senses that a genuine relationship may be developing with the chilly yet intriguing Roberte. We see her as Auguste sees her, standing in the caramel sunlight, looking up at the carvings; she is as beautiful and severe as any stone saint. Later that day, at a café, where Roberte has encountered Auguste as she returns to the hotel, he delivers another disquisition, apropos his book. "A man always believes his eyes better than his ears," he remarks in conclusion, and smiles to himself; the line is a quotation, it appears. And so it is: Auguste, a comprehensively cultured young man, is making an allusion to the story of Candaules, as recounted by Herodotus. He has his laptop with him; a few keystrokes bring up a picture, which he shows to Roberte: Jean-Léon Gérôme's *King Candaules*.

Cut clumsily to another laptop: Roberte, in bed, beside Pierre, is reading the relevant pages of Herodotus on her laptop. She reads aloud the words spoken by Candaules to Gyges, his bodyguard: "It appears you do not believe me when I tell you how lovely my wife is." The king's name, according to Herodotus, meant "dog throttler," Roberte tells her husband. This is one of the very few enjoyable moments of this generally unenjoyable film: the way Imogen forms the phrase—*l'étrangleur de chiens*—as if the words had a taste of exquisite sourness; the tiny clenching of her eyelids here, expressive of a perverse frisson, is wonderful. When, soon afterwards, a neighbour's repulsive dog is found dead, a few days after taking a nip at Roberte's ankle, not for the first time, we of course suspect Pierre; but wrongly, as it turns out. Vermeiren's little joke. Yet perhaps things will nonetheless end badly for Pierre, the wife-displayer, as things ended badly for Candaules. Auguste dislikes Pierre and is falling for Roberte, and it's not impossible that Roberte has some feelings for Auguste, though what Roberte is thinking is no more visible to us than are the frigid depths of the ocean.

But no, we are being misdirected: it is Auguste who will suffer in the end; the depraved husband and wife will carry on as before, untroubled. The allusions to Aphrodite, the promiscuous and pitiless goddess, were a clue. When mortals couple with deities, the story rarely ends happily for the mortal. Erymanthos, son of Apollo, merely observed Aphrodite making love with Adonis, but that was enough to get him blinded.

•

It gratified Thibaut that others could see what a fine woman he now had as his lover. He had never experienced jealousy, he told her. And he had never wanted children, so a wombless woman was not—as it had been for Loïc—something less than a woman should be. He even professed to find the scar attractive. True beauty was found in irregularity, he declared. "Marks of life" excited him, as mere "pretty girls" generally did not, he claimed. Every week, as an art dealer, he encountered so many pretty girls. His world swarmed with eye-pleasing young women. "So perfect, so tedious," he sighed. One of his ex-lovers, formerly a war-zone reporter, had lost an eye; she wore a patch, "like a pirate." Another, once a champion equestrienne, had a "fabulous scar" across her midriff, having been kicked by a horse. He had, however, known some conventional beauties intimately, he admitted. Some varieties of "standard beauty" were irresistible, like some kinds of cheap music. Thibaut's ex-lovers were plentiful; he was easily bored, too easily, as Imogen was informed at the outset.

The time she spent with Thibaut was eventful and pleasurable. She learned things from him; his mind contained a vast catalogue of art, and all of its information seemed to be available to him instantly. His eye was good; he had discernment. Every month there was an expedition with Thibaut. He lived for these adventures, he told Imogen. He had a need, a physical need, for new experiences; as an actress, she would understand this. The trips were enjoyable. In a village near Udine she met the last living descendant of an artist who had worked in the studio of Paolo Veronese; this very old man owned a sketch that he believed to be in Paolo Veronese's hand, as did Thibaut. A fearsome woman in Portugal had a chapel in an unused wing of her villa where the cobwebs were as thick as lace curtains; she owned a still life that her family displayed as the work of Josefa de Óbidos, which it almost certainly was not.

One evening, Thibaut told her about the *maison de maître*. He made a proposal, which he expected her to reject. She understood the ploy: he could not bring himself to break with a woman who had endured what Imogen had endured, so it was necessary that she should be the one to leave. To that end he had revealed the secret. Imogen had to know everything about who he was, he told her. But, to his well-suppressed astonishment, she agreed to the suggestion. And Thibaut was dismayed by the consequence, by the pleasure that she found in that place, a pleasure that seemed to exceed even his own. "I am not what you need," he told her afterwards, as though he had been wounded and was asking permission to leave.

•

It was not her intention to put me to the test. "I know you love me," she said. If nothing else, it would be a new experience; instructive, even. From what she had told me, I thought that I could imagine the scene. "I'm not sure I need to see it," I said. Imagining it and seeing it are quite different things, she answered. "Perhaps I need you to be there," she said. Then she apologised for using that word. "I would like you to be there," she clarified. "But if the idea makes you unhappy, I'll say nothing more about it." It might be difficult for me, she knew. Nothing between us would be changed if I declined to attend.

•

It is rare to find a man who genuinely loves the female body, Imogen said. Certain acts of intimacy tend to be performed out of a sense of duty, or as a means of securing credit. Many men, being limited to a single shot, are intimidated by female potency, or never get round to discovering it, she said. The image of the woman as receptacle was strangely durable. "But was there ever a more stupid idea than penis envy?" she wondered. Balzac had a dread of ejaculation, she told me: it was a waste of his creative energy, he believed. He once lamented that a masterpiece had been lost to French literature in the course of the preceding night—he'd had a wet dream, and had thereby squandered a short story. We looked at Rodin's statue of Balzac; I'd never noticed before what was happening, or what seemed to be happening, underneath the cloak. "A snowman in a bathrobe," was how a contemporary had described it, she told me.

•

As befitted the meeting place of an esoteric cult, the *maison de maître* was not a building that one could happen upon by accident: a gravel track, branching from a minor road, descended through woodland that hid the house from view. A kilometre along, we came to a high wall and a gate. Flanking the gate were lanterns that had panels of ruby glass. A password had to be given at the entryphone, then a sequence of numbers typed on a keypad. The timing was melodramatic too: we were instructed to arrive at midnight.

The house: a large, tall-windowed structure of grey stone, with a short flight of steps leading to the door, at which stood a very tall young man, sub-Saharan African, dressed in the livery of a footman, circa 1800—a long coat of heavy material, red and green trimmed with golden braid, over breeches and white stockings. We stepped into a hall that was lit by a pair of crystal chandeliers; chamber music, eighteenth-century, came from hidden speakers. Arrivals were greeted and directed by a handsome man, fortyish, in tuxedo and bow tie. He was overgroomed: not a strand of the eyebrows disrupted their line; the virile jaw had been shaved to a plastic smoothness; the exquisitely manicured hands gave off a citric perfume. His manner was courteous but unsmiling. I imagined that he imagined himself to be a force of moral liberation; a debonair intellectual roué; a saboteur; a cynic and a poet. The property had been rented for the occasion, as it had been several times before, for the same purpose. It was possible, Imogen told me later, that the man who conducted himself as the master of ceremonies was not in fact the host: the true host, Imogen had heard, was passing himself off as one of the staff—perhaps the saturnine waiter who dispensed the champagne.

A large room in the basement had been set aside for disrobing.

There was little conversation in this ante-room. The atmosphere was not that of a party. With the demeanour of a surgeon preparing for an operation that was not certain to succeed, a woman put on a high-collared gown and long black gloves, all of black satin. Another assiduously checked every zip and buckle of her costume, as if securing armour. Other women were more or less naked, but for a web of gauze and ribbons. A man put on a domino mask and a black cloak; this was the entirety of his attire. His companion too wore only a cloak and mask—but a more elaborate creation, with plumes of thin purple feathers arching out from the eyes. One by one the participants departed, solemnly. Taboos were about to be broken.

Afterwards, I remarked that the woman with the long black gloves had suggested to me the image of a surgeon. There had indeed been a surgeon in the room, Imogen told me, but the protocols of the gathering forbade identification. One of the men was a writer of crime novels. A high-society lawyer had also been present, and a politician. Whenever the newspapers run stories about such debaucheries, the cast always includes a politician and a lawyer—or a judge, best of all.

•

I could try to describe what I saw at the *maison de maître*. I could describe the light on the bodies, the radiant and delicious flesh, the blood-flushed skin. I have read accounts of gatherings like the one at the *maison de maître*. "An Adonis sat on the edge of the bed, while a line of women took turns with him," reports one participant. And: "My friend was being ridden by a honey-skinned goddess, a woman too gorgeous to be envied." A soundtrack could be supplied, with mingled sighs and cries and moans of surrender, possession, release. Perhaps I could fashion a few elegant sentences from the couplings of the finest bodies. Some of the bodies were indeed magnificent. The scene could be transformed into a tableau that had some quality of art. But the reality, for me, was not an aesthetic experience, nor was it the realisation of any fantasy. There was no revulsion either, and no shock. A degree of fascination, I admit. But most strongly, at first, I believe, what I felt was a kind of anxiety, though everyone, as far as I could tell, was having pleasure—a great deal of pleasure; in a few cases, a pleasure akin to derangement.

•

At the *maison de maître* I had this thought: a cinematographer would be able to make an erotic scene of this, but if one were to watch it on a TV screen, as images generated by the undirected eye and circuitry of a CCTV camera, the squalor would prevail. Intoxicated by the flesh, these people do not see what the machine would see. Were they to observe it from the distance of the mechanical camera, purely as images, they might find these contortions ridiculous. This is what I thought: detachment would reveal the reality of it. The image would be evidence. But I also thought: the images would not be true to the experience; the desiring eye sees more than the machine.

•

As though opening a locket, I often return to the sight of Imogen in the garden of the museum, after we had spoken, before the guided tour. She sat on a bench, reading the leaflet. She seemed to be reading every word of the text. Having finished it, she looked around; her half-smile appeared simply to be indicative of her pleasure in what she was seeing. She went down to the pond. At the edge of the water she stooped; the carp must have been at the surface. Something in the sky caught her attention: she turned her head, raising a hand to her brow, against the sunlight. She could not have been aware that she was being observed, I am certain. What I was seeing was Imogen alone, Imogen herself. When I talked to her, she became someone else: she became who she was for me, as I became who I was for her. She looked at her watch. I can see her now, the innocent Imogen, looking up at the sky again, smiling at something only she could see.

•

I woke up one night to see Imogen looking out of the window, at the bright and enormous moon: "Let's go out," she said, as if it were the start of the day. There was something actorly about the impulsiveness, but I was easily persuaded. We dressed and went out, to the park, and what we saw seemed unforgettable, as it has proved to be: the zinc-coloured grass, the trees with leaves of writing paper, the delicate shadows. There were times at which I thought that I was fully myself only with Imogen, and others—sometimes in the course of the same day, the same hour, the same minute—at which it seemed that I had become, temporarily, someone who was not truly himself, but whom it was more satisfying to be.

•

Despite the terrible sufferings of his final weeks, Philip II of Spain died an exemplary death, in uncomplaining submission to the will of God. In the final days, relics from the Escorial's collection of several thousand items were placed on the death bed, for the king's contemplation and comfort. The knee of Saint Sebastian was brought to him, and a rib from the body of Saint Alban. The latter was of particular potency—through its power, the pope had declared, the soul of the king would be liberated from Purgatory.

•

A wedding party. The arrival of a bride was imminent. Around the front door of the hotel, half a dozen young women waited, each in a peach-coloured satin dress, strapless. One of them was flirting with the doorman; she angled her back towards him, so that he could admire the head of the tattooed dragon that lay on the nape of her neck. When the bridal car came into view she hooked a finger into her dress and extracted a smartphone. The car was a low-slung vintage Citroën, black, immaculate, with pink and white ribbons stretched across the bonnet and a bouquet lashed to the radiator grille. Suddenly, every bridesmaid was armed with a smartphone or camera. The driver, in full chauffeur rig, disembarked swiftly, to open the door for the bride. As she was being assisted from the vehicle, her father exited from the opposite side. A small girl in a bright pink dress was ushered towards the car, to take up the train of the dress. But the train had become caught on some part of the door. The chauffeur took action: kneeling on the tarmac, he started to disentangle the fabric. The father intervened. Becoming angry, the bride protested that damage was being done. The bridesmaids lowered their phones. At last the dress was free. A bridesmaid descended, to restore the train to its optimum shape. The father of the bride took the arm of his daughter, but the bride would not move. After a brief exchange of words, she withdrew into the car. Her father spoke to the chauffeur, who in turn explained to the assembly: the arrival would have to be restaged. The car drove away; two minutes later it returned. This time the dress flowed smoothly out of the vehicle. One of the bridesmaids turned her back and raised a hand, to take a photograph of herself with her friend, the bride, coming up the steps behind her.

June

Thirty-two visitors.

•

"I need to have a rethink," says William. "I don't have what it takes for this lark." Yesterday he was out in a rough sea. Nothing exceptional for every other member of the crew, but too much for William. For an hour he clung to a stanchion, throwing up. At one point he vomited in the wrong direction and splattered himself from face to waist. The others carried on working through the mayhem. Gary, the hard man, ex-army, was ripping up fish while telling tales of the really bad seas he'd been caught in. Waves as high as houses, in total darkness. In the end, William was sent to his bunk. "Disgraced," he says, though everyone was laughing about it by the time they came back to port. He had the look of someone who had lost half his blood, and it was a full day before he lost the feeling that everything was still moving. "So I'm out," he tells me. And the drugs are an issue too. "It's the only way these blokes can do what they do," he says, "but I don't want any of that. If I started, I wouldn't be able to stop."

•

On the website of a newspaper that likes to present itself as the champion of deep-rooted British values, we are invited to admire the body of "reality TV star Michelle" as she "tops up her tan in Marbella." More: we should study the "perfectly tanned and toned figure" of eighteen-year-old Zoë, who looks "full of body confidence" in her cute pink bikini. Sylvie "flaunts her pert posterior and amazing abs" in her "latest workout snapshots." A semi-famous actor, a "notorious party animal," is seen departing from a club with two "leggy blondes," who have no names; we should envy him, it appears, but we must deplore the semi-famous actress who is looking "the worse for wear" as she clambers into a limo at two in the morning. We should also regret that a certain TV presenter, 35, seems to be struggling to lose weight after the birth of her first child, a full six months ago.

•

A birthday present from Francesca—a book about decorated skeletons. "Saw this and thought of you," she writes. The skeletons reside in various German churches, some of them in resplendent made-to-measure tombs with glass panels for ease of viewing, some behind screens in side chapels, some in storerooms, under piles of surplus seating. When northern Europe was first being menaced by Protestantism, these bones were removed from the Roman catacombs, given saintly names, and dispatched across the Alps to the jeopardised territories, where they were adorned with fabulous costumes and festooned with jewellery. The bedazzled faithful, in adoring the glamorous relics, would thereby be reconnected with the martyrs of the true church; the marvellous skeletons, with amethysts for eyes and ribs wrapped in gold leaf, were harbingers of the glory of the Heavenly Jerusalem.

•

Francesca, on her first visit to the museum: we stood together in the mirrored room, each with a candle, and she made the flame dance around the faces of all the little Francescas who stood in ranks around us. She turned slowly, and the assembled Francescas turned slowly in the foggy glass. "My team of ghost girls," she said.

•

I remember the day we met up with Francesca and her boyfriend in Rome; they had arrived the previous day, and we were leaving two days later. Francesca was our guide for the day, a role she occupied with aplomb. We walked down the road from the Campidoglio. Francesca read aloud the inscription on a lintel, first in Latin, then in translation. *Nicola, whose house this was, was not unaware that the glory of the world in itself is of no importance.* I can see Imogen's marigold dress. She and Francesca walked ahead, arms linked. The boyfriend, with me, kept glancing at the two women, as though concerned that Francesca might be sharing secrets, or that Imogen might be giving her advice that was contrary to his best interests. At the Bocca della Verità, after Francesca had whispered something to him, he stood before the huge stone face and placed his hand in the mouth, which supposedly would shut like a trap if a lie were to be uttered.

That evening, having noticed a look transmitted by the boyfriend to a young woman at a neighbouring table, Imogen said to me, as we walked back to the hotel: "This one is going to break her heart."

•

After Imogen's departure, Emma was inclined to wonder why I had not paused before embarking on an affair that would have been so unlikely to produce a good outcome. For Emma, all decisions should be preceded by careful consideration of outcomes. I was unworldly, in some ways, she told me; my choice of career was evidence enough; a man of my type would have been particularly susceptible to a woman of Imogen's high voltage. She saw *Le Grand Concert de la Nuit* but not *Chambre 32*. Emma was appalled by the idea of *Chambre 32*. She could never watch it. Why would she? Why would anyone watch such a thing? Imogen, she suggested, was akin to an overpowered sports car that its middle-aged owner regrets buying within the year, after a near-death experience. With *Chambre 32* Imogen had gone too far, my sister said; I could only agree.

•

Sometimes, on days of acute happiness, Imogen would suddenly stop and look around, her elation having reached such a pitch that it compelled her to halt and take note of everything, to embed in her memory every detail of the locality in which the mood of the day was invested. In Rome, walking towards Santa Maria della Vittoria from San Carlino, she stopped; turning, she surveyed the street—the buildings, the road, the sky; she looked to the left and to the right, slowly, two or three times each way; I had walked on.

A passing man, misreading Imogen's frown of concentration as perplexity, crossed the street to ask if she were lost. His dog was kitted out in a tight satin coat, Italian azure, and adorned with the badge of the national football team. For a couple of minutes the man stayed with Imogen, watching the contortions of a vast cloud of starlings.

We were in her room, late at night; the pain had risen. She could not recall the man and his dog. She clamped her brow with a hand, trying to press some memory out. "No. Nothing," she said. "Starlings I remember. Many many starlings." She could not remember San Carlino. "Describe, please," she said. "Take me back to Rome." I remember the tone—like a happy woman, addressing a friendly bus driver.

•

In her dark episodes, Imogen's head was full of remembered phrases. They repeated themselves, dozens of times, and she was powerless against them. Her head felt like "a drum full of dirty clothes," she told me. One day, the phrase "Why ever would he do such a thing?" asserted itself. No meaning could be attributed to it. It was a memory, she knew, but she could not tell whose voice was speaking.

I slept on the floor. In the middle of the night I woke up to see her sitting on the bed, staring at the window. Her eyes were haunted. "We would be damned," she was hearing, over and over again. This time, she knew the source: these were words she had spoken as Beatrice.

•

The train came to a standstill between stations, on a raised section of track. Houses backed on to the rail line, and we looked down into an unfurnished ground-floor room. Under a bare light-bulb, a man and a woman were talking, a pace apart, face to face. The dirty glass of the window, struck obliquely by the late sunlight, had a grey cast, which made it seem as though the couple were standing in a deep dusk that was confined to that room. The light-bulb was on. The man had his hands on his hips and the woman's arms were crossed; they looked like actors in rehearsal, in a scene of disagreement. But then the man moved a hand to the woman's cheek and left it there; he leaned forward to kiss her. The kiss was gentle and long. I glanced at Imogen; she was smiling and crying. In a fit of impatience, she ground away the tears with the heels of her thumbs. "This is ridiculous," she apologised.

•

When I took refuge in the yellow and silver chamber, only one other person was in that room: a man of my age; his chest was pale and doughy; his limbs disproportionately thin. He lolled in an armchair, splay-legged, recovering from his exertions, it appeared. In one hand he held a purple scarf, which lay over his thigh; his penis had shrunk into its nest. As I came in he nodded to me, then he shut his eyes. Subdued and sweet-tempered music was coming from the adjoining hall. "*Ah, j'adore l'épouse de monsieur Haydn,*" murmured the lolling man; he amused himself immensely. A chaise longue stood in the corner of the room. That was where I sat. I too closed my eyes, to listen. The floor was highly polished parquet. At the sticky sound of skin on varnished wood, I looked towards the door. A woman

approached, a large woman; she was wearing a black domino and a
belt of small black beads; nothing else. She stood in front of me and
smiled; she had a pretty mouth; carmine lipstick; bright and even
teeth. Her eyes regarded me as though I were a friend whom she
was pleasantly surprised to have encountered here. She stood with
her feet almost touching mine. My arms would not have reached
around her. Her hips and shoulders were broad, her thighs strong
and smooth, her breasts hefty; a fertility figure. She said something
that I did not understand, then placed her hands flat on her stomach;
her fingers pointed downward, directing my gaze to the naked cleft;
a small red stone glittered there, in a fold of glistening skin. Again
she spoke; she smiled, with a radiant confidence in her ability to
excite desire. Her hands rose to her breasts; the nipples were pierced
by tiny silver arrows. I wondered how it would feel to embrace this
body, a body unlike any that I had ever touched, but it was an almost
theoretical curiosity. She bent down, bringing her face close to mine.
"*Saisir le jour*," she murmured, as if suggesting a little excursion. A
perfume of cherries and champagne came with her breath.
I demurred, but with warm thanks. "Ah, English," she commiserated.
As she looked down to my lap, her lips formed a wry pout, as though
to say: "Your body is not in agreement with you." The recuperating
man was watching us from the other side of the room. In English
he called out, in a voice of some grandeur: "The day will not be
seized." The mighty woman turned to look at him. An amiable
exchange ensued. She crossed the room and held out a summoning
hand, which he took.

•

Waiting for Imogen, I sat in the garden of the *maison de maître,* by the wall of jasmine. People were leaving now. Behind me, many of the windows were open, but barely a sound came out of the house; now and then a cry. The air was placid and warm. An ordeal had been completed. The scene was a pastoral nocturne. The grass sloped down to a stream, where the silhouettes of willows and chestnuts made areas of deeper darkness against the sky. A pallid statue stood in the gloom. Beyond it, another pale shape emerged, rising from the grass by the trees; a woman—a wide streak of hair divided the figure's back. A second body arose, not to its full height. Kneeling, the second figure pressed its face into the thighs of the first.

There was a second bench, a few yards from mine. Suddenly a woman was there. She wore a dress that was long and white and translucent, and silver sandals. Fortyish. From a shoulder, on a slender silver chain, hung a small silver box, kidney-shaped, from which she took a brace of cigarettes. She offered one to me, without speaking, and I, without speaking, declined. In silence we sat in the fragrant and motionless air of the night. Still the two bodies by the trees were conjoined, face to groin. My companion's gaze paused on them, and paused on the statue with the same indifference, and on the trees, the moon, and the bandages of cloud above it. With closed mouth, she slowly exhaled. She leaned back, to regard the sky directly overhead. Infinite boredom suffused her face. An hour earlier, I had seen her naked in an upstairs room; her ankles and wrists had been shackled to steel bars; a younger woman stood behind her, holding some sort of electrified wand.

The situation in the grass was changing. The kneeling figure—male, it was now clear—had stood up and was putting on a robe; the woman lay down, and disappeared from view. Leaving the robe untied, the man walked towards the house. Seeming to recognise my companion, he raised a hand, and she reciprocated. He was perhaps a decade older than her, with slicked grey hair. On reaching the bench, he stopped and extended a hand to the woman, as if inviting her to join him for a waltz. Her smile was that of someone who has heard a once-amusing story too often; she stood up, and wished me good evening. The man bowed to me.

A few minutes later, Imogen came out. From the footfall I knew it was Imogen, without turning to see. She slid her hands onto my shoulders and whispered: "All right?"

"Indeed," I said.

She stood squarely in front of me, to look steadily, then she put her arms around me.

•

Might an image, in being written, in being expelled on to a page, be attenuated by this exposure, if not purged completely? Writing as an inoculation? The image: Imogen on the black couch, in the light of a single candle, her arms at her side, motionless; eyes closed; a recumbent tomb-figure. A young man, athletic, came into the room. Looking at me, he gestured towards Imogen, as though inviting me to precede him through a doorway. She turned and held out a hand to me, like a woman who was about to jump; I was invited to annihilate myself with her.

•

A call from William, barely audible against the noise. He's walking to Mousehole, he tells me. He has a hangover to walk off. Two miles there, two miles back, but in this wind a mile feels like twice the distance. "Listen," he says. What I'm hearing, he tells me, is the bushes beside the road, shrieking. The sea looks like a ploughed-up field with snow on it, he says. Ahead of him a woman is walking with a spaniel, and the dog's ears are horizontal. "This is what it's all about. Feel the energy," he yells. Energy is what drew him to the edge of England. It flows through the earth, down to the southernmost point. That's why England's southern pole is William's destiny. Evidence: he has been offered a job. This is the reason for the call—next week, he becomes a driver, delivering for a supermarket. "Hours are crap, money's not great, but what the hell, eh? Turning the corner, my man. Onward and upward."

•

The second encounter with William: spotting Imogen from the opposite side of the road, he crossed immediately, jinking through the traffic.

She greeted him on our behalf. It might have been evident that I was not delighted; Imogen was staying for only a few days, and I felt I had rights to her company. She too, I think, would rather not have had the interruption, but she dissembled perfectly. "Hello, William," she said.

"Hello Imogen," he answered, with bright familiarity, as if this bit of banter were some sort of private joke. "All right if I join you? Just for a minute," he asked. "Today I can pay," he added, dredging a palmful of coins from a pocket. "Had a good morning," he explained. He was carrying a backpack, which he kicked under the chair he had selected, on Imogen's side of the table. When he sat down, a waft of beer fumes reached me. "All clear," he said, tapping the scar on his brow.

Imogen commended the neatness of the stitching.

"And what about you?" he asked her. "What are you up to?"

In the previous week she had been doing a voiceover.

William could not have been more amazed, but immediately the amazement was replaced by reconsideration. "That makes sense," he told her. "You've got a nice voice," he said. The niceness of the voice, and the nastiness of some other voices, gave him material for a minute or so. I seemed to have become invisible.

The waitress, the same one as before, came to the table, and William ordered a coffee, as casually as a regular. "Good name, Imogen," he said, reattaching his attention. "Never met an Imogen before. Great name." He could not recall a David either. He knew a Dave, but he was a Dave, not a David, which was not the same thing at all, he told us, just as William was not the same as Will or Bill or Billy. William had a theory, a theory that experience had validated: that there is an affinity between people who share a name. In giving a certain name to their child, parents were recognising, albeit unconsciously, the qualities that this name represented. Thus the essence of every John was his John-ness, just as everything labelled gold was gold. Davids were dependable, he complimented me, whereas Daves had a tendency to be dodgy. Obviously the parents of almost every Dave originally called the boy David, but when David chose to become Dave he was correcting a mistake that the parents had made. This is not quite how the theory was expressed—William's explication was less succinct. He was interruption-proof.

A few yards from where we were sitting, a signpost had been

149

knocked out of the perpendicular by a car. Noticing it, William was prompted to recall an interesting fact that the father of a friend, a policeman, had once told him: that it was better to drive into a brick wall than into a tree, because a brick wall will collapse when the car hits it, whereas a tree will spring back, worsening the impact. Years later, William had remembered this advice, and "given the choice of a tree or a wall," he had driven at the latter; and, just as the policeman had said, the wall folded over the car bonnet, causing only minor damage to the driver. "But I'm a good driver," he wanted us to know, as if we might be looking for a driver to hire. He liked driving, but couldn't afford his own wheels at the moment. When he had got himself sorted out, he might get a driving job, he said. He wasn't stupid, he wanted us to know. He had the brains for a "proper job," but he was never going to wear a suit and he wasn't good at being bossed around. Or he might train to be a plumber, because he had the sort of brain you need for that kind of work, and he was good with his hands. But it wasn't easy to find someone to take you on, so it was likelier that he'd go for the driving option. Once he had taken his father's BMW, not strictly with permission, and he'd gone for a drive on the motorway at night. He'd done a hundred miles in an hour. It was an out-of-body experience, he told us. He'd been totally in the zone. It was like watching a video of himself demonstrating how to drive safely on a motorway at a steady one hundred miles an hour. The owner of the car wasn't his real father, he clarified; glancing at me, he became aware that he was in danger of losing his audience. "Another story," he said, checking his cup. "Now I'll get out of your way," he said, standing.

He seemed not to be expecting anything, but Imogen opened her bag and took out a ten-pound note. "Fuck me," he said, holding the note in both hands, at arm's length. "Pardon the language. But—"

"Take it," she said.

"You won't win," I told him.

He folded the note in half and slotted it into a pocket of his bag. "This means I'll be back," he said. "You know that, right?" His eyes were watering.

When he had gone, I took issue with Imogen's generosity. "He'll spend it on drink," I objected.

"Maybe," she said. "If that's what he needs."

I made some other uncharitable observations.

"Would you like to be in his place?" she asked.

"I'm not sure I know what his place is."

"Whatever it is, it isn't one we'd swap for ours."

•

Some people of "wild imagination" would be at the *maison de maître*, Imogen warned me. Was it because I lacked imagination, I asked, that she thought I might benefit from this experience? It was not a question of administering a corrective, Imogen said. And a lack of imagination could be regarded as a strength. This was when Imogen talked about Simone Weil, a writer she admired greatly, she told me, though Simone Weil was as unlike Imogen as it was possible to be. The imagination, Weil maintained, is coercive: it imposes itself upon the real and leads us away from the true. "Not to imagine—that's the supreme faculty," Imogen paraphrased. One should aim, Weil had written, "to obliterate from one's self one's point of view." Imogen was inviting me to observe, to attend. There was no connotation of subservience; on the contrary. "I submit myself to your mercy," she said, with a gesture of prostration that was not entirely parodic.

●

A school group this afternoon. One of the teachers, new to the school, recently returned to the area in which he grew up, tells me that he was moved by the display of spar boxes, in particular the box of Lake District minerals. Almost forty years had passed since he last saw that box, and the sight of it brought back to him, suddenly, a memory of being at the museum, aged seven or eight, with his sister, who had convinced him that the cluster of green pyromorphite crystals was in fact a lump of kryptonite, the stone that could vanquish Superman. He had no recollection of room seven, however; it must be assumed that his parents had steered him away from it.

●

On Alfred Street this afternoon, as a woman passed me, I was struck by an unusual perfume. Violets and something smoky were in the mix, but that was as much as I could distinguish; the scent disappeared in seconds. Even if I were to be handed a bottle of the perfume, however, I would not be capable of separating the elements of the compound. Imogen, however, would have named them immediately, like someone with perfect pitch separating the notes of a complex chord. At Val's house, one of the guests was wearing an intricate scent. Imogen inhaled a draught of the delicious air, and said to the woman, outright, as if she had been walking with a group of friends and suddenly come upon an amazing view: "My God, that is wonderful." The woman leaned towards her, to offer a more concentrated dose. Closing her eyes, Imogen began to name the ingredients: bergamot and grapefruit; rose, frankincense and sandalwood; coffee, kiwi, honey. As she named them, I could discern each element. "Quite a nose," said the woman. A conversation on the topic of perfumes ensued. Val looked on. Almost on first sight, it was clear to me, Val had arrived at a conclusion: this woman is a performer, always. And perhaps, on this occasion, Imogen was a little bolder than usual, for the benefit of Val, a woman who put so much work into her own sincerity.

•

Agamédé—the scene in which she removes the stopper from the phial of perfume that the Count has given her, a unique perfume composed for Agamédé on his instruction, blending the rarest and most intoxicating extracts. With an expression of great seriousness, like a chemist assessing the result of an experiment, she raises the opened bottle to her nose. Her eyes are overwhelmed by the torpor of surrender; then comes the smile—that drowsy, aroused, arousing smile.

•

The party at Val's: a gathering for a select group of thirty or so, belatedly for Samantha's birthday—some from the yoga group, a couple of colleagues, some from the pottery class, and others whose connection was never clear. Samantha's social life was much richer now, thanks to Val. We had been invited, I assumed, partly in order that Imogen could be assessed.

A profusion of multi-ethnic snacks and dishes had been arrayed on a table below the alcove that housed the little brass Buddha. We were making our selection when our host appeared beside us. She wanted Imogen to know that she had enjoyed *Devotion*. In particular, she had loved the costumes; and the childbirth scene was so powerful—"unbearable," even. Samantha joined us, allowing Val to assist a guest who had a question about what she was eating. Then Conrad passed by, with a "How's it going?" Had Imogen not been there, he would have moved on. We had met before. He found me uninteresting, whereas my former wife was cool, or coolish, by virtue of having walked out of a mainstream marriage to become his mother's lover. But I was dull; just as he, with the good-bad haircut and the affected slouch and the limited edition T-shirts, was a conceited and pampered adolescent. Beside him stood a huge-eyed wraith of a girl: this was Katrin, of whose prettiness and brilliance we had heard, via Samantha. Katrin mouthed a hello and offered Imogen a hand. Her hand had about as much weight as a playing card. "I've heard a lot about you. About both of you," said Imogen, giving Conrad a smile that deflected his gaze. She had remembered which instruments Katrin had mastered, according to Val: guitar, piano, flute, cello, accordion. "And you write songs, I hear," she said. Katrin looked to Conrad, and Conrad nodded; the shyness was uncharacteristic. "Conrad writes the words," answered Katrin in a tiny voice. "I can't sing," Conrad told Imogen; it was almost disarming, the way he said it—as if the inability to sing were a clinical diagnosis, of no great seriousness, but mildly embarrassing. There was a brief discussion of their tastes in music and the way they worked together, then Imogen said: "Would you let me hear something?" Again Katrin looked to Conrad. "You mean, like now?" he asked. "Why not? Who knows when we'll next see you?" Imogen pointed out.

Leaving Samantha to circulate, we followed the youngsters to Conrad's room, at the top of the house. Guitars hung from brackets: a Stratocaster, a Telecaster, a Les Paul, a custom-made Spanish guitar—so many guitars, all of them gifts from the guilty father, now living in California and earning inconceivable quantities of dollars. We listened to a song that they had recorded onto Conrad's laptop; a beguiling little piece, in the voice of a homesick traveller, with some simple strumming behind Katrin's voice, which was quiet but true. The second song was a sweetly innocent serenade, in which the singer invited a new arrival in town to come for a walk. "Wonderful," Imogen pronounced, and Katrin, sitting on the floor, with her arms around her knees, looked abashed. I excused myself to return to Samantha.

"She's a hit. Well done," said Samantha, with a smile that seemed to imply that I had somehow executed successfully a complex subterfuge. Val, I observed, had taken note that Imogen and the youngsters had not returned downstairs with me. The creatives were bonding. Within moments of their reappearance, Val rejoined us. Katrin and Conrad were so talented, she informed us. With brisk affection, she ruffled her son's hair, asserting her claim.

When Imogen and I were taking our leave, Conrad and Katrin came over. Katrin, closing her eyes, pressed herself to Imogen; I received a handshake from Conrad. By association with Imogen, I had been transformed in his eyes; and vice versa.

•

Samantha was glad to hear that I had met Imogen; the new relation-ship might remove the last deposits of guilt. The betrayal was in her mind much more than it was in mine. Whatever wounds there had been had healed by this time. I was reasonable, but my reasonable-ness never fully convinced her. On the contrary, she took it to be the manifestation of a deeply buried anger—an analysis with which Val, I am sure, would have concurred. But I was no longer angry; perplexed, but not angry. There was, however, a widening distance between us. She had assumed a manner that was new; a softer self-presentation; it owed something to Val's brand of serenity.

•

If a soul is to know itself, it must engage with, or look into, another soul—this from the dialogue of Alcibiades and Socrates, which may or may not have been composed by Plato. "One eye looking at another, and at the most perfect part of it, with which it sees, will see itself," we read. The soul is visible in the pupil of the eye, in the form of a girl—the word *kore* means "pupil" or "little doll," I have learned. Kore is also another name for Persephone, whose myth may be read as an allegory of the soul's imprisonment in the underworld of the flesh. The Eleusinian Mysteries, the most celebrated secret rites of ancient Greece, were dedicated to Demeter and Persephone. The details of the Eleusinian Mysteries are unclear, but it is known that initiates were required to drink *kykeon*, a blended barley drink which some believe to have had psychotropic effects, caused by the presence in the barley of *Claviceps purpurea*, the rye ergot fungus.

•

At the *maison de maître*, what I saw in Imogen's gaze: solicitude; gratitude; surrender; blindness and oblivion. The body was satiated, quelled, sacrificed. When she opened her eyes again, she was like a woman waking after surgery. It was like falling back into life, she said.

•

"My aim is to enable my clients to focus on the here and now," says Val, in this week's bulletin. It is no easy thing to focus on the here and now, she acknowledges. Our thoughts "tend to roam in time and space." Often they are in the past, reliving a painful memory or a pleasurable one. Often they are in the future, daydreaming or making plans. Sometimes, Val concedes, it is necessary for our thoughts to be somewhere other than where our bodies are. "We need to examine and make sense of what has happened to us," as she points out. And we need "to shine a light onto the path that stretches ahead of us." And yet, she alleges, many of us spend too much time with our minds focused on some place beyond where we are. In "obsessing about the past," we run the risk of "regret-addiction." Worrying about the years to come, we squander our time in a place that may exist only in our imagination. "For much of our lives, we are like people with binoculars pressed to our eyes, oblivious to our surroundings."

•

Epicurus to Idomeneus of Lampsacus: "I have written this letter to you on a happy day to me, which is also the last day of my life."

•

Afternoon tea and cakes with my father and Rose, in the crypt of St. Martin-in-the-Fields, which they discovered on their last trip into town; it's handy for the theatres, and not too expensive, and not too noisy, Rose explains. "Phil struggles if there's a lot of noise," she tells me, flittering her fingers around an ear, by way of illustration. For Rose, my father has always been Phil, whereas for my mother he was always the full Philip; "a rebranding exercise," as Emma would have it.

Rose thinks I require pepping up; I need to meet someone. She wants to know why I haven't signed up for any online agencies. Some of them are really good. The way they analyse your character is amazingly accurate, she tells me; it doesn't matter what your interests are, they'll find someone who's "compatible." A friend of hers—Amy, she says to my father, to ensure that he's following—found a really lovely man last year; they hit it off right away, and now they are getting married; they both like birdwatching, she says, as if no nut could be harder to crack. "I'll give you the website," says Rose, consulting her phone. I promise to investigate.

The phone holds much evidence of the improvements that Rose has made to the garden. Rose's phone is the latest model; she is as comfortable with the technology as any teenager. And she is a tremendously efficient woman; the garden is impressive. But Eastbourne is the sunniest town in the whole of the UK, so any idiot can make things grow there, she says; the self-deprecation is not feigned. Eastbourne is changing so quickly, she informs me. Property prices were good when they moved there, but now they've gone mad. Rose cites examples of the madness of property prices in Eastbourne. Most of the talking is done by Rose, as is increasingly the case. My father's hearing is worse this year than last. "A blessing, in some circumstances," he says. They are in town to see a show, a musical. A treat for his birthday. Rose is a big fan of musicals, and Phil has come to love them too. "As long as there's dancing. He really likes the dancing. Isn't that right, love?" My father concurs. "You get prettier girls in musicals. Good legs," he says, and Rose raises an eyebrow, delighted by his incorrigibility.

"What about you?" Rose enquiries. "What are your plans?"

I tell her that I'd thought I might wander over to the Soane museum.

She smiles. The ageing son is a hopeless case. "Don't forget what I said," she says on parting, tapping at an imaginary keyboard.

•

My father understood the relationship with Imogen: I was going through what many men of my age go through, a low-level crisis exacerbated by the divorce, which had unsettled me more than I cared to acknowledge, he believed, or so Rose has told me. I don't recall ever discussing the divorce with my father; I kept him apprised of developments, no more than that. He could see what drew me to Imogen: she was nice-looking, and had money. A woman with money is as attractive to a man as a moneyed man is to a woman, despite what people say, he maintained. But social class is a different matter, and with Imogen I had strayed a little too far from my proper

159

territory, even if my territory, like my sister's, is no longer wholly congruent with his. And actresses are flighty by nature, as everyone knows. As for the idea of having a girlfriend who was often not even in the same country, never mind in the same city—no wonder it didn't work out. Rose, who is of a more romantic temperament than her husband, as she has often said, sees things slightly differently: actors don't make good long-term partners, that much is obvious, but they are exciting and unusual people, so it was not surprising that I had taken a chance when the opportunity arose. And for men, it goes without saying, a pretty face goes a long way, Rose observed. Rose has a pretty face, still. For a woman in the latter part of her sixties, she is remarkably pert; she suits her name, though my sister, in the early days, when Rose was barely acceptable, was of the opinion that she was less a rose than a Christmas-tree ball—a bright and shiny void. Some respect, however, had to be given to Rose's mercantile skills. She had, after all, made a success of her shop, the shop into which our father had walked one day, in search of a birthday gift for his daughter, thinking that an item of leading-edge kitchenware might be just the thing. Fractiously divorced the previous year, Rose was perhaps susceptible to the attractions of a dependable man, and my father was a man of manifest dependability; a man, moreover, who seemed to genuinely appreciate the quality of the merchandise on offer; he was clearly very fond of his daughter too; and a well-preserved specimen into the bargain. Rose, for her part, was a highly personable woman; in the course of the first conversation—on what must, I imagine, have been a slack day at the shop—it was established that she was the owner of the business, that she was freshly single, and that she enjoyed nothing more than cooking. Within a few weeks he had been given proof of Rose's prowess at

the stove. This, my sister was convinced, was the principal explanation for Rose's success; our father, she thought, had not eaten anything more nutritious than ready-meals since our mother had died.
And there was the sex, of course. On the evening of our introduction
to Rose, a remark was made from which we were clearly invited to
infer that some highly satisfactory sexual activity had been taking
place. On subsequent evenings we observed, as intended, significant
glances and small smiles. City-breaks were mentioned; Bruges was
a preferred destination—very pretty, and much better value for
money than Paris, Rose advised. The innuendos were unseemly. But
my father seemed happy, and still does.

•

Even if Rose had not been Rose, even if she had been a woman of
our father's age, rather than one who is less than a full decade older
than his daughter, Emma could not have approved. A new wife
within a year of the first one's death—the hastiness was indecent. A
longer period of mourning was our mother's due; for a woman of
our mother's selflessness, a posthumous repayment of four or five
years should have been the bare minimum, as Emma sees it. The
new relationship signified too urgent a need; a lack of robustness.
And then Rose is so unlike our mother. The dissimilarity is such
that it has made Emma wonder, at times, about the depth of our
father's attachment to our mother. At what point in the year of being
alone, Emma asks herself, had he become someone who could marry
a woman like Rose? My sister is often aggrieved on behalf of her
mother. Neither of us has any memory of any disagreements between
our parents, but our mother's life was not her own: she was allowed

to do nothing except have children, and raise them, and then take a job that must have bored her senseless, typing letters all day. A "negative inspiration" for her daughter, as Emma has put it. When at last our mother stopped working, she began to read books, for the first time since her marriage. Her enthusiasm for the novels of Willa Cather was indicative of previously untapped resources. Too late, she confessed to Emma that she would have loved to travel across America, coast to coast. "Dad is like me—not much in the way of imagination," said Emma once. "Mum was different—or she would have been." She doubts whether Rose has read a book of any sort.

•

From time to time, when Imogen was a girl, her father would reveal some idiosyncrasy of character that might have surprised many of the people who knew him, she told me. In the depths of a wardrobe lurked some dandyish shirts, which for some reason he had not been able to discard; she could not imagine him wearing such things, at any age. He confessed to a liking, not quite extinct, for the music of Charlie Parker. And she remembered being shown a picture of Lord Berners, taking tea at home, with a large white horse standing on the carpet beside him, drinking from a saucer. "A chap it would have been fun to know," her father commented.

It was possible that her mother had been a source of fun in the years before Imogen was old enough to intuit, from her father's one memorable use of the word, that he wished their life were in some way different from what it was. Her mother seemed to lack all capacity for frivolity. It was possible, as Imogen came to understand, that her mother was no longer the person she had been when her father had fallen in love with her. Photographs, however, showed little evidence that Charlotte in her early twenties had taken life more easily than she did in later years; she smiled in some of them, but the smile suggested camera-readiness rather than light-heartedness. Still, it was possible that something had been lost in motherhood. She might have cast off the last of her youth, to take on the dignity and seriousness that was required of a woman of her newly acquired standing. If that is what had happened, the thoroughness of her assumption of the role was remarkable. She had grafted herself perfectly onto the tree of the English family. No one could ever have evinced a deeper respect for the ways and the history of the Goughs. "The high priestess of etiquette," Imogen called her, preparing me for what was in store.

•

In the library there used to be a photograph that was taken at the house in 1944, on the tennis court. About twenty people were in the picture, some of them dressed for tennis, most not. For years the only points of interest, for Imogen, were that the boy sitting cross-legged at the front was her father, and the woman standing behind him was her grandmother, of whom she remembered little other than that she could sing nicely, kept a retinue of King Charles spaniels, and perfumed herself heavily with rosewater. But one day she asked her father about the woman who stood at the far left. This was Veronica, and she was very much not dressed for tennis. Her dress was a Fortuny silk gown, a thousand-pleated thing that fitted her body like a flow of syrup. Her face was in the shadow of her hand, and the picture was rather grainy, so the photograph did not truly show how gorgeous Veronica had been, her father told her. Even people who could not abide Veronica could not deny that she was a stunner. Her father had met her only two or three times, and never forgot the amazing dress that she was wearing on one of those days. It was ultramarine, and had tiny glass beads on the seam. Corsets could not be worn with such a dress; indeed, he later learned, it was designed to be worn without underwear of any kind. Veronica was a scandalous woman. The young man standing beside her, who at the time was engaged to the young woman on the far right of the picture, was later discovered to have been simultaneously intimate with Veronica, who had come to the party as the companion of another young man (back row, middle) and at one time or another was known to have been involved with at least three more of the men who appeared in the photograph.

At some point the picture was removed from the dresser. Imogen found it, after some searching. We looked at it together. "Which were the ones who sinned with Veronica?" Imogen asked her mother. "I have no idea," her mother answered, not looking. Neither did she know where Veronica belonged amid the ramifications of the Gough family tree; the connection involved multiple marriages and divorces and was too complicated to be memorised. Veronica was reputed to have had the finest legs in all of London, Imogen's father had told her. A young man was said to have shot himself for love of her, or in despair at her faithlessness. He had survived, but was badly damaged in mind and body. If one had placed that woman's lovers end to end, Imogen's mother commented, they would have spanned Hyde Park.

July

WILLIAM CALLS, buoyant. Unloading the van this morning, he noticed a woman on the opposite side of the road. At exactly the same moment as he noticed her, she looked across at him. She was getting into a car and she looked over the roof, right at him. The way she blinked made him think that she had recognised him. She had long dark hair, parted in the middle, and her face was very pale. Her nose was distinctive too—narrow and straight. Her mouth was small and pretty. The resemblance to the woman in the London café was uncanny; and she definitely gave him a look. "It was like déjà vu, but more solid than that. You know what I mean?" he says. He didn't try to talk to her. There wasn't enough time anyway; they looked at each other, and then she drove off. That was enough. "I'll be seeing her again," William promises me.

•

Replete with assurances that she would make a most dutiful and faithful wife, most of Adeline's letters give the impression of having been composed in accordance with rules set out in a manual of letter-writing for young ladies. Their artlessness seems artful. The letter of June 18th, 1854, however, has the freshness of spontaneity. It makes reference to a walk by the river, a walk that seems to have been of great significance in the development of the relationship. A kiss was bestowed. At the close of her letter, Adeline writes: "I fear that the love I feel is beyond my control." We know, from Charles's reply, that the letter was written on paper that had been scented with lavender oil. Many of Adeline's letters were perfumed with lavender or violet oil. After her death, Charles would take the letters from the box in which he kept them, and would breathe the remnant of their scent, I told Imogen. Supporting the letter on her upturned fingertips, as though it were a wafer of glass, she lowered her face to the paper and closed her eyes. If someone were to bottle the perfume of second-hand bookshops, she would buy it, Imogen said.

•

We came across William in the park, on a Sunday afternoon. He was lying on the grass, basking, with his feet raised on a backpack. It appeared that he was asleep. It's probable that I hoped that he was, but just as we reached the part of the path that was closest to where he was lying he suddenly opened his eyes, as if he'd picked up our scent, and looked straight at us. He waved and stood up, hoisting the bag onto his back. The weight of it made him stagger. Still waving, as though he had something to give us, he lumbered up to the path.

He apologised to Imogen for having talked too much last time. "Tell you the truth," he said, "I was a bit out of it. Anyway, I just wanted to say sorry. Thank you. I'll let you get on," he finished, stepping back.

We were in no hurry, Imogen told him. There was an unoccupied bench a few yards further up the path. "Let's sit down for a few minutes," she suggested. William and I followed her; he looked at me and shrugged, as if to say that the matter was out of his hands.

The bag, we learned, held everything he owned. A friend had let him sleep in the bath for a couple of nights and now he was going to try Melville Street. Asked about his family, he told us that his mother and her husband had moved to Hull, the husband's home town, because they could buy a palace in Hull for the price of the dump in Abbey Wood. William would not be going to Hull. "Practically Norway, isn't it?" he said.

With Imogen he had a conversation about families. When she told him something about hers, he listened with no apparent resentment, but as if she were from a foreign country. It seemed to impress him that she was unapologetic about her good fortune. Fathers and stepfathers were discussed: his stepfather, a decorator, was an arsehole who expected to be waited on hand and foot; his real father was an arsehole too, but an occasionally interesting arsehole, who played drums with a pub band whenever his motor skills were up to it, which wasn't often, because of the drink. Nearly all of the conversation was between Imogen and William. The common touch did not come easily to me; I could hear a note of condescension in my tone, whereas in Imogen's there was none. William wanted to hear more about her family. I relapsed into the background. When I glanced at my watch, William noticed the movement of my hand, though he was looking at Imogen, engrossed. "You have to go," he said, in rebuke to himself.

"I do," I said, and told him where I worked.

"I know the place," he said. "Never been there. Free, is it?"

I regretted that it was no longer free.

"Pity," he said.

167

Imogen tucked a note into a pocket of his bag.

"Way too much," he said, removing it.

"Take it," she said.

He did not resist. "You are one lucky man," he told me.

•

When Imogen took my hand and told me that she might want to choose the day of her death, I saw no self-pity in her gaze. We talked about suicide. "People take it as an affront," she said. They deplore it as an abdication of responsibility, or a display of ingratitude, a rejection of the greatest of all gifts. It is regarded as an act of desertion: the suicide leaves the living to fight on, in the battle of life from which the coward has fled. "I learned something the other day," she said, smiling brightly, as though the subject were trivial. Louis XIV had ordered that the corpses of suicides should be dragged through the streets face-down, then hanged or chucked onto a rubbish heap. "I would prefer a more conventional send-off," she said.

•

I have made arrangements to end my life before the impairment of my mind makes any decision impossible, she wrote. *These arrangements may require the assistance of a third party. My mother has consented to be that third party, though it is contrary to her wishes. She has consented to my decision out of love for me. I am fully aware of what I am doing.* I signed the document, as its witness. Reading it, the following week, Imogen said to me: "I hope I can be the person who wrote this."

•

My sister has joined a book group. I should do likewise, she tells me, because book groups are always packed with women, many of them interesting. Emma's group is entirely female, and a couple of them are unattached, in their late forties, early fifties. Lots of empty nesters go to book groups, apparently, and many of these empty nesters are newly single. Her two eligibles are examples of the phenomenon: no sooner had their children left home than their marriages fell apart. The women are making up for lost time, says Emma. Their *joie de vivre* is a rebuke to my lassitude. Even better: one of them is an archaeologist. A pity I don't live closer. The archaeologist is highly intelligent and "warm." This is the kind of woman I need to meet, Emma tells me.

•

In the park this afternoon: a dark-haired girl, thirteen or fourteen years of age, sitting on the grass, alone; she had no phone, and no book; she simply sat on the grass, gazing across the park, arms crossed. A solemn-looking child. On the basis of almost no evidence, I characterised her as someone who was solitary by choice. Her face bore no resemblance to Imogen's, but I think what made me halt was a reminder of the photograph of Imogen at that age, sitting on the fence of the paddock, deep in thought, unaware that her brother had aimed the camera at her. On the back of the picture, in pencil: *Imo, away with the fairies.* Three decades of life were left to her. And suddenly, looking at the solemn girl, I experienced a surge of tenderness, as if the two girls had become the same child. A moment of rich sentimentality, halted when I became aware that I was being observed by a man of my age, who was misunderstanding what he was seeing. A mistake that anyone would have made.

•

At the paddock, Imogen recalled an afternoon, in summer, when she was twelve years old. She was standing by the fence when her mother called, and for some reason, at that moment, the three syllables of "Imogen" struck her purely as a sound, like a word of a foreign language. "Imogen," she realised, was not an inseparable aspect of who she was. It was not like the redness of a strawberry. She let her mother call her three or four times. It was an interesting experience, listening to the syllables as they flew into the air. It was like a special kind of nakedness, she told me, though she was not certain that this image had occurred to her at the time. A day or two later, she had a similar thought about the apple tree. Sitting on a bench that had faced the apple tree towards which we were now strolling, young Imogen had murmured to herself: "Apple tree. Apple tree. Apple tree." Over and over again she had murmured the words: a meaningless jingle, a pleasant sound that had nothing of the tree in it—"Apple tree. Apple tree. Apple tree. Apple tree. Apple tree."

•

Three people for this afternoon's guided tour. At the door of the room that had been Adeline's, I removed the key from my pocket and paused before inserting it into the lock; a touch of suspense. This was where Adeline died, I announced. For the remaining fifty years of his life Charles Perceval had left the room untouched, with the clock set permanently to 1.10pm, the time of her death. Some changes have been made in the interim, but much of the furniture and many of Adeline's belongings are still here. Adeline's wedding dress attracted immediate attention. The veil—an exquisite piece of Burano lace, as delicate as frost—was marvelled at. I pointed out the pastel portrait of Adeline with the blood-red roses, and the locket that contained a loop of her hair. Various items—a set of brushes, a necklace, earrings, books, a cameo—lie on a faux-medieval table, in an arrangement of simulated abandonment. The saint with the dragon, I explained, standing at the print beside the bed, was Saint Margaret of Antioch, who was swallowed by Satan in the form of a dragon, but escaped by bursting out of his stomach, which had been unable to tolerate the cross that Margaret was carrying. Saint Margaret, one of the so-called "helper saints," was often invoked during labour, as were Saint Barbara and Saint Catherine of Alexandria, whose images are on the opposite wall.

I remember Imogen in that room. She was the last to leave the portrait; she stared at it as if it were of special significance to her; as though Adeline were an ancestor.

•

At the piano, she stopped playing in the middle of a phrase. "This is rubbish," she said. "It's Beatrice playing, not me." She held her hands in front of her face and looked at them as though they had become unrecognisable.

"It sounded fine to me," I said, which was true.

"It was awful," she said. "Prissy." Her mood was darkening.

•

One night she rang, and told me: "The fog is coming down." That morning, talking to someone in the street, she had experienced the "slippage" that always preceded a slump: a fraction of a second before speaking, she had heard a pre-echo of the words that she was about to speak. In a day or two, she knew, the "chemical deluge" would begin. She would not allow me to visit. "There would be no pleasure in being with me," she said. "I have to be alone. For everyone's sake. But it'll pass," she reassured me. For a month I did not see her. Whenever I phoned, her voice was a slow monotone. She could not sleep; when she tried to read, sentences became comprehensible only after three or four attempts, or sometimes not at all. She apologised for not making sense, but she did make sense, though the words came effortfully. "I love you," she once said, after a long silence, as though she had lost her memory of almost everything except this fact.

•

Each role was to an extent an alias, but at times, she said, she felt that her own self was an alias: Imogen Gough was a role, and she had no idea who was playing her. Every time we speak, we assume a character; the words are our costume. "Even with you," she said, as though admitting an infidelity. It was the nadir of a day. Weeping, she asked: "But why would you want to live with me? I'm nothing." She was squinting at her reflection in the window of my bedroom, as if trying to make out who was there.

•

In the archive we have the journal that Charles Perceval wrote, spo-
radically, in the years following the death of Adeline. Parts of it are
barely recognisable as writing—the script on these pages is like a
graphic representation of his misery. In places it appears that, at
some later date, on reading what he had written, he had decided to
obliterate his confession: whole paragraphs have been scored over,
creating a screen through which only fractions of letters can be read.
I showed Imogen such a page. But some passages were clearly written, and eloquent. Charles Perceval describes the horror of the
moment in which the lid of the coffin was lowered into place; he
watched as Adeline's face was removed from sight forever. "The
light will never fall on her again," he wrote. At the graveside he gazed
down at the coffin, transfixed, as the clods of mud drummed on the
wood above her face. That night, whenever he closed his eyes he
saw her staring into the darkness, under the earth, a mile from where
he lay. Every day, for many weeks, he returned to the grave. He felt
that he had been changed into a being without substance; he was a
spectre whom people mistook for a living man; he was an entity for
whom memory was more real than the world through which he
moved. During his watches of the night, the face of dead Adeline
would appear. He saw the simper of the decaying lips; the rotted
eyelids, like leaf mulch.

•

We talked about what had been said at the hospital and what she
had read. "I know where this is going," she said. The day before, in
the morning, she had gone out to buy bread. The noises of the street
had seemed strange, as if the sound were coming through some sort

of membrane, as if she were no longer fully part of the same reality as the traffic. "I'm already fading out," she said. At about nine o'clock I persuaded her to take a walk. It was a splendid evening—the longest day of the year was a few days away. We did not talk much. The scene was beautiful: turquoise water; golden sky; handsome buildings; shadows thickening underneath the trees. She laughed once, quietly. Then, locking her face into a frown of fortitude, she announced: "In this scene I play a woman who is thinking positively. I contemplate the beauty of my surroundings; the river is a metaphor, as goes without saying."

•

The only way William can make all his deliveries in the allocated time is to drive like a lunatic from house to house, and I'd be amazed how often people forget to be at home, and how many of them moan because they've been given bananas that aren't as big as they like their bananas. And some of the shift managers don't know the first thing about communication. But none of this really matters, because "a great thing has happened." He was dropping off an order at lunchtime yesterday, in Wherrytown, at an address he'd not been to before. The customer turned out to be a childminder—he had to weave his way past half a dozen toddlers to get to the kitchen. "A lot for you to look after," he remarked as he followed her, bearing his stack of crates. Her name is Suzanne, he knew from the paperwork. "They're not all mine," she answered, and at that moment he entered the kitchen to find himself face to face with his pale and dark-haired woman. Every day he had been hoping to see her again, and here she was, at last. It was clear, just from the way she said hello, that he would like her very much if he could get to know her; which was as expected, of course. On her lap sat a girl, three years old, William guessed, a cute kid, and smart, he could tell from the attention with which she watched him unpack the crates. He gave the girl a wink, and risked a light stroke of the cheek, which was well received by her mother too—it was obvious that the woman was her mother. He is almost certain that she's unattached: no ring, and she "gave off a single-mother vibe." On the basis of two minutes in the kitchen, he came to the conclusion that her friendship with the other woman is close. "I've got a toe-hold," he tells me. It would not have been a good idea, we agreed, to tell the woman that he had seen her before, and that he could give her the exact date, time and location of that first sighting.

•

Today: ninety-three visitors. A boy, twelvish, in the mirrored room, pointed into the army of duplicates and barked: "You there—what's your name?" As if somewhere in the infinite ranks of pointing boys there were one who was not the double of all the others.

•

At a café on Place de la République, Imogen told me that she had once had lunch there with Antoine Vermeiren, who had revealed that this unlovely part of the city was one of his "holy places." He had pointed across the square to indicate where the city's first diorama theatre had stood, the theatre of which Louis Daguerre was the creator and proprietor. Antoine explained how the diorama had worked, with its revolving auditorium and the lighting effects by which the illusion of movement was created. So Daguerre must be regarded as the "grandfather of cinema," Antoine stated. And that was not all.

One morning in 1838 or 1839, in Boulevard du Temple, just a few metres from where Imogen and Antoine were sitting, a man had stopped to have his shoes cleaned, and had thereby become the first person ever to appear in a photographic image. On that particular morning, in his studio above the diorama theatre, Louis Daguerre had directed his lens towards Boulevard du Temple and captured forever what the lens had observed. It is known, from Daguerre's annotation, that the picture was taken at eight o'clock in the morning. The year is uncertain, but the time is not. Boulevard du Temple would have been busy at that hour, and yet the daguerreotype shows a scene that resembles an empty film set. There are no carriages or carts on the road; the pavements are deserted. This is because Daguerre's process required an exposure time of several minutes; people going about their business would have moved through the frame too quickly to leave any trace on Daguerre's photosensitive plate; they dissolved into the air. Only one of the many people in Boulevard du Temple on that particular morning stood still for long enough to make his mark.

The picture is in front of me. There he is, near the lower left-hand corner, with one foot raised to rest on the shoe-black's box; the shoe-black himself is a less distinct form, so shadowy that he is often overlooked. Some people believe they can see other figures in the picture: two women with a pram have been discerned; there may be a face at a window. But the standing man is the only vivid presence. His legs are as precise as the nearby saplings, so he must have held the pose for some time. Imogen wondered about him: would anyone stand stationary for five minutes or more, on one leg, to have his shoes cleaned? And his position within the image, so discreetly yet conspicuously placed, in silhouette against the whiteness of the pavement—it made her suspicious. Surely the standing man had occupied his place in the scene by design? He was an accomplice, not someone who had merely happened to pause there. This seemingly artless picture, this veritable relic of a morning's moment in Paris, may not be what it appears to be.

•

"I have seized the light. I have arrested its flight," proclaimed Daguerre. But, just as the body of the standing man has been reduced to bones and dust, decay has reduced the material of his image. Silver and mercury composed the scene on the metal plate; oxidation of those chemicals has destroyed much of the picture. The *Boulevard du Temple* at which I am looking, I have learned, is a facsimile, a daguerreotype made in 1979, from a photograph of the original daguerreotype taken in 1937 for the American curator and art historian Beaumont Newhall, who had found the picture in the archives of the Bayerisches Nationalmuseum. It was framed with two other daguerreotypes—a still life and a second image of Boulevard du Temple—which Daguerre had presented to King Ludwig I of Bavaria in 1839.

•

William told us about his recurring dream. He found himself in a town that he recognised immediately from other dreams: he was on a cobbled road, and in front of him rose a high wall, built of large yellow stone blocks, with an archway in it, spanning the road that he was on. Through the arch, the cobbled road led to a church with a tall spire. Halfway along, he could turn left into an alleyway which ended at a terrace; if he turned right, another alley, wider than the first, wound down to a place where cars and coaches were parked. From the car park a road curved up to the church, passing a shop that had a mannequin in armour outside. Every time this dream occurred, everything was in precisely the same place, so he knew that he was not making it up—he must have been to this town. But he had no memory of ever having been in such a place. Perhaps he had been there with his parents, when he was a child. If that were the case, it was odd, he thought, that his parents never appeared in the dream. He was always alone, looking up at the spire, with birds and clouds above it. But in the dream he was very happy, and he was happy when he woke up, for as long as the atmosphere of the dream town persisted. He would love to go back there, he said, but he had no idea where it was, other than inside his head.

Imogen responded in kind: sometimes she had a dream that bore some similarity to William's. It involved her mother. The setting was not constant: it might be a city street, or woodland, or a room at home. What defined this dream was that Imogen and her mother were talking to each other, seriously, at length, and the conversation would culminate with her mother using a word that sounded French, but which Imogen had never heard before. Her mother might point to something and say the word, or it might be that the word signified something abstract, such as a mood or a quality of light at a particular hour of the day. However it was used, the word always struck Imogen, in the dream, as being a sound that fitted the idea or the object perfectly, just as the song of a bird belongs to the bird. When she woke up, however, the word was no longer there. She had only the sense that something wonderful had been revealed to her, momentarily.

William nodded deeply; he understood, as a pupil understands a master. They looked at me. "Sometimes I dream that I've become the director of the British Museum," I lied, playing my part.

•

"Our entire history is only the history of waking men," wrote Georg Christoph Lichtenberg. The private life of this brilliant man is scandalous to us, yet it appears that for the people of Göttingen it was a subject for gossip only. In 1777, in his thirty-fifth year, Lichtenberg met Maria Dorothea Stechard, a "model of beauty and sweetness." She was twelve years old. She lived with him from 1780 until her death in 1782. Her death affected him, "like nothing before or afterwards," but in the following year he began a relationship with his housekeeper, Margarethe Elisabeth Kellner, seventeen years his junior, whom he married in 1789. Always in poor health (severe scoliosis of the spine), he felt that his death was imminent and wanted to ensure that Margarethe would receive a widow's pension. His death was not imminent: he died in 1799. Margarethe, having borne six children, outlived him by almost half a century.

•

This evening, a moment in which Imogen was acutely absent. The rain stopped, and a crack opened in the aubergine-coloured sky, uncovering the sun. The pavement gleamed, and for some reason the gleam brought to mind the sand at low tide, late in the day, shining pale green and pewter, and Imogen stopping, seizing my hand, amazed.

•

William made another delivery to Wherrytown today, a couple of hours earlier than the previous delivery. There were just three children in the flat with Suzanne. "Things a bit quieter today," he remarked. Suzanne smiled; the invasion was due in an hour, she told him. "Same crew?" he asked. The answer was positive. "That explains the crisps," he said; the delivery included a substantial quantity of crisps. No further information was volunteered, and William was content to leave it at that. The nameless friend is a regular visitor, he deduces. "Softly, softly," we agree.

•

In the hospital, after the last operation, Imogen raised the gown to reveal the stoma. I can see her face: the fear and helplessness. It was as if we were comrades and she had suffered a mortal wound. I had brought a card from Francesca and Geraint; they had enclosed a photo of themselves, waving at the camera, at Imogen. "It would be good to see her again," she said. She would never see Francesca again. She looked down at the bag. It was like a cross painted on the door of a house in which the plague had struck, she said.

•

We were talking about Charles Perceval, one day during the making of *Devotion*, and Imogen said that it was not difficult to imagine that, as a doctor, he would have found solace in the experience of Mass, whether or not he truly believed. Participation in the chorus of the faithful would have been a release from the terrible privacy of his work. The burden must be intolerable at times, she said: knowing that a patient will soon die, no matter what the treatment; carrying the weight of the patient's faith; having to temper the truth, according to the patient's strength of mind. "No patient wants to know the absolute truth," I have read. But Imogen demanded to know everything that the doctors knew, unmitigated.

•

Today—sixty-three visitors.

•

Val's thought for the month: when two people are falling in love, they learn about each other by listening. "We talk about ourselves— 'This is who I am,' we tell the newly significant person." This process of listening and learning is "key" to the thrilling early weeks of the relationship. And from this process, if we are fortunate, arises a special and enduring intimacy. But this intimacy is not without its dangers. Familiarity might not necessarily breed contempt, but it can entail a loss of respect. We need to be on our guard, Val adjures us: "*I* and *You* must not be lost to *We*." In order to prevent the loss of *I* and *You*, we should take measures "to keep alive the sense of discovery" that brought us together in the first place. Val has a method to recommend. It is simple, but effective, she promises. All that is required is for the long-term couple to set aside ten minutes each week to listen to each other. Yes, ten minutes is enough, it seems. Person A talks for five minutes, about whatever it seems important to talk about, and Person B listens, without interrupting. After five minutes, they swap roles. Easy. The sofa is the recommended venue for these relationship-sustaining monologues. The ambience must be comfortable, relaxed. "There should be no element of confrontation," we are told.

•

In his seventieth letter to Lucilius, Seneca writes: *mere living is not a good, but living well. Accordingly, the wise man will live as long as he ought, not as long as he can.* In the same letter we read: *You can find men who have gone so far as to profess wisdom and yet maintain that one should not offer violence to one's own life, and hold it accursed for a man to be the means of his own destruction; we should wait, say they, for the end decreed by nature. But one who says this does not see that he is shutting off the path to freedom. The best thing which eternal law ever ordained was that it allowed to us one entrance into life, but many exits.*

•

As might be expected of a graphic designer, Loïc was "an intensely visual person," as he told Imogen. And yet the visible changes that had been inflicted on her body were not of paramount significance to him, he insisted, on the night of his confession of inadequacy. The scar was discreet, and barely troubled him. She was still an immensely attractive woman, he reassured her. What troubled him, he admitted, was the "inner destruction." Though he loved her, he was conscious that he had begun to withhold something of himself. He was ashamed of this. It disturbed him, that he should be so disturbed by the "alteration" that her body had undergone. It was a deplorable weakness, he knew; a weakness that was especially contemptible when regarded in the light of Imogen's courage. And he did regard himself with contempt. He hated himself, he insisted; by way of demonstration, he wept a little. But he had an obligation to be truthful. Sexual energy had ebbed out of the relationship. The body cannot lie, he told his lover; this nugget of wisdom, she sensed, had been used before, in other terminal discussions. In conclusion, his love had changed; it had not waned, but it had become something else.

For Imogen also, the sex was very much not what it had been, she informed him. She was tired; areas of sensation had been lost; and there was pain. Loïc understood. But in time the pain would disappear, he told her. Of course she was tired; the tiredness too would go. Recovery would take time. "You are always impatient," he told her, as if this had been a major aspect of her allure. He had done some research into the experiences of women "in the same situation" as Imogen was now in. Many of them, he had discovered, reported that sex was better than ever.

A doctor—a male doctor—had told Imogen the same thing, she told Loïc; she found it hard to believe.

The research was unimpeachable, insisted Loïc. Problems were common in these situations, of course, but their resolution was often "a matter of psychology." What she needed, he said, was a new relationship, with a better man. So Loïc contrived to place himself again in the centre of the stage. It was as though he regarded her cancer as a test of his mettle, and he had failed the test. He would still be her friend; he insisted on it, though he had let her down as a lover. Loïc did not stint on the self-accusation. The self-scourging made him feel better about himself. But the penitent garb would soon be discarded, Imogen knew, as she cast him out.

Loïc had been pleasing to the eye, and talented, but now it dismayed her—amazed her, even—that she had failed to discern the feebleness of the man. "So now I'm on the lookout for someone with a post-surgical fetish," she said.

•

Another Wherrytown delivery for William, mid-morning; again, the three small children are there, but not the alluring friend and her daughter; again many packets of crisps. Today, because the weather is so good, they are having a picnic, Suzanne tells him. One of the children claps his hands; another yells her approval. "That'll be great, eh?" says William to the kids; it can do no harm to advertise his niceness. As he sorts the paperwork, he scans the photographs that are stuck to the fridge with magnets. He sees a picture of the friend and her little girl, sitting on thrones of sand; both are laughing; this is definitely a woman he could love, William tells me. He nods at the photo and remarks, as Suzanne signs the invoice: "She seems like a terrific kid." Suzanne glances at the picture, then at him, then at the photo again. "Oh yes," she answers, "Tilly's a star." A small smile in her eyes suggests that he has given himself away. He leaves still not knowing the name of Tilly's mother, but he is getting closer, says William. "The arrow is on its way."

•

Some months after we were there together, Imogen returned to the *maison de maître*, for what would be the last time. She decided it would be the last time as she was leaving the house. Her body had lost much of its strength and appetite, she told me, but this was not the principal reason for her decision. The principal reason was the loneliness, which was more intense than ever. Only once had she not left the *maison de maître* in a state of something like desolation.

•

Encounter with Samantha and Val, outside the bank. They are going to Berlin at the weekend; Conrad and Katrin are playing there, Samantha tells me. A recording contract has been discussed. I offer my congratulations. Samantha is glad to hear that William's life is on track. I commend Val's new glasses: retro black horn-rims, with big lenses. She seems amused by my ingratiating performance. It's a strong outfit, I almost tell her. She does look good: the bold black frames and wild grey hair; the burgundy sweater and pitch-black coat. "Well—have fun," I say. "We will," Samantha promises, as Val takes her arm.

August

"HOW'S THE RESEARCH GOING?" Samantha asked, some time after Imogen had left. It was assumed that, in the apparent absence of any new relationship, I would now immerse myself in the Perceval project. A new tangent had opened up, I told her: Cornelius Perceval, it appeared, had been in some way involved with Thomas Beddoes' experiments with air-based therapies. The story of the Percevals was of no interest to Val; as if the subject were of some intimacy, she disengaged herself. We were sitting outside, and Val cast onto the street her look of benign and mellow wonderment. When I said that I thought the Percevals book would take two or three years to write, Val turned back to me and smiled. In her eyes, for a second, appeared a nuance—the very slightest nuance—of pity. A few years on, still no book. Credit where credit is due.

•

What has happened, I wonder, to the perpetually walking man? We saw him many times, always walking, always in the same garb, whatever the weather: black boots, black waterproof trousers, black anorak, with the hood pulled up. On his back he carried a large black bag, of the kind used to carry newspapers for delivery; the bag invariably appeared to be full, and he bore the weight of it on a wide webbing strap that ran across his forehead and pressed the hood over his eyes, like a cowl; one could see the strain in his neck; he stooped, and every stride was effortful, as though he were wading into surf. William knew him, and cautioned against engagement. What the man's story was, he didn't know, but he had "brain issues," said William. "Not right in the head. Not at all right," he told us. William had spoken to him twice, which was once more than enough. He had come across him by the Abbey one night, talking to himself as if in conversation with half a dozen people—"Like he was walking with an invisible gang." The man heard voices all the time, it seemed. When William suggested that he might benefit from medical attention, he was rebuffed. There was no point in talking to any "expert," the man had answered, because the voices were real things, not things that he was imagining. If the man ever interrupted one of the voices, it would wait for him to finish and then resume where it had left off. This was proof of the voices' reality. There were other proofs too. The voices said things that the man knew to be false, for example. Therefore they were independent of him. Sometimes they used words that he would never use himself, or whose meaning he didn't know.

Only once did we come across the walking man not walking. On a very warm Sunday evening, near the station, he was sitting against a wall. The bag was beside him, but the hood of the anorak was in its customary position, obscuring the top half of his face. He was leaning against the bag, motionless; his hands dangled on his knees. Imogen crossed over to him. As she took out a banknote, he abruptly looked up and swore so fiercely that she stepped quickly back, as if from an animal that had tried to bite. She placed the note on the pavement, near his feet; he kicked it away, then stood up, turning his back; he raised the bag and put the strap across his forehead.

Though upset, Imogen made light of it. "A lesson there for Lady Bountiful," she said, taking my arm. The man was walking off, projecting great anger in every lurch of his stride.

•

Emma's phone, she tells me, can provide her with a report on how well or poorly she slept the night before. She puts it under her mattress when she goes to bed and in the morning it displays a graphic that informs her, for example, that she was restless at 3am. If I were to avail myself of this technological marvel, it would reveal my sleep patterns to me, and thus, perhaps, in ways unexplained, help to combat the insomnia. I explain that I don't need a phone to reveal my sleep patterns. I know when I'm not asleep, thanks to the bedside clock, at which I find myself staring three or four times per night. "One day you'll join us in the twenty-first century," she says.

•

"Contact is imminent," William calls to tell me. This morning, driving along the seafront, he saw four women and a gang of small kids walking towards him, on the promenade: Wherrytown Suzanne, Tilly's mother, and a couple of others. There was a queue of traffic at the approach to the junction, so he was moving slowly; as he crept closer to the women, William was sending out the mind-rays—*Look up, look up, please look up.* Suzanne looked up. She could have looked anywhere, but she looked straight at his van, as if the message had hit its target and she could see the trace of its flight through the air. So he waved, and Suzanne smiled, as he passed them. In his mirror, he saw Suzanne say something to Tilly's mother, then Tilly's mother turned her head, in the direction of the van, and they both laughed. It was not a discouraging laugh, says William; very much not.

•

Today: fifty-seven.

•

Coming back through the park, I stopped at the stand of sunflowers, recalling how strongly Imogen had disliked them. They always made her think of *Village of the Damned*, she said, though there are no sunflowers in *Village of the Damned*. When I had passed them earlier in the afternoon, the flowers had been in sunlight; now they had been in shadow for a couple of hours, and their heads had moved. The face of the largest flower was parallel to the earth. Looking at it, I had the thought that everything in the park had moved in that time. More: a flower is not a thing, the thought continued: what we call a flower is not a fulfilment of what the flower is—it's a phase in a process, as the seed is a phase and the mulch is a phase. The flower is not a thing but a category. I stared at the drooping sunflower. Everything is always arriving, the thought continued. Now I write: light is withdrawing from the floor and walls; the blood surges into and out of my hand. I add a full stop; an unnatural thing.

•

An evening at the cinema. Losing interest in the film, I looked across the row: every face attentive, lit by the reflected light of the projected images; a communion of sorts. Here, in the darkened hall of the cinema, we submit to the torrent of the visual. At home, armed with the remote control, we do not submit. Walking back, an acute attack of something like homesickness, remembering conversations with Imogen after seeing a film—no specific conversations; just the fact of them. She would have noted proofs of technique that I had not noticed. The timing of a turn, of a smile; once she was struck by the way an actress had picked up a glass, I recall; I cannot remember which film that was.

•

Déjà vu: a boy crossing my path on a skateboard; the air at a particular temperature, with a particular strength of breeze; the hue of the sunlight in the upper reaches of the chestnut trees; and then what I think was the trigger—the clatter of a lorry's tailboard. The sensation of displacement was so strong, my blood pressure seemed to plummet; a one-second dose of vertigo. A moment later, today resumed.

William one morning saw a magpie land on the pavement in front of him. It flustered its wings for a few seconds, before becoming very still, as if to ensure that it had gained his attention. Exactly this thing had happened before, he knew, but the uncanny instant was no sooner felt than lost, leaving no clues. There never are any clues, as William said to me. The moment feels like a repetition, but one can never work out what is being repeated. But in the case of the magpie he could work it out. It was not really an instance of déjà vu. The bird was familiar, William realised, simply because every day was in fact like every other day. He was sick of this place, and the people of the town, for their part, were sick of the sight of him. He had become too familiar. Some gave him money every now and then, but most looked at him and moved on, sometimes with sympathy, as if that might in some way ease his situation. "But when did feeling sorry ever help anyone except the one who's feeling sorry?" he asked. Resting his head on the back of the bench, he looked into the sky. "Nobody round here will give me a job. Not a proper job. They know me. I'm the layabout." So he had decided to leave. He'd been talking to someone who had a van, and they were going to drive around, grabbing work where they could—"picking fruit, digging holes, whatever." They would sleep in the van if they had to, and just keep going until the wheels fell off. "I've enjoyed talking to you," he said, and gave me a hand to shake. "I hope we meet again," he said. "And if you ever see Imogen, say hello." Then William was gone, for a long time.

•

After a month of silence, Imogen rang, late on a Sunday morning. I can hear her voice: the tentative tone as she said my name. Something was wrong, I knew at once. "The curse has struck," she said. Loïc was taking care of her, with other friends of whom I knew little more than their names. Her mother would be arriving the day before the operation. "She's been working on my morale," Imogen reported. Certain avenues would now be closed, this was true, her mother had conceded. But there were worse things than childlessness, she had pointed out, Imogen told me, laughing. And adoption was always a possibility, her mother added, as if this were a last resort for the tragically desperate.

•

She could name several people who kept their distance after it had become known that there would be no recovery. Some, who would have described themselves as friends, phoned to declare an intention to visit, and were never heard from again. On the other hand there was Sue, who rang within hours of hearing the news from someone whose agent had also been Imogen's. A couple of years before we met, Imogen and Sue had been in a production of *Twelfth Night*: the staging was inane; the director a conceited dolt; the audiences lukewarm. They had spent a great deal of time together, drinking and moaning, but had barely been in contact since then.

Sue arrived on the following Saturday, and was in tears before she had locked the car; she had not been prepared for so severe a decline. "I don't know what to say," were her first words, and in that instant of honesty Imogen's affection for her was reawakened.

There was no need to say anything, Imogen told her; it was enough that she had arrived.

Sue held out her arms, in a way that asked if an embrace would be appropriate. Others had stood back, as though some sort of quarantine were in effect. She held Imogen lightly, and not for too long. It was a warm day; they went into the garden and sat on the bench by the pergola.

In the interim, Sue had widened considerably. In her younger days she had appealed to directors who wanted a cheeky and tomboyish kind of girl; now she was usually the cuddly mum. "Pleasant and capable," she said. "But low on the fuckability scale. My fuckable days are done," she proclaimed, slapping her thighs, as if gratified to have finished with the exertions of youth. Hearing what she had said, she flinched at her tactlessness.

Imogen reassured her: the situation should be ignored as much as possible, she said.

"I talk too much," said Sue. "I always talk too much. I should be listening."

"What can I tell you?" said Imogen. "Here I am. It's bad, but there's nothing to be done."

"Don't you want to talk about it?"

"Not really," Imogen answered. "I'm glad you're here. Tell me what you've been up to."

Work had not been plentiful of late, Sue reported. She was up for a TV part, playing a headmistress who turned out to have been fiddling the school's accounts to pay for her shopping binges. The script was based on a true story. The woman had been coming to work in a Burberry coat, with a Vuitton handbag, but she managed to convince her colleagues that they were high-grade fakes. Even when she took her third exotic holiday of the year, it seems nobody had wondered where the money was coming from. "Could be a lot of fun. But not as much fun as your sexy costume drama," she said, meaning *Le Grand Concert*. "I loved it."

They talked about *Le Grand Concert*, though Imogen felt no connection with it now; it belonged to a different life.

"You know what happened to Tony?" Sue asked, alighting on a happy thought. A reminder was needed: Tony was the insufferable director of *Twelfth Night*. The news was that he had married an Argentinian woman, who had stabbed him in a fit of jealousy. "A superficial injury, sadly," said Sue. She reminisced about that terrible production, of which her memory was rather more full than Imogen's. It was a pleasurable distraction, a story. Imogen's feeling of separation from the past, she told me, felt rather like wisdom; the fabled wisdom of the dying. And when, shortly before leaving, Sue asked if Imogen was angry about what had happened, it was not a lie to answer that anger would be pointless. Disappointment was what Imogen felt, she told her friend; a terribly heavy, at times unbearable disappointment.

"If I were you, I'd be smashing the furniture," said Sue.

"The stuff in this house is too sturdy for that," Imogen answered. "And one must think of the heirs."

Sue's farewell was frank. "I suppose this is the last time we'll see each other," she said.

"I think so," Imogen answered. "The funeral doesn't count. I won't know if you're there."

"I'll be there," Sue promised; and she was.

Again they embraced. Sue said: "I am so glad to have known you." Without looking back, she walked down the drive to her car.

•

For yesterday's delivery, Wherrytown Suzanne switched her time-slot back to midday, which William took to be another encouraging sign—it seemed possible that she had chosen the lunch period in order to bring about another encounter with Tilly's mother. And indeed there she was, in the kitchen, ready to lend a hand with the unpacking. "But I did not play it well," William tells me. The opening gambit was fine, he thought: a casual but friendly "Hello, Tilly" for the little girl, who was sitting at the kitchen table, with the other kids, scribbling. It did not surprise the child that he knew her name. He gave her mother a quick smile. "Nothing too obvious, nothing heavy," he reports. After a remark on the weather, he went back to the van for the rest of the stuff. When he returned, Suzanne had taken one of the children to the bathroom. He was left with Tilly's mother, who took a bag from him and asked what time his shift had started. Suddenly he felt as embarrassed as a twelve-year-old when the prettiest girl in the class talks to him in a new way. His first delivery had been at seven, he told her; he said something else about his working day. "That's tough," she sympathised, and he told her it was OK, that he likes driving. And then he said, with a nod towards the children: "But it's not as much fun as this." He heard himself, and was embarrassed. She knew what he was telling her: "I like kids. I don't mind that you've got one. I'm a better class of bloke. I'm the caring type." She did a half-smile, which was her way of saying that "fun" was not exactly the right word. Then Suzanne came back, so he couldn't do anything to dig himself out of the hole he'd created. "I sounded like I was desperate to clinch a job," he tells me. I advised him not to worry; his comment had not been taken in the way he had imagined, I was sure.

•

Supposed relics of Saint Stephen can be found at some three hundred different shrines, I read. The division and distribution of saintly corpses was permissible because on the Day of Judgement all the extant pieces would be gathered supernaturally, and the flesh restored.

•

On holiday with Benoît, in Sicily, Imogen went to the catacombs in Palermo. She described to me the ranks of mummified bodies, leaning out of their niches to watch the visitors pass by. Their teeth erupted through skin that had turned into flimsy bark; their mouths made the shapes of screaming and of idiotic laughter; they clasped their desiccated hands, as though in attendance at a funeral. Benoît, horrified, fled back to the street; he had been suffocating. Imogen, though horrified too, remained for an hour; she made herself walk along every corridor, inspecting every face. Better this, she had thought, than tombstones carved with roses and angels, and verbiage about peace and eternal rest. Benoît thought otherwise: the idea of the dead was what mattered, not their bones. The function of the tombstone was to summarise what was important to the living.

On the tombstone of Frederick Montague Gough (1823–94), and his devoted wife, Emilia Edwina née Willoughby (1837–1928), fifteen lines are needed to list the deceased man's virtues and achievements; of Emilia the stone tells us nothing but that she was a devoted wife and mother, and had enjoyed a long life. Behind Frederick and Emilia stands Imogen's stone, next to her father's. Name and years, that is all, as requested; not even "Here lies." Her body, the remnant of her body, Imogen herself, is in the soil below my feet, I told myself; the image was intolerable.

•

The anniversary visit. "Imogen had so many friends, but it is a long time since I heard from any of them," says her mother, as we stand on the threshold of the room that had been Imogen's. The remark is not made to elicit pity; it is the presentation of a fact. "Only for us is today unlike any other day of the year," she says. The room has been repainted and the bed removed, with most of the furniture. I see nothing that had belonged to Imogen. "I couldn't keep it as it was," she says. "That would have been morbid." Sunlight and Imogen's absence fill the room.

We go downstairs, to talk in the living room. She brings tea, and we sit on opposite sides of the low walnut table. Her bearing is diplomatic. The depth of the air above and around us impresses itself upon me; our bodies are small objects, in a medium of perfect transparency.

"Some of my neighbours are better disposed towards me nowadays," she tells me. "I am the local lady of sorrows." The quick smile of irony is reminiscent of her daughter's. She lifts her teacup, on its saucer; she takes a sip, and replaces it, soundlessly. Her calves, demurely slanted, side by side, form an exemplary shape. "Most people are sympathetic. Nearly all," she decides, having scanned a mental register of her acquaintances and found among them an exception or two. The vicar is not a friend, she tells me. "He admires me, in a way. I have suffered, and that is commendable in itself. But he cannot approve." No matter what the judge and jury may have thought, the vicar sees sin. "In his eyes, I am a criminal. A suicide takes from God a power that is rightfully his. So the vicar would rather not talk to me." The women tend to pity her. Some have pitied her for a long time, she says, because she is a widow, and because her daughter was problematic. "But their daughters are so dull," her mother sighs. "Imogen was not dull. She did things that I wish she had not done, and I'm sure you feel the same way," she says, "but she was never dull." I agree; a rueful smile is called for, and suffices; we are the ones who knew Imogen, her look says; words are superfluous.

She receives invitations quite regularly, albeit not as many as when her husband was alive. "People warmed to him more than to me," she informs me. "He was the warm one and I was the cold, or the cool. That is how we were seen. My manner does not encourage people to approach. I am aware of that. It's how I am made," she says, as though discussing an object of unusual and mildly intriguing design. She finds a way to decline most of the invitations, "which is best for all concerned." Small talk and gossip have never interested her. "I am like Immy in that respect, at least," she says. Everyone knows that on the whole she prefers her own company, now more than ever. "I read a great deal," she tells me. "Crime novels, mostly. I am not an intellectual person. I watch a great deal of television. Too much. And I interfere with the garden. But I tire easily. Which is to be expected at my age. But since Imogen died, I tire more easily."

We take a stroll through the garden. She indicates places where alterations have been made since I was last here, and talks about Jonathan's plan to convert one of the outbuildings into a restaurant. Only local produce will be used; Helen will manage the business. "An enterprising couple," she remarks. We go as far as the little lake with the yew tree and hellebores and bleeding hearts—the "glade of gloom," as young Imogen named it, she tells me. I admire the glade. I assume that we will now return to the house, and that I will leave soon after, but she produces a small surprise. "I am going to walk a little farther," she announces, turning to face me. She thanks me for the visit, for my "loyalty." Smiling, she shakes my hand and says: "Well, on we go." The dismissal has taken thirty seconds. The meaning of the handshake is unmistakeable: *There will be no need for you to come here again.*

•

Imogen imagined the ideal final scene: her mother would administer the releasing dose on a Sunday morning, so that the church bells would be the last thing that Imogen would hear. We studied a selection of exit lines, genuine and apocryphal. "Tell them I've had a wonderful life" was one that she particularly admired, but she decided to compose her own: "No bloody way I'm doing this again," she would murmur, as the bells chimed.

•

Legend has it that Mary Magdalene, having been set adrift in a boat that had neither a rudder nor sails, with her brother Lazarus and their sister Martha and several other followers of Jesus Christ, came ashore on the coast of Gaul at the place where the town of Saintes-Marie-de-la-Mer is now situated. Soon after, Mary withdrew to a mountain cave, now known as La Sainte-Baume, where she was to spend her last thirty years in prayer, contemplation and penance. Maximinus, another occupant of the rudderless boat, became the first bishop of Aix. When Mary was near death, angels transported her to Maximinus, in whose arms she died; he interred her body at the place of her death, which became known as Saint-Maximin. Eleven hundred years later, monks in Vézelay claimed to be in possession of her relics, but in 1279 the saint's remains were discovered in Saint-Maximin by Charles of Salerno. The Magdalene had appeared to him in a vision, telling him that her body would be found in a coffin marked with her name, with a green shoot on her tongue and an amphora of bloody soil from the foot of the cross beside her. The skin of her forehead would be uncorrupted, because Christ had kissed her on the forehead in the garden of Gethsemane. All this was duly discovered, on December 9th, 1279. Construction of the basilica of Saint-Maximin-la-Sainte-Baume began soon after.

According to the *Golden Legend* of Jacobus da Varagine, the Magdalene was a wealthy woman; her family weren't merely residents of Magdala—they owned the whole town, and a piece of Jerusalem too. That's why she fell into sin, I told Imogen, as we looked out over the vast garden of the Gough family's home. Throughout her years of penance, the Magdalene was lifted up by angels, "at every hour canonical," to receive heavenly nourishment. "Heavenly nourishment sounds good," said Imogen. Eating was no longer a pleasure for her. I continued to read. The figure of Mary Magdalene is a conflation of several different stories; the penitent prostitute is not in the Gospels. And if all the relics of Mary Magdalene were what they were claimed to be, the woman would have had no fewer than two heads and eight arms. The arm in Fécamp, I read, was damaged when Saint Hugh of Lincoln took a bite out of it; one is permitted to ingest the Eucharist, argued Hugh, so why not the flesh of the Magdalene? "Please tell me you're making this up," Imogen said.

•

Saint Teresa: "The pain was so sharp that it made me moan many times; and so great was the sweetness caused by this intense pain that I would never wish to lose it . . . It is no bodily pain, but spiritual, though the body has a share in it—a great share, indeed."

•

That stupendous afternoon in Sainte-Chapelle—standing in the indigo light of the stained glass, Imogen remarked that she imagined that the spectacle of this building might be enough to make some doubters wonder. We were looking at the window that shows the rediscovery of the relics of Christ and their relocation to Paris, carried by the saintly King Louis, in penitential garb. I mentioned Pascal's wager: if you win, you win an infinite and infinitely happy life; if you lose, you lose nothing.

"So you then start acting as if you believe in God?" she asked.

"Or you could say that you apply the faculty of reason, then start living a Christian life."

"In the face of overwhelming evidence that it's nonsense?"

"One could argue that the idea of evidence is of no weight. The supreme entity cannot be confined to our categories of thought."

"Well, I could manage the acting," she said. "Repentance is the bit I'd struggle with."

•

According to the *Encyclopaedia Britannica*, the first sect that is known to have made use of images of Christ were the Carpocratians, a Gnostic group that took its name from Carpocrates of Alexandria. The Carpocratians claimed that one of these images of Christ was a portrait created by Pontius Pilate. It seems that they also venerated images of Plato, Pythagoras and Aristotle, among others. The earliest account of the Carpocratians appears in the *Adversus Haereses* of Irenaeus (c.130–202), in which he alleges that they practised sorcery and indulged in licentious behaviour. Clement of Alexandria (c.150–210) similarly accuses the Carpocratians of immorality. At the *agapai* or love-feasts of the Carpocratians, claims Clement, the participants "have intercourse where they will and with whom they will." Epiphanius of Salamis, writing two hundred years later, repeats the allegation. Carpocrates, he writes, taught his followers "to perform every obscenity and every sinful act." The justification for these orgies, supposedly, was that the Carpocratians believed that in order to ascend to heaven the imprisoned soul must pass through every possible condition of bodily life. It was in order to release the soul from the cycle of reincarnation that they gave themselves up to "all those things which we dare not either speak nor hear of."

•

William glum: Suzanne has reverted to the mid-morning delivery time; thus no mother of Tilly. He is inclined to take this as an adverse judgement: evidently he did not impress. No reference to the missing friend was made by Suzanne, nor by William. He has to find a way of speaking to her again, with nobody else around, he tells me. Perhaps he should simply come right out with it and ask Suzanne if she could pass on his number. "What would you do?" he asks me. The assumption seems to be that anyone who managed to attract a woman of Imogen's calibre must know a thing or two about strategy. I counsel patience. He has felt all along, from first sight, that it was going to happen. "It will, in its own time," I tell him. William considers the advice. "Yes, you're right," he decides. Two minutes later, he has another idea: next time he has time off in the middle of the day, he could station himself for an hour or two within sight of Suzanne's flat. Many people would be inclined to describe that as stalking, I advise.

•

Last year's visit to Imogen's mother—fine weather; coffee on the terrace, at the iron table. An elegant old coffee pot, delicate cups, a tiny jug of cream, petits-fours, borne on a black and gold lacquer tray. Seated against the backdrop of the house, she presented a superb appearance. A grey cashmere sweater, roll-neck, was combined with black slacks; on a wrist hung a loose chain-link gold bracelet; the make-up was subtle and perfect—a little enhancement of the lips, lashes and brows, and some high-quality creams for the complexion, I imagined. If ever the fire alarm went off, she'd touch up her hair and lipstick before leaving the building, Imogen once said. In the evening there was some function in the village that she was obliged to attend, she told me. "It will be tiresome," she said. "But one should not withdraw into one's shell." We talked about the responsibilities that came with the house and her position. Then she said, in a tone of instruction: "But you know, David, every woman has to be an actress." She smiled as if a camera had been pointed at her, and made a small supple-wristed flourish of her hand. For a moment, she resembled her daughter too closely.

•

For Imogen's mother, the films of Antoine Vermeiren exemplify traits of French culture with which she had no patience whatever, notably an over-indulgence of artists who seem to believe that they are under some sort of obligation to shock. Her daughter's attachment to Vermeiren was explicable chiefly as an over-extended protest against the values that her English schooling had for some reason failed to inculcate. In itself, acting was an inappropriate activity for a person of Imogen's background, though as a semi-Frenchwoman her mother could of course appreciate that cinema was capable of being an art form, albeit an art form of a minor order. Perhaps she would have been able to come to terms with her daughter's career had she been an actress in the style of Grace Kelly, said Imogen— someone soignée and enigmatic; dressed by Dior; the type of actress who would look perfectly at home in a scene set in an opera house or a Mayfair gallery. It was at the Royal Opera House that her parents had met: Gerald, having stepped out into the street to clear his head of the tedium that had accumulated during the preceding hour, found himself standing in close proximity to Charlotte, who similarly was accompanying her mother that evening. He offered a light for her cigarette; a conversation ensued, in which Gerald, perceiving at once that this attractive young woman was something of a connoisseuse of the ballet, gladly assumed a chiefly receptive role. With little difficulty he evinced a more positive attitude to the evening's entertainment than he had felt until this moment. She disclosed her place of employment; this too signified refinement. At the next opportunity Gerald paid a visit to the gallery in which Charlotte's elegance was utilised in a vaguely secretarial capacity. Though possessing no more knowledge of the contemporary visual arts than could reasonably be expected of any young woman of her class and expensive education, she was, as photographs attest, a striking presence. Potential customers liked to look at her; her face, her manner, helped to put them in a spending frame of mind, or at least in a mood to linger, as Gerald did.

•

Some of what I saw at the *maison de maître* excited me. This must be confessed. Looking at people whom I did not know—this could be arousing. Watching Imogen, however, there was torment; but also admiration, even wonder at such abandonment. Perhaps I was witnessing a kind of courage, I told myself.

•

Imogen's gaze at the *maison de maître*: as if looking up from the depths of a pit into which she had fallen, and seeing the light of the sky. The same gaze on waking, one morning near the end.

•

As I'm falling asleep, an idea presents itself: of people preserved on the page, lustreless, like pallid specimens in formaldehyde. The idea expires a moment later. Words do not preserve the person; they are not held in a colourless medium of language. Another image arises: an object calcifying in a stream of mineral-rich water; a bottle becoming encased in stone. In the stream of memory and retelling, the reality of the past is transfigured. The image of the bottle does not satisfy. Better, perhaps, to think of the restoration of a building.

Bit by bit, the old fabric is replenished. Stonework is renewed, damaged glass repaired, carvings are recut, rotten timber replaced. In time, little of the original remains; it becomes impossible to tell what is new and what is old. Thus each recollection of a moment, of a conversation, reinforces some part of what is being remembered, and in the process of reinforcement something is replaced. With each retelling, the past becomes more solid and less true. Then, on the brink of sleep, another image—the body-casts at Pompeii. Words take the place of the dead, filling their vacancy, just as plaster poured into the voids within the hardened ash took on the forms of the dead of Pompeii, whom we can almost imagine alive.

•

William joyful. This afternoon, his day off, he was sitting on the seafront, reading his book, when suddenly he had a strange sensation, as if the pressure of the air had changed. The sound of his pulse had become more prominent than the voices of the passing people and the gulls. He looked up, for an explanation. He saw Tilly first, twenty yards away, running, and then her mother in mock pursuit, ten yards back, making the empty buggy veer from side to side, as if it were out of control. When might such an opportunity come again? William waved, and Tilly's mother saw him immediately. She raised a hand, but the chase could not be abandoned; they passed him, and it seemed that the wave would be the end of it. But then a swerve, and a call to Tilly, who turned and came to her mother, to take her hand and clamber aboard. They came up to him. "How are you today, Tilly?" William enquired, and by way of answer the little girl showed him her arm, adorned with a bracelet of pink plastic beads, a gift from her mother that morning. William complimented Tilly on her jewellery and footwear. Behind him, an ice-cream van was parked. "Would Tilly be allowed—?" he asked her mother, indicating the van. "Yes!" shouted Tilly; already the child was his ally. Ice cream in hand, Tilly wandered; her eating technique was beguiling—a precise quarter-turn of the cone for every lick. "She is very methodical," her mother commented, before asking: "What are you reading?" William handed over the book—the mysteries of Stonehenge. The subject appeared to be of interest to her; she read the back cover, then began to flick through the pages. "Jenna," she said, interrupting the browse to hold out a hand. "Not working today?" she asked. Within a couple of minutes there was something that William had to say. He knew that it might be better not to say it, but the words were inside him and they could not be held down; it was as if he were holding his breath and the only way to get oxygen into his lungs was to get rid of the words. So he told her, "completely out of the blue," that he very much liked the colour of the shirt she was wearing, which he did—it was the colour of thunderclouds. Jenna blinked, and frowned, and looked at him. "Are you trying to pick me up?" she said. "No," he told her, which was the truth, but it would not be possible, at that moment, to explain why it was true. On some other day, with enough time, it would be possible; but he was afraid, now, that there would be no other day. "Really?" said Jenna. She was looking at him steadily; she might be annoyed; she might not. "Really," he answered, laying a hand over his heart. And she said, narrowing her eyes, as if about to threaten him: "Oh, go on. Give it a go."

•

Even after Imogen had gone to Paris, she marked this day, Francesca's birthday. The year of her departure for Paris, she sent a shirt. It was an amazing colour, Francesca reported—a metallic blue-green, or maybe more a greyish ash blue. Imogen had enclosed a postcard. On the front was a picture by an artist called Nattier, whose penchant for this soft green-blue-grey was such that his name has been given to it. On the postcard, Imogen wrote that the young lady depicted on the other side was known for her "great appetite for learning." The card came from the Louvre, so the painting must have been Nattier's portrait of Marie Adélaïde, a daughter of Louis XV. Madame Campan refers in her *Memoirs* to Adélaïde's "immoderate thirst for knowledge"; she refers also to Adélaïde's bad temper and domineering manner. In the absence of any eligible monarchs or high-born heirs, Marie Adélaïde preferred not to marry. Madame Adélaïde, as she was known, "found solace in music," I have read.

•

The costume designer for *Le Grand Concert de la Nuit* made effective use of Nattier's blue. It's the colour of Agamédé's dress, the one on which she is lying when she looks up from the bed and smiles, having seen in the shadows of the coffered ceiling what appears, to us, to be a beetle moving in a hole in the timber. We see a movement that is perhaps a twitching of the beetle's wings. Slowly the camera zooms into the ceiling, and we see that the beetle is a human eye; the young Guignan. At the third or fourth blink the angle is reversed, to show the coupled bodies: the rough reddened back of the Count; the pale skin of Agamédé's legs against the blue-green velvet.

•

Today, the long-awaited call. With great regret, it has been agreed that council funding for the Sanderson-Perceval Museum is an expense that can no longer be justified. "In an ideal world we would not countenance such a decision, but we can no longer afford to maintain the cultural resources that we have hitherto provided for the city." Closure will not be immediate, however, and might even be prevented. Third parties are being invited to submit plans "for the future operation of the museum." These are hypothetical third parties.

•

The only photo I have of myself with Imogen is one taken by Francesca, in a restaurant in Rome. She is leaning towards me, with her head resting on my shoulder; there may be an element of parody in the pose, but Imogen's affection for Francesca is evident in the smile; but my smile could be that of a man who had been in the dentist's chair only an hour earlier. There is one other image: we appear together in a few dozen frames of *Devotion*. At 49.25, a servant opens a door for the lady of the house—the most evanescent of cameo roles, my reward for assistance given. Freeze the film at 49.27 and there we are, momentarily, her face and mine in a single image.

•

Text from William: *A lot going on. She's great, the kid's great, everything's great. You have to meet her.*

September

THERE IS A PHOTOGRAPH OF IMOGEN with Benoît, an attractive couple, sitting at a café on Place Plumereau; it was taken by a friend of Benoît's, a colleague from the university. Imogen is looking at Benoît, laughing wholeheartedly, and leaning back from him a little, with a hand raised to her lips; it appears that Benoît has just said something outrageous and funny. He is looking directly at the camera, with the slightest of smiles, and an eyebrow insouciantly raised; his remark has had the desired effect, it seems. The date is printed on the back of the photo; within a few months, Imogen and Benoît would have separated. She had no memory of the occasion of this photograph; what the picture showed did not accord with her memory of those months. She did not doubt the veracity of the image. Her laughter was a fact, but it was a fact that had no reality for her. The picture was almost incomprehensible because, as the date proved, it had been taken a few months after the death of her father. She remembered her grief, the burden of it. Yet here she was, at a café on Place Plumereau, laughing with Benoît. On that date, three elements of her life had coexisted: the bereavement; the end of the relationship with Benoît; the preparations for *La Châtelaine*. But it was only when reminded of their coexistence, by a piece of evidence such as this, that the three elements were brought together again. As they existed in her memory, they had already become three separate stories.

•

William is now certain beyond all possibility of doubt that Jenna is the pre-ordained soulmate. Yesterday evening she proposed a visit to Tintagel. She has a passion for King Arthur, she revealed. For Jenna it's irrelevant that there's no historical connection between any King Arthur and the castle at Tintagel. Tintagel is a magical place; the name in itself is magical. And King Arthur is a magical being. She believes in him the way some people believe in Jesus, she confessed to William, knowing that he would understand, though some of her friends think she's too New Agey about all this stuff. If it were all nonsense, she points out, why would the story still be so powerful? A trip to Tintagel is a sort of pilgrimage for her, she told William; she goes there every year. He took this as an invitation to tell her more about his theory of energies. What he really wanted to tell her was why it was that he had known, the instant he first saw her, that this was the woman he was destined to be with. But he knows he should not say anything about the London woman. There is a risk that Jenna will take it the wrong way, and think that he has taken a shine to her because she reminds him of another woman, an unforgettable other woman, which wasn't the case at all—the café woman was just a sign, an omen. But he told her his idea about graveyards. Jenna thinks it all makes perfect sense.

•

At the Cluny museum, some time after the *maison de maître*, we looked at a tapestry in which David, on the balcony of his palace, gazes in the direction of the bathing Bathsheba. Putting my hands together in a gesture of prayer, I intoned: "Have mercy upon me, O God, according to thy lovingkindness." Psalm 51 was written after Nathan the prophet had confronted the adulterous king. Imogen did not know the story. Having seduced and impregnated Bathsheba, David summoned her husband, the general Uriah, in the hope that the reunion of husband and wife would lead Uriah to think that he was the father of the child that Bathsheba was now expecting. But Uriah decided to remain with his troops, so David ordered that he be placed in the front line of battle, whereupon Uriah was killed, leaving David free to marry the widow. Their child died, in proof of God's displeasure. Their second child, however, would survive; he was Solomon.

Imogen blinked and smiled, as if I were a machine that had disgorged information at the touch of a button. "What would I do without you?" she said. Then: "I'm not joking." We walked to the Métro arm in arm.

•

Yes, Imogen once answered me, she had known several actors to whom the adjective "insecure" could be applied; she could name one—a well-known actress—who had confessed that she needed applause in the way that one needs a mirror. Imogen, however, did not feel that she was an insecure person. On the contrary, she said, she was absolutely secure in the knowledge that there was no secure entity behind the name of Imogen Gough.

•

At the St. Agnes cemetery, Imogen was moved by one gravestone in particular. A male and a female hand, clasped, were carved into a niche in the vertical stone. The last line of the husband's epitaph for his wife: *For nine years we were such friends.*

•

Interviewed for the release of *Maintenant et à l'heure de notre mort*, Imogen named *Au hasard Balthazar* as her favourite film. In all of cinema, she told the interviewer, there was nothing as affecting as the death of the donkey Balthazar, and that was because the animal had not been aware that it was in a film. There is too much acting in most of the films she had made, Imogen said to me, towards the end. That was why *Chambre 32* and *Maintenant et à l'heure de notre mort* were the ones she liked most, or disliked least. They were the films in which the acting had been reduced to a minimum. The interviewer had encouraged her to talk in superlatives, but she said the same thing to me: *Au hasard Balthazar* was her favourite film, and the death of Balthazar was the most moving scene she knew. "Apart from this one, of course. This one takes the biscuit."

•

"If your father had been alive, would you have done it?" asked Imogen's mother, of *Chambre 32*. It was possible that she would not, Imogen admitted to me, but not to her mother, who would never watch *Chambre 32*. Of the films she had made with Antoine Vermeiren, her father had watched only *Les tendres plaintes*. He understood that nudity might be justified on artistic grounds, but there would have been a terrible indecency in seeing his own daughter naked. The arts in general were not really his thing, he confessed, as Imogen told me. He appreciated their value in principle; knowing his limitations, he was content to leave actual engagement to finer sensibilities than his, such as his wife's.

•

Lichtenberg: "Imagination and fantasy must be used with caution, like any corrosive substance."

•

Emma calls, with an invitation: a barbecue. "Sue will be there," she tells me. It is necessary to refresh my memory. "Sue. Durham Sue," she elucidates. Sue will be down in London for a week, staying with a daughter. For many years she has lived in Durham; once every two or three months Emma speaks to her; once every two or three years they meet. My sister has an admirable ability to sustain friendships that others would let lapse. It's simply a question of making a bit of an effort, she has told me. I have maintained no friendships for as long as Emma has maintained a dozen.

Emma lists the other guests. As if as an afterthought, the roll-call ends with: "And Becky will be there as well."

This name too is not immediately meaningful.

"You met her last year," Emma prompts. "Nick's birthday. Tall woman. Fair hair. Glasses. You liked her."

"I did?"

"Yes. She's a teacher."

"Well, I do like teachers, that's true." All that comes to mind is an inchoate image of a large woman, of severe manner, with an aura of low-level resentment; I have no recollection of any conversation.

"Tall. Unusually tall. Come on. You can't have forgotten."

Another element of her identity seems to arise: "Divorced, messily?"

"She's divorced, yes," answers Emma.

"Would this be some sort of matchmaking manoeuvre?"

"Not at all."

"I see."

"David, do you have any sort of social life?" she asks. "Going to the supermarket does not count."

"I'm fine," I assure her.

"You're becoming a hermit. Do you want to spend the rest of your days on your own?"

"I'm fine, Emma."

"As far as I can tell, nothing is happening in your life," she protests.

My life is not eventful, but is not quite the tundra of tedium that she imagines, I tell her.

"OK, so what are you doing with yourself? Have you even started that book?"

"I have notes. Many notes."

"As I thought. I don't suppose you've applied for any jobs?"

"No."

I am a defeatist, Emma tells me.

The museum sector is not as ripe with possibilities as is the world of commerce, I point out.

"You have been too long at that place," Emma tells me, not for the first time.

"You may be right," I concede.

"You need to stir yourself."

I promise to stir myself.

"And you'll come? You can stay over. You must stay over."

"I'll make a note of it."

"Please, David, come. You'll meet some nice people. You never know, you might even enjoy yourself."

I am grateful for the invitation, I tell her, and I appreciate the attempt to fix me up.

"I am not trying to fix you up."

I remind her that I met divorced Becky last year, and that evidently she did not make much of an impression on me; and vice versa, I'm sure. All we have in common is that we're unattached, and the clock is ticking audibly.

"She's a nice woman," says Emma. "And she liked you."

"I am touched," I answer.

"You're not going to come, are you?"

"Almost certainly not."

Talking to me is like trying to get fire from a wet log, Emma tells me.

•

"A human being has so many skins inside, covering the depths of the heart. We know so many things, but we don't know ourselves. Why, thirty or forty skins or hides, as thick and hard as an ox's or a bear's, cover the soul." Meister Eckhart.

•

William has cleared the last hurdle: Jenna's parents have met him, and he seems to have passed the audition. On leaving, he was hugged by the mother. They are affectionate people, with each other and with their daughter, William reports. It's the second marriage for each of them, and both were into their forties when Jenna was born. One gets the impression that they've never stopped feeling grateful for their good fortune, says William. They had tea in the garden, by a huge fuchsia that reaches to the sill of Jenna's room. She might have been named Fuchsia if the choice had been her mother's; it would not have been the right name, William tells me. There's a fine display of roses too; they were planted when Jenna was born. William enthused about the roses, genuinely, which went down well with the mother, and Jenna's father seemed to like him too, because William made it clear that he appreciates Jenna as she should be appreciated, unlike Max, Tilly's father. Max was a "complete waster," Jenna's dad disclosed as soon as the opportunity for a quick man-to-man arose, over the washing-up. Unknown to Jenna, Max had been a man with a problem: whenever he saw a betting shop, he was compelled to unburden himself of whatever cash he happened to have to hand. He was a roofer, a man with skills, and should have been earning decent money, but instead he was getting deeper into debt with every month. Eventually he owned up; his parents and Jenna's bailed him out; he swore that he was a reformed man, that Jenna and Tilly could depend on him. Then he did the same thing all over again. "So she kicked him out," the dad told William. The story, in outline, was already known to William, as Jenna's father might have assumed. But he wanted William to understand that his daughter was not to be trifled with. "You're not a waster are you, son?" he asked, giving William the sort of look one might get in the police cells. "I am not," swore William, and that seems to have been good enough, because he was given a hand to shake. The other hand, William had noticed earlier, was half a finger short of its full allocation. "Lost at sea," Jenna's father explained, noting the direction of William's glance. When he was younger, he had worked on the boats and a rope had whipped a bit of his finger off. Barely any of his old mates have full hands; he counts himself lucky for having lost only a semi-finger. His closest friend had drowned at the age of thirty-eight; Jenna's father had seen it happen, and that's when he had decided to get off the boats; he was the same age as his friend, and had been starting to feel too old for that life anyway. William sensed that this was a moment in which he could lighten the mood while showing respect for the hard men: he confessed to the ignominy of his brief career on board. "Nowhere near tough enough," he admitted. The honesty of the self-judgement seemed to enhance his standing. "Well, son, tough isn't everything," said Jenna's father, and right on cue Tilly came running into the kitchen, for a ride on William's shoulders.

•

The reflection of myself in the blank screen of the TV, sitting in the light of the floor lamp, glass in one hand and book in another—it brings to mind Imogen's description of her father, as she saw him one evening. She came downstairs, looking for her brother. The trees were moaning in the wind, she remembered; rain dashed against the windows like hail. On her way to the games room, she passed the open door of the living room. A faint light came out of it, from a single lamp, set beside one of the wingback chairs. This was the chair in which her father would sit to read the newspaper. When he was there, she liked to read at other end of the room, on the drop end sofa; sometimes her brother or mother would be there too, but there was a particular pleasure to sharing the long room only with her father. They would call to each other—"All right there?"—as if in rowing boats on a lake. It was his custom to have a glass of whisky at this hour; a single drink, from a cut-glass tumbler. On the evening of the downpour, when she looked into the room, the newspaper was on the table next to the chair, with the decanter; her father, tumbler in hand, seemed to be watching the clouds that were sliding over the moon. She went to him. "Quite a night," he said. The weather is all they talked about, as she recalled. That evening, her mother was elsewhere, playing bridge. This was not unusual. Her father could not comprehend the appeal of bridge; only people in prison had a valid excuse for playing card games. His wife had her pastimes and he had his; her interest in vintage cars was as negligible as his interest in bridge, as was to be expected; this was understood by everyone. But a sadness had settled in him. The sadness was very visible on this particular evening, Imogen told me. When she looked back into the room later, on her way to bed, he was still in the wingback chair, looking at the night sky, with the glass in his hand and the decanter beside him; the decanter was emptier than it had been. His hand rose, to put a little more whisky into his mouth, as if topping up the liquid in a machine.

The second measure of whisky became a habit. Sometimes she would look across the room and see that he was holding the newspaper but not really reading it. He did not drink like a man who was suffering deeply; whatever troubled him, it seemed, could be eased with two glasses. Perhaps it was only the cares that come to all people as they grow older, Imogen thought; and there must be other cares that come with this house. But perhaps, too, it occurred to her, as she looked at him, he was nostalgic for the early days of his marriage. This was nothing more than supposition. For all she knew, the early days had been much like these. Her parents' respect for each other had always been evident, she said, but the marriage often appeared to be more a pact than a romance. She could not recall having seen her parents kiss, except on birthdays and at Christmas and other special days, and those special-occasion kisses had always seemed to be kisses of thanks more than anything else.

•

Imogen's mother recalled the day she had come to the house with Cressida, before she and Gerald had become engaged. They had travelled in Cressida's car, a stately Rover that had been discarded by Cressida's father upon his acquisition of a sleek new Jaguar. The Rover was a thoroughly unfeminine thing, but it was comfortable and Cressida had a taste for eccentric gestures. Other young women of her milieu were driving Minis, but it amused the lissom Cressida to be the pilot of this ponderous vehicle. Her dress that day was a violent shade of turquoise, and had been made by Cressida herself; it was "indecently short," Imogen's mother told us, and Cressida's limbs were of uncommon perfection. Men of all varieties had a tendency to fall for Cressida without further ado, even though she was as fickle as a cat, as was evident within two minutes to any unsmitten pair of eyes. "I suppose I was setting him a test," said Imogen's mother.

The two young women arrived in the village some time ahead of schedule: the car was powerful and Cressida drove quickly—too quickly, as if assured that her beauty, in combination with the heft of the car, bestowed invulnerability. Within sight of the gates, however, the Rover failed. A terrible din erupted; many pieces of metal had broken free underneath the bonnet and were rioting. Cressida stopped and turned off the engine. The din lessened, but ominous sounds continued; an explosion might be imminent. There was only one thing to do: fetch Gerald. Leaving Cressida to stand watch, at a safe distance, Imogen's mother ran up the drive. The hero returned with her. "I see, I see," he repeated, as she described the symptoms; the situation was grave, it appeared. He greeted Cressida with a handshake, appraised the legs with a discreet glance, then advanced fearlessly upon the stricken vehicle. "Stand back," he ordered, before opening the bonnet. His head disappeared into the jaws of the Rover; he reached in. From the movement of his arm, it was apparent that things were being dismantled. He recoiled, in reaction to a terrible discovery. He leaned further in, to scrutinise the damage. "Is it ruined?" asked Cressida. Gerald stood up, stepped back, and turned to face her. His demeanour signified a poor diagnosis. He took a step forward, and answered, sombrely: "Get back in the car, and drive up to the garage slowly. Very slowly indeed," he said. "And when you get there ... [long pause] ... put some bloody water in it." At which Imogen's mother, seizing the initiative, exclaimed: "Water? Water?" She rolled her eyes, appalled. "We've given it petrol. We've given it oil. Is there no limit to the monster's appetites?" Gerald, she told us, laughed as loudly as a burst balloon. "Then he looked at me," she said, "and I knew that I didn't have to worry about Cressida and her legs." She reprised the response that she had given Imogen's father, pressing a hand to her chest, aghast at the car's gluttony. This, I think, was the last time I heard Imogen laugh.

•

For a while Imogen had thought that her dying might bring about a new frankness in the relationship between herself and her mother. She imagined sessions of truth-telling, by which each would attain a fuller understanding of the other; a deepened affection might result. There would be episodes of weeping and embracing. Imogen would reveal the person she had come to believe herself to be. She would endeavour to explain, without apology, the things she had done, or most of them. Perhaps her mother, in return, would explain how life with her husband had come to be something other than the life she had hoped for. She might admit to having ceased to love him. But whenever it seemed that the moment for candour might be presenting itself, Imogen said nothing. She foresaw her mother's reaction: denial and withdrawal. "I would have hoped not to become a widow so soon," she might answer, in her door-closing voice, as Imogen characterised the tone with which her mother annulled any conversation that seemed to threaten turbulence. "People talk too much nowadays," her mother had said once, removing herself from the vicinity of the television. Imogen remembered this, and other declarations of distaste for garrulous people. What, she came to ask herself, would be the benefit of any self-revelation? Did she think her mother's disapproval would suddenly be converted into its opposite, in response to her daughter's courage? A tacit truce had maintained the equilibrium of the family; why jeopardise it now, when there would be no time to repair the damage that might result? So, instead of opening themselves to each other, they waited together. There would be no conventional coda to the story, in which long-suppressed issues were at last acknowledged, if not resolved entirely. The silences lengthened at the approach of the last great silence, and the past was allowed to become extinct.

•

In a photograph that had been on display in the library for as long as Imogen could remember, a dozen men stood behind a table on the terrace; her great-grandfather sat at the table with his wife, and three other women who were the wives of two of the men, plus a widowed sister of the great-grandfather's wife. No jollity was in evidence: everyone seemed to be aware that a rite of commemoration was being conducted. "The self-conscious deceased," she called them. The young man in uniform, standing between the windows, was a clue to the date, as was the man with the empty sleeve, beside him. The roses in the picture were in bloom. The man in the uniform would die before the flowers did; a shell exploded and his life was finished in a moment as brief as the opening and closing of the camera's shutter. Nothing of his body was ever found. This was the last picture of him, Imogen had been told. The very tall man, the one whose expression was that of a man glaring defiantly at his firing squad, had also been a soldier; he had been awarded a medal. The man with the illegible face became an MP after the war. A magistrate was in the photo as well.

Imogen's brother, as a boy, would gaze upon this picture as if to find instruction there, she said; here were represented the English and manly virtues. It was his destiny, gladly accepted, to preserve the house in which were enshrined the values that gave this picture, for him, its potency. He would regard his life as a failure if the house were to pass out of the family. But Jonathan would not fail. The great story would be maintained. The rare breeds, the organic methods, the management of the properties—Jonathan knew what he was doing. "Unlike me," said Imogen, as we drove towards the house, for my introduction. Her mother had still not abandoned hope that she might one day ensnare a man with some sort of pedigree, she warned me, although the odds were becoming longer with every year. "But a museum director—at least that's someone who has respect for the past. And the age gap won't be an issue. It was the same with her and my father. The stability one gets from an older man," she said, commendingly.

•

Ruminations from Val on the topic of separation—more specifically, the damage to one's self-esteem that can ensue from the ending of a long-term relationship. She speaks from painful experience. On the eve of her fortieth birthday, her husband announced his departure. She took the rejection badly, she admits: consumed by self-pity and rage, she became caught in "a cycle of negativity." She felt that she had been judged and found wanting; she had failed "as a person." A friend suggested that she might benefit from talking to someone who could see the situation from the outside, dispassionately. Initially resistant, Val eventually acceded, having acknowledged that she could not recall her last wholly sober evening. Her therapist, a "wonderful woman," brought light to the darkness. Through their long conversations, Val came to see that the crisis of separation can be the making of a person; unhappiness could bring about "growth and a new depth of self-awareness"; in refusing to surrender to "self-limiting beliefs," one might become "newly empowered." With the help of the inspirational therapist, Val changed her life. "Both personally and professionally," she remade herself. Through this process of enlightenment, she came to understand that certain aspects of herself were not, after all, intrinsic qualities of her "true self," but instead were "behaviours" that she had acquired by "emulation." The worst thing that had ever happened to our author turned out to be the best thing. "Desertion became liberation." It was as if she had been confined under electric light, but now was living in sunlight, she tells us. But it cannot be denied: the aftermath of separation is often a "hard road." One must pass through Denial, Anger, Depression, Guilt and Loneliness before Acceptance—or even, if all goes well, Forgiveness—can be achieved. Each of these stages is "crucial to the healing process."

•

The end of life is nothing more than the point beyond which one ceases to exist, said Imogen. The end is merely a border, yet we think of it as a destination, as if life were a story, with the last day as the conclusion to which everything had been leading. But life is not a journey. The day of her death would be less significant than this one. "This is more important," she said, turning out her hands to the street. We were at a café in Place Larue. Students passed by, and tourists on their way to the Panthéon; we sat in the sounds of conversation and traffic. "All of this life," she said, gratified that we were in it. We were a pair of happy particles, active today in this corner of the city, she announced. Starlings rushed over the roofs; she looked up, smiling into the sunlight.

•

"God does not inhabit healthy bodies"—the words of Hildegard von Bingen (1098–1179), polymath abbess of Rupertsberg and Eibingen. Her writings on medicine and science are gathered in *Physica* and *Causae et Curae*. Three other volumes—*Scivias, Liber vitae meritorum* and *De operatione Dei*—record her mystic visions, which were retrospectively diagnosed by Oliver Sacks as being "indisputably migrainous," though it has also been proposed that their hallucinatory qualities might be attributable to ergot poisoning. In 2012, Pope Benedict XVI named Saint Hildegard as a Doctor of the Roman Catholic Church; of the thirty-six saints to have been elevated to that rank, only four are women.

•

Jenna's family has been in Cornwall for centuries, William reports. The men had all been miners and fishermen until recently—her father was breaking with tradition in becoming an electrician. His grandfather had been a wild man, apparently. Jenna relates that great-grandfather Isaac was said to have thrown a man down a mine shaft because of something he'd done to a young girl. "You'll love her," William tells me. "She's got some amazing stories." She can show me some hedges, not far from where she lives, that are six thousand years old, says William, understanding the allure that ancient hedges would have for me. We agree a date.

•

From the window of Imogen's room we watched as her mother walked down the central path. At the sundial she stopped; she put her hands on it, as though taking hold of a lectern, and looked down. She seemed for a moment to be reading the inscription, and considering its meaning: *Utere, non numera.* Then it appeared that she was only using the sundial for support; her arms were locked onto it, and her shoulders rose and fell with the depth of her breathing. She looked up, towards the copse; a minute passed before she moved on.

"I cannot remember ever seeing my mother cry," Imogen remarked. She remembered her mother taking the call that told her of her own mother's death. "Je vous remercie," she said, and replaced the handset precisely, as if it were a piece of antique porcelain. That is all Imogen could remember her saying to the person who had called; she had said very little, Imogen was certain. Imogen and her brother were sitting at the far end of the room. Standing in front of the children, their mother announced: "I have to go to Meudon." After a pause the explanation was given. She went upstairs. A few minutes later, at Jonathan's suggestion, Imogen followed, expecting to find her mother in tears. She was not in tears, though she had loved her mother and had spoken to her every week. Already she was packing a suitcase, as if she had been ordered to leave the house forthwith.

And when her husband's heart failed, without warning, she did her weeping in private. On the day of the funeral she was the perfect image of resolve, of grief turned inward. She was the head of the family, and it was imperative that nobody should see her cry. At the graveside, her face was rigid with dignity, Imogen told me. Even in Imogen's last days, her mother did not weep. I can see her, holding her daughter's hand; she looked into Imogen's face, transferring fortitude from eye to eye. When it was over, I was called back into the room. She kissed Imogen's brow, then left me with her. Still she was not crying. A minute later, I heard a howl; one long cry of heartbreak and fury, then she screamed Imogen's name.

•

"We want you with us for as long as possible," Imogen's mother told her.

"Even if I'm no longer me?" Imogen asked.

"You will always be you," she said. But it appeared that she had anticipated this conversation. Leaving aside all questions of feeling, she said, putting an end to one's life was a difficult business. There were risks. An accelerated death might be more painful than allowing things to run their course.

It would be quicker, Imogen countered. There was no achievement in staying alive as long as possible.

The debate continued into the early hours. A debate is what it was, Imogen told me. There were moments when it was as though it were the case of a hypothetical patient that was being analysed. Of all the roles that Imogen had played, the bravely dying woman was the one that would make her mother proud, Imogen said to me.

When it had been accepted that dissuasion was not possible, there remained the problem of execution. Assistance might be required.

"Of course," her mother agreed.

Imogen suggested that I might be the one who would do the deed.

Her mother's response was immediate: "Impossible," she said. There was nothing to discuss: she had brought Imogen into the world; she had to be the one to help her out of it.

•

Her mother produced a sheet of paper on which the salient facts had been noted; the elegance of her handwriting made the page look like a letter of invitation or thanks. As she had said, there were risks: a chemical death was not a straightforward business. But fifteen grams of Nembutal in concentrated soluble form should provide a peaceful end; phenytoin sodium could be used to increase its potency. It would not be easy to obtain these substances, but it could be done. As for the legal questions: she knew what charges might be brought, and what her defence would be. She had researched the precedents. "Not that the defence is of any relevance," she said. Because she loved her daughter, she would do what was asked. It was her duty, too. "There is no nobility in suffering," she said.

•

Her mother confessed that she had gone to the village church and spent an hour on her knees. As she had not been there since her husband's funeral, she suspected that her prayers weren't given top priority. She'd imagined a ticket machine, like the one at the super-market delicatessen counter. "Ticket number 56,000,890," she said, and they both laughed. Her mother's laugh, rarely heard, was a brief and light chime; it would have worked well in Restoration comedy, said Imogen.

•

The imprecision of Imogen's sense of chronology bemused her mother. How was it possible to be able to memorise whole pages of a script, yet be unable to place the events of one's own life in anything but the most approximate order? There were twenty obscure film directors whose biographies Imogen knew better than she knew the biography of herself. Asked to put a date to a significant family incident at which she had been present, Imogen might be wrong by a year or more. One evening, at the table, her mother mentioned a storm that had brought down some of the chimneys. Imogen remembered that night: the shattered masonry; the flooded garden. It had happened shortly after Benoît's first visit, she recalled. Her mother corrected her: it had happened after Benoît's second visit. Corroborating evidence was produced; she made reference to an incident involving Imogen's father and Benoît and a waterlogged field. Imogen deferred to her mother's memory of the sequence of events; her mother was always right. For Imogen, her mother said, the past was like the sea—always in motion, impossible to map.

•

Imogen sat in the bay window, with a blanket over her legs; she had fallen asleep. When she woke up, I brought a glass of fresh water. "Thank you, Doctor Perceval," she said. A widower had written to Charles Perceval, to tell him that his wife, near the end, had said: "It is not unpleasant to die in the care of Doctor Perceval." I had quoted this line to her in the mirrored room, Imogen reminded me; Adeline's body had rested in the mirrored room, encircled by candles, I had told her, and Charles had watched over the open coffin for two days. Immersed in grief, unable to be a father, Charles Perceval gave up his son. He shunned society, and ceased to take Communion; for half a century he lived alone. But in time he resumed his medical practice, and became known for the tact with which he eased the dying out of life; in his bag there was always a bottle of ruby-red laudanum.

I held Imogen's hand; I could feel every bone. The window was open; the sound of a tractor came in with the warm air.

•

It was said of Cornelius Perceval that he dissected a cadaver as skillfully as Bernini had carved marble. I invited inspection of the case of knives; the blades, as could be seen, would still be serviceable. Bottles of calomel stood on a shelf by the pencil portrait of Cornelius Perceval, alongside bottles of quinine and rhubarb compound and laudanum, and a miscellany of other redundant medications. I directed attention to the toxic "blue pill." Perceval was a liberal prescriber of the blue pill and other doubtful curatives, I told the group. In 1811 he wrote to his son: "I know as well as any man how to discover the disease, but I do not know how to cure it." He had become a "therapeutic nihilist," I pronounced. This phrase often makes an impact, and Imogen seemed to make a note of it. We examined the portrait of the irascible Cornelius Perceval. His ire was frequently roused by the arrogance of his wealthy patients. A letter to his wife, on display, complains of his being obliged to enter a gentleman's house by the servants' door.

•

Jonathan opened the door, and I saw the body: it was Imogen; it was not Imogen. The body's indifference to us, to everything, was brutal. Already the lines were disappearing from her brow. Imogen was absent from this flesh, but the body had a monumental presence; a horrible beauty. It was possible to believe, said Jonathan, that she had at last been taken to a place that was full of light and peace.

•

Having made the calls that had to be made, Jonathan came into the library. "Helen not here?" he asked; there seemed to be no urgency to finding her. Helen had gone outside, I told him. Standing at the window, I had watched her walk slowly away from the house, down the central path and through the pergola; she was now out of sight. On the sill stood the photograph of Jonathan and Imogen at the party for his ninth birthday, in feathered headdresses, with streaks of dark paint across their cheekbones. He picked it up and looked at it. "Mother's back with Imogen," he said. "I don't think she'll be down for a while." He apologised for leaving me alone, but he had to go to Helen, he said. Not a sound came from upstairs. The whole house was occupied by death; it had become the house of the dead woman; the air in every room had changed. I picked up another picture: the one of Imogen and her father by the cedar tree in the garden of the Musée des Beaux-Arts. The young woman in the photograph smiled at me; her face bore no resemblance to that of the body that lay in the room above.

•

William told me one afternoon, not sober, that when he was still at school he'd been sent to talk to someone about his drinking. He had liked this woman so much that he'd increased his intake to make sure that he would be sent to talk to her again. "She was posh too," he said. "Posh and nice." He'd experienced some unpleasantness that morning; two episodes of abuse, and several nasty looks. "A lot of people use their eyes like weapons," William said, putting the backs of his hands over his eyelids, with the forefingers pointing out. But eyes and ears are receivers; they are lenses and microphones, wired to the computer-brain. "Input, not output. That's what I'm all about," he said.

•

Lunchtime stroll. Almost back at the museum when I became diverted by an altercation between two dogs, one a mud-coloured mongrel of medium build, the other a strange lamb-like creature, slighter than the mongrel, with blueish-white fleecy fur. The barking was what had drawn my attention; only after noting the oddness of the lamb-like dog was I struck by the appearance of its owner, a woman with a sleek bob of silver hair, streaked with dark strands, and a close-fitting knee-length coat, carmine. The pets were reeled in, skittering and barking, while apologies were exchanged. Then the lamb-dog and its owner were coming towards me. She turned to look over the town, presenting a strong profile; I could imagine such a face on an allegorical figure—of Justice, perhaps. Her posture was remarkably upright, and her stride purposeful. The dog was at her side now. Its gait was light—a graceful prance. The woman took a treat from her pocket and lobbed it onto the pavement. As I was about to pass, the dog looked up and, meeting my gaze, sprang at me, not aggressively. "I'm sorry," said the woman, bending down to scoop the dog towards her. She reproached her pet for its lack of manners; the dog's name was Bianca. "Nothing to apologise for," I said, and asked about the breed. "A Bedlington," was the answer. Having obtained permission, I stroked Bianca. I remarked on the softness of the fur, and the woman said: "I think we've met." She frowned. "I'm sure we have," she said, and in the next instant she supplied the answer: five or six years ago she and her husband had taken the tour of the museum. "It was fascinating," she said. Bianca was pulling at the lead. "We must go," her owner apologised. "She's a lovely little beast, but she has no patience whatever." The longest conversation for several days.

October

In regent street I am struck by a powerful scent—someone in the crowd is wearing a perfume that Imogen sometimes wore. The smell is that of snuffed candles. "Odour of Sanctity," she called it. No specific memory ensues. The momentary transit of a ghost; a spectre of aromatic air.

•

Online, a recent interview with Antoine Vermeiren; he goes to some length to ensure that his interviewer properly appreciates the philosophical heft of his work. We must understand that our words for "theory" and "theorem" are rooted in the ancient Greek *theoría*, meaning "contemplation, speculation, beholding, spectacle." And *theoría* is related to *thea*, "a view, an act of seeing," from which the modern "theatre" is derived. The first theorists, he maintains, were those who undertook journeys—arduous and perilous journeys, often—to witness an event or spectacle in honour of the gods. Vermeiren's scholarship is plausible. He adduces an unnamed text by Aristotle, a work that survives only in fragmentary form. "We go to the Olympian festival for the sake of the spectacle, even if nothing more should come of it," he says that Aristotle writes. And: "We go to *theorise* at the festival of Dionysus."

•

It seems that the aristocratic class played little or no part in the Bacchic Mysteries of pre-Imperial Rome. The orgiasts, I have read, were commoners, even slaves. We know little about the form of these Bacchic rites, but it is said that initiates were obliged to undergo terrifying ordeals. In 186 BC the Roman authorities outlawed the cult; when revived by Julius Caesar, the Bacchic Mysteries took a tamer form. The original Mysteries were vulgar and bestial. Much of the flesh on display at the *maison de maître*, however, was prosperous; tanned, toned. An opera audience stripped bare.

•

At the *maison de maître* there was a lithe young woman whose breasts had been augmented surgically, but tastefully. The breasts were keenly molested, but what made her particularly attractive to many, I suspect, were the noises. Her yelps and howls seemed to gratify her partners. At climax, she vented a geyser of obscenities; the climaxes were frequent. She thrashed and flailed; she drummed her heels and screamed. Her pleasure seemed to depend largely upon the mirrors: she watched as if enthralled by her own wildness. Her hair was loose—thick curls, the colour of brass, that reached halfway to her waist; a Pre-Raphaelite maenad.

Antoine Vermeiren was thinking about a comedy based on the myth of Orpheus, he told Imogen, during what might have been their last conversation. Orpheus would be an uxorious middle-aged man, a ballad-singer, mourning for the wife he had lost, through his own stupidity. After years of moping, he would put himself out in the world again. He would become a party animal, or pretend that he had become one. A gang of highly sexed young women would tear him apart, perhaps not metaphorically.

•

A provocative writer argues that the notorious Messalina, wife of the emperor Claudius, was reviled by her contemporaries not for her promiscuity but because she fell in love. The man in question was not her husband: he was the senator Caius Silius, described by Tacitus as the most beautiful young man in Rome. On August 23rd, 48 AD, the day of Messalina's death, she attended a *bacchanal* in celebration of the wine harvest; she was attired as Ariadne; Caius Silius—with whom, it was alleged, she had entered into a marriage contract, having renounced her husband—played the part of Bacchus, the lord of the orgy. Claudius, on hearing of this outrage, ordered the murder of his wife. Messalina's unforgiveable crime, this writer maintains, was that she had abased herself in loving Caius Silius. A Roman matron owed devotion to her household, and to nothing else; the submission of love was a dereliction of duty, a more grievous offence than mere fornication. This writer refers to the wayward Messalina as an "adolescent." At her death, he states, she was twenty years old. Other sources make her a decade older. Some of these sources, however, might themselves be unreliable. Much of what we know, or think we know, of Messalina's depravity comes from chroniclers such as Tacitus, Suetonius and Juvenal, who were not her contemporaries. The legend of Messalina is largely a posthumous creation, disseminated by people whose motives were at least in part political. But Pliny the Elder, to whom we owe the story that the insatiable young empress, in competition with a prostitute, once bedded twenty-five men in succession, is perhaps a more dependable witness; he was born just a few years later than Messalina.

•

Said the exquisite Guillaume to Imogen: "It is only with you that I know who I am." He was offering himself to Imogen "without condition," he announced. Such self-repudiation was "what love demanded." The declaration took place in a location he had chosen with care: a superb restaurant, deeply rural, recently opened and thus known only to the few, for now. As befitted the occasion, he ordered an extravagant bottle, a Clos Saint-Jacques. Everything was at Guillaume's expense: the meal and the room at the idyllic hotel, which he had reserved as a surprise. A deep wound was being inflicted on his bank account; the symbolic significance of the gesture was understood. Just as he was renouncing his cash, he would renounce his freedom. In the expectation, of course, that Imogen would renounce hers.

•

Surveying the orgiasts from the gallery of the *maison de maître*, a man of my age, of louche demeanour, turned to me and remarked, as if addressing a fellow connoisseur in the presence of some stupendous but troubling work of art: "*C'est sublime.*" Perhaps there was some truth here, despite the posturing. The beautiful is purely pleasurable, according to Schopenhauer, whereas the sublime gives rise to a mingling of pleasure and pain. The sublime is resistant to contemplation. In Schopenhauer, there are gradations of the sublime. At the weaker end of the spectrum might be the sight of sunlight on a barren mass of boulders; there is no danger, but the scene establishes a hostile relationship to the will of the observer. Sublimity increases with the threat of destruction. A vast desert, in which the observer would certainly die, is more sublime than the boulders, but to be exposed to a storm in the mountains, amid lightning and torrents and rockfalls, is more sublime still. Only the infinite extent of the universe exceeds it.

•

For a moment, at the *maison de maître*, I could imagine seeing myself from across the room: a bogus anthropologist, making observations. I imagined how it would be if my employers were to learn of this: the disgrace, the shame, though I did not feel ashamed at that moment. What would I say? "An error of judgement. A lapse. That is not who I am." But a photograph would prove the contrary. *If that's not you, who else might it be?*

•

Imogen wished that she had been able to make films of the kind that Robert Bresson had made: films that had the sadness one finds in a town, in a landscape or a house, rather than the beauty or sadness one finds in a photo of a town, a landscape or a house, as Bresson himself had put it.

•

An ancestor of Adeline's had been clerk of the kitchen in a bishop's household, and the blood-red roses in the bishop's garden had thrived, it was said, because they had been planted in soil that had been mixed with earth from the grave of a saint; a portion of that soil had later been carried to the Hewitt house—hence the splendour of its rose garden. Imogen was standing beside me when I showed the group the pastel portrait of Adeline with her blood-red roses. I would have talked about the church commissioner who called on the Hewitts, demanding proof that they had destroyed their "images." The commissioner was shown a garden wall into which the fragments of a broken sculpture of Saint Margaret of Antioch had been incorporated. What the commissioner didn't know was that the head of Saint Margaret was in effect a door—in the cavity behind it, the family had stowed a reliquary and other forbidden items. This, I might have suggested, could serve as metaphor for the family's resistance to the new church: outwardly, they observed the new rite; in private, they remained faithful to the old ways. For five years, they had given sanctuary to a relative who had been expelled from her convent; she had lived in the space beneath the roof, the solitary occupant of the Hewitts' clandestine nunnery. The Hewitt house was in the vicinity of Redruth, which I will pass on my way to William and Jenna; but not a stone of the house remains.

•

The screaming of foxes wakes me, and what comes to mind is another night, with Imogen, in the garden of her house. "Listen," she said, pressing my arm to make me stop. We heard foxes, and a conversation of tawny owls, far off. "Male," she said, pointing left, after the first call and reply; "female," pointing right, like a conductor. Leaves hissed in the breeze. I can picture the scene: the moon cross-hatched in the branches; the low dust-coloured clouds. "The concert of the night," she murmured, as we listened. Walking back to the house, slowly, she told me about Arianne, who had left Paris, and almost everything of her former life, to live alone in the Pyrenees. Few were invited to her mountain cottage. Imogen visited her, after the first operation. The retreat was embedded in huge silence; the whistle of a marmot might be the only sound for an hour. Griffon vultures patrolled the air. Imogen talked to Arianne about sky burials. The idea of being "strewn about the mountains" appealed to her, but only for as long as she was with Arianne, she said. The tranquillity of the mountains had taken possession of her for a while. She imagined that people had once gained a comparable benefit from hermits; they caught contentment off them, which may or may not have lasted. "But this is where I have to end," she said, and pressed my arm again.

•

The door is opened by William. As on the day of his departure from my house, an embrace rather than a handshake is what the situation demands. With a hand on my shoulder, he guides me to the living room, where Jenna and Tilly await. Jenna stands as I enter the room. "Pleased to meet you," she says, giving me a hand that is cool and small; it's as though I were William's employer and she needs to make a good impression. Tilly, sitting on the floor, regards me uncertainly, but her smile, when her mother introduces me as William's friend, is bold and delightful, as William had said.

And Jenna is indeed pale, but not unusually so; her hair is dark and long, her mouth small, certainly; and her nose could be described as narrow and straight. For some reason William has omitted to mention her voice: it's deep, with a throaty and grainy quality, and lovely.

Jenna had thought she would cook stargazy pie in my honour. People use all sorts of fish for it, but Jenna's family always observes the classic recipe. The heads of the pilchards are left sticking out through the crust, he warns me. "Like they're gazing at the stars. It's kind of grim."

"It's so the oil can flow back in," Jenna explains. She tells me the tale of the pie's creation, in celebration of the courage of Tom Bawcock, the fisherman who went out in a terrible December storm and came back with enough fish to feed the entire village.

"And who never existed," William interrupts, teasing.

"Maybe, or maybe not," she says, with loving disdain.

The fish are local. William tells me about the revival of pilchard fishing in Newlyn, thanks to Nutty Noah. They catch them the old way, using ring nets, at night, when the fish come up to feed. "It's madness," he says. "They can pull in four tonnes in an hour."

"You'd think he'd been at sea all his life," says Jenna. "Instead of two days."

"More than that," William corrects her. "Four at least, my lover," he says. The sudden Cornish accent gets a laugh from Tilly; it is soon apparent that William can get a laugh from Tilly whenever he chooses.

At the table, at William's urging, Jenna tells me stories of her family. She ranges through the generations: the great-aunt who'd had six sons in a row, then six daughters, then three more boys; the great-uncle whose voice was the loudest anyone had ever heard; the relative who had come through many years of deep-sea fishing unscathed, give or take a fracture or two, only to drown, drunk, in the bath. While she talks, William looks at her with admiration, as if the stories were of her own invention, and mostly new to him. She is persuaded by William to produce her phone, on which the course of their relationship is charted in a hundred pictures.

At eleven, Jenna begins to yawn. She apologises: it has been a long day, and she has an early start in the morning. We look out of the window at the lights on the hill. In summer, she tells me, every house is lit up at night; in the dead of winter, they are nearly all dark. She often works for Londoners in the holiday months. "Some of them, you wonder why they have children. But they pay good money," she says.

"Not all of them," says William, putting his arm around her.

Jenna gives me a hug. She hopes to meet me again.

"I'm sure you will," I answer.

"Oh, you will, definitely," says William.

As soon as Jenna has left us, William asks, as if a lot depends on the answer: "So? What do you think?"

"She's terrific," I tell him, candidly.

He looks towards the window. "OK," he murmurs, and for a moment, despite what I've seen of them together, I think he's about to tell me that he is having doubts. But what he says is: "In that case I'm going to give her the bended knee routine. If she says Yes, you're the best man. Or the best I can manage."

•

In one of her letters Adeline makes reference to an ancestor, John Hewitt, who died at Clyst Heath. His throat was cut by a German *Lanzknecht*. On August 5th, 1549, nine hundred Cornish prisoners were killed in this way at Clyst Heath, by order of Lord William Grey, who had one thousand German mercenaries under his command. Grey and his Germans were fighting the Catholic insurrectionists of Cornwall alongside the king's troops. The king's chronicler, John Hayward, recorded that the nine hundred prisoners were bound and gagged before their throats were slit, and that the slaughter lasted a mere ten minutes. On hearing of the atrocity, an army of two thousand Cornishmen advanced on Clyst Heath. Nearly all of them died there, in the bloodiest day of the Prayer Book Rebellion, an uprising that cost the lives of ten percent of the population of Cornwall, by some estimates. Speaking of the battle of Clyst Heath, Lord Grey stated that he had never "taken part in such a murderous fray." Two years earlier, he had led the massacre at the battle of Pinkie Cleugh, the last pitched battle between Scottish and English armies. Unlike at Pinkie Cleugh, there is no memorial at Clyst Heath. A rugby pitch marks the place where the nine hundred were executed.

•

A lustrous early morning in the park; windless; cloudless; cool. Long shadows of the trees on the pale gold grass. A sense of pause; the withdrawal of autumn is under way. Sitting on the bench, I recalled taking Imogen onto the terrace, in the wheelchair. The sun was still touching the hill; washes of mist lay in the hollows. She said something, so quietly that I did not hear her clearly. Smiling, her face in the light, she repeated: "One more day." She said it as if life were an addiction that she lacked the strength to overcome. She took off a glove to hold my hand; her skin was as cold as tap water.

•

A scene to which intense happiness is attached, like a label: in Cornwall, above a cove. The spray was being thrown up to the cliff tops; from time to time it touched our faces; the water boomed and seethed on the rocks below. Huge ribbons of foam a long way from the shore. The sea in flux everywhere. A sumptuous sunset. Vast clouds filled the sky—an endless troop of them approaching over the sea, mighty turmoils of white and pink above the roseate water. I see Imogen in her big Aran sweater; her hair disarrayed. We sat for an hour or so, and barely said a word.

•

The date of Imogen's birth. Every year, unless work made it impossible, she came home for her birthday. It was an observance that she felt obliged to maintain, and not just for her mother, she told me. At a break in the rain, in the late afternoon, we went outside. Above the hills, the sky was a mess of steel and iron colours, but the water on the paving stones was like a golden paint. Bright water dripped around us as we walked through the pergola. One of the horses was at the fence; a thin steam rose from its back. She stroked its muzzle and pressed her face to its neck, savouring the smell of the animal. Hans was the horse's name; he was Imogen's favourite; at times, when Hans raised his head into the sunlight, it was possible to believe that contented-seeming Hans had a consciousness of his contentment. At some point before we returned to the house, we talked about birthdays, about the religions that acknowledge no anniversaries. Imogen had worked with someone who had told her about an ex-boyfriend whose mother, a Jehovah's Witness, though appalled by the idea of birthday parties, had spent a fortune on her daughter's wedding; soon after the wedding, the ex-boyfriend had abandoned the Witnesses, and was consequently disowned by his family. When we celebrate an anniversary, Imogen remarked, we are like people standing together in the middle of a river, holding hands to brace ourselves against the current. Now I throw another page into the water.

•

From the terrace, with Imogen's mother, I watched Imogen and her brother, walking towards the paddock; he gestured grandly; plans were being explicated. Jonathan was a strategist, I was told; a young man who was prepared to embrace change, whenever change was necessary, as it now was. And Helen was invaluable too. "Invaluable" was the adjective that Imogen's mother used. The profundity of Helen's pedigree had already been impressed upon me. "Her people have been here since Stonehenge was new," Imogen had joked. In addition to being handsome and well-finished and infinitely English, Helen had proved to be an astute businesswoman; she had negotiated effectively with various buyers for their produce, Imogen's mother told me. The estate was in safe hands with Jonathan and his wife, I was assured. "Imogen has been swimming against the current all her life," her mother said. "But one cannot do that forever." It seemed that I had some potential as a sensible influence, an antidote to the wilfulness that had been characteristic of Imogen since childhood. My appreciation of the house and of its history might help to weaken Imogen's resistance, she seemed to imply. There was something in the way that Imogen attended to her brother, as he swept an arm across the scene, that seemed to indicate that a change had begun, her mother thought. "One day she will come back," she stated.

•

Returning to the living room, to find me studying the portrait of her mother, Imogen's mother remarked: "Imogen always detested that picture." We considered the painting of Éloïse. The grandmother's hair, fiercely wrought, was framed by the splendid autumnal foliage of the garden in Meudon; the texture of the hair was indistinguishable from the texture of the leaves; her fingers, flatteringly elongated, seemed to have no bones; her face had little more definition than a pillow. She was extremely proud of her hands, Imogen told me; she treated them every morning and every night with an esoteric unguent derived from Madagascan vanilla orchids. They were aristocratic hands: she had reason to believe that her bloodline flowed back to an unnamed mistress of the duke of somewhere or other, a duke for whose existence, according to Imogen's father, there was nothing in the way of proof, of any kind. "Le Duc de Mirage," her father called this elusive ancestor. Like her father, Imogen found it hard to love Éloïse. And Éloïse, for her part, found it hard to love the grandchildren. She seemed to care most deeply for her clothes (as Imogen remembered her, she would dress for the family visitations as a normal person would dress for an evening at the opera), her garden, her dogs—she always had a Bichon Frise or two—and the memory of her husband, Michael, the brilliant diplomat and debonair Englishman, whom she had met in Paris after the liberation and promptly married. Imogen's father, though treated with respect, was conscious that Michael had set a standard that he could never match. No man could ever match the élan of Michael. He had been killed in a road accident, aged fifty-one, and Éloïse had vowed never to remarry. It was genuinely a vow. She had taken a decision, and Éloïse never went back on a decision that she had made, as she often reminded her family. It was one of her principles. To remarry would have been to traduce the peerless Michael. For the rest of her life she would be an exemplar of noble widowhood. Two or three times a year her family were welcomed—"perhaps not the right word," said Imogen—to her splendid house. It was necessary for the family to go to Éloïse, because Éloïse would never leave Paris. This seemed to be another point of principle. She conducted herself, Imogen said, like an actress who had abruptly, in her prime, abandoned her profession and withdrawn from the public gaze. What she did with her days was a mystery. As far as her granddaughter could tell, her principal occupation, other than inspecting the gardener's work, was browsing the innumerable fashion magazines to which she subscribed. Reference was sometimes made to her visitors, who were understood to be women of leisure and a certain distinction, but none of these visitors were ever seen, or had names that Imogen could recall. The garden was vast. Play was permitted in a small and precisely delineated zone of greenery and in one room of the house, a room that was almost devoid of furniture and never warm, even in the height of summer. The whole house was chilly, as Imogen remembered it; the air was like the air in the depths of a cave.

The creator of the portrait, Imogen's mother explained, had been a long-standing friend of her mother's gardener, who had one day asked if his friend Gaston, a "successful painter," might be permitted to work for a few hours amid the wonderful flowerbeds. Permission was granted, subject to stringent conditions, and Gaston duly arrived one August afternoon. The garden delighted him, as did the dogs: he confessed to being "enamoured" of the Bichon Frise. Further ingratiation was achieved by presenting Éloïse with a sketch of her pets. "My mother was unaccountably charmed," said Imogen's mother. The dogs were brought to Gaston, for more thorough scrutiny. A double dog portrait was the upshot. "A frightful thing," she told me. But Éloise, when she looked at this painting, seemed not to see the maladroit brushwork—she saw only the images of her beloved dogs. Then came the portrait of Éloise herself. "My father had died, bear in mind," Imogen's mother confided. "For some unfathomable reason, it was only when the portrait was finished that it occurred to my mother that this man might have something else in mind." She laughed. "What's so amusing," she said, "is that he was not merely a mediocre painter: he was a comprehensively unattractive specimen. A tiny man, with green teeth and puny legs. And absurd hair. Like a bird's nest soaked in oil. Whereas my mother was a fine-looking woman. Not that one would know it," she said, waving her cigarette at the picture. "Imogen was rather like her, in some ways," she remarked, in a tone of conclusion.

"Oh yes?" I said.

"Yes," she said, and that was all.

•

A strange dream, in which I confessed everything to Val. We were at her house. Val and I had withdrawn to the bathroom, because every guest was obliged to confess to her in the bathroom; it was a condition of the invitation. Val held my head between her hands, as if it were a pot that was filled to the brim with water. Her hands shook with the effort of holding it. The explanation was obvious, she said: I took pleasure in my humiliation. Waking, I gave some thought to the proposition. Dreams, however ridiculous, often have the power of truth, if only for a moment. But no humiliation was intended by Imogen, and none experienced. Some anguish, yes; but no humiliation.

•

Queuing in the post office, I noticed, at the counter, the pretty white dog—Bianca. I recognised the dog first; her owner's hair was hidden under a soft woollen hat, midnight blue. The coat, of matching colour, was somewhat longer than the red coat; its length directed attention towards the elegant shoes. Turning from the counter, she noticed that I was in the queue, and smiled. As she exited, we both mimed "Hello."

•

Imogen had fallen asleep, I thought, but then she spoke: she had just seen, with wonderful precision, a downpour in Cornwall. The rain had been so heavy that we'd had to stop the car, by a phone box. The red of the phone box was the only colour within the rain. Then, in the direction we were facing, the sun came out, and for a minute we were in the midst of brightly glowing water, through which we could see nothing. The deluge did not fade out: it ceased in a matter of seconds, like a badly executed special effect. A boy in a blue anorak was revealed, standing on the other side of the road, looking up at the sky, laughing, incredulous; his shoes disappeared into water as he stepped off the kerb.

"But where was that?" Imogen asked.

I recalled a downpour that had made the car tremble. I remembered the sudden sunlight before the rain had stopped, but no phone box nor any boy. "Near Zennor," I answered.

In the last weeks, drowsing, she often experienced scenes of similar intensity. Sometimes, I think, they were more dream than memory, though they had an aura of recollection. Without opening her eyes, she described an evening that had returned to her: a long walk after a meal, in a small town; a river; a busker by a spotlit building. We had strolled along a street of shops in which none of the streetlights were working. "Do you remember? Where was that?" she asked, looking at me.

"I don't know," I answered. "Am I definitely there?"

She closed her eyes again; she clenched her eyelids. "I'm not even sure I'm there," she said.

•

In the park, passing the bench where I sometimes sat with William, where Imogen and I sometimes sat with him, I remember the day he talked about the sound that a mass of small leaves made in the wind. It gave him a "great contentment," he said. He told me that for a couple of years, when he was at primary school, he had lived near a canal, and on the edge of this canal there was a tree that he used to climb. In the wind, this tree made a sound "like an avalanche of sand," he said. On blustery days he would often lie below the tree, relishing the sound it made. He was happier then than he had ever been since, he thought. What was it that happened in our heads when we remembered a sound, he wondered. "The memory of a sound isn't really a sound, is it?" he said. "You're not actually hearing anything."

•

On a Sunday morning, hearing bells from over the hill, Imogen said to me that the best of her childhood was in that sound. On Sundays at home, in this room, reading, she had been happy, and her happiness was at its fullest when the bells were ringing. If she were allowed only one recording on her desert island, it would be the sound of those Sunday mornings. Many times she had walked with her father to the crest of the hill, just to listen to the bells, she told me. Once she had seen tears in his eyes. She had tried to believe that this was because he too was moved deeply by the wonderful sound.

•

"Thank you for escorting me to the edge," Imogen said one morning. She looked at our hands, and smiled. "One body fewer. It doesn't matter. I can say that. It seems to be what I feel." But she was not sure that she was prepared. Rather, a mood had settled on her, like black snow, she said. Her laugh was a retching cough.

•

The sunlight drenched the blossom of the apple trees. It was so beautiful, it was like dying, said William. Imogen asked him what he meant. "Everything is energy," he answered, as if this were something that many people knew. "Everything is frequencies. That's what all of this is," he said, circling a hand above his head. The hand went round and round; he had been drinking. The whiteness of the blossom was frequency made visible. The blossom would not last long, but its energy would last forever, he said. Some of the energy of the tree had penetrated his brain; it was so powerful that it had wiped out all of his thoughts. That is why it was like dying. "I see," I said; he sensed that I was uneasy with him, whereas Imogen was not.

•

Some Roman tombstones have holes drilled into them; to honour the occupant of the tomb, and to provide nourishment in the afterlife, relatives would pour water, wine and honey into the hole, so that the liquid could flow through the stone and onto the ashes. But we should be wary of attributing to all Romans a set belief on the subject of the afterlife, Francesca warned. Some believed in ghosts and spirits, and others did not. Among the latter, there would have been many who nonetheless maintained the traditions by which the dead were kept alive. She told us about a Roman tombstone that is inscribed with a text addressed to the person who has stopped to read it. There is no life beyond the tomb, the text tells the reader; the dead are dust and ashes, and wine poured into the grave will make mud of the remains, nothing more.

•

"Inspirational stuff," said Imogen, reading of the last hours of the life of Cato the Younger, as recounted by Plutarch. *Then the sword being brought in by a little boy, Cato took it, drew it out, and looked at it; and when he saw the point was good, "Now," said he, "I am master of myself"; and laying down the sword, he took his book again, which, it is related, he read twice over.* Later that night, *he took his sword, and stabbed it into his breast.*

•

Imogen discovered, in a box of miscellaneous old photographs, a small picture of a young woman sitting at the library table, on which a chess board had been set. From the young woman's dress, and certain details of the room, it seemed that the picture dated from around 1920. She was smiling, apparently at something that was happening to her left. Her expression suggested an attractive and clever character. Most of the chess pieces had been removed from the board. Imogen liked to think that a male opponent had just conceded defeat. The fairness of the young woman's hair and the clarity of her eyes gave young Imogen the idea that she was German. Matilde, she named her, because neither her mother nor her father had any idea who the young woman might really have been. Nobody knew who she was. For some time, this was wonderful. Matilde was a woman of mystery. Her name was Matilde in the way that a painting of a beautiful unknown woman might be given a name: Flora, Venus, The Veiled Woman. When she was sent to school, Imogen took the photograph of Matilde with her. The meaning of the image began to change. Matilde had been brilliant and beautiful; she had visited the house, and sat at the table at which Imogen had so often sat. Now nobody at home knew anything about her. Somewhere her body was lying in the earth. Her gravestone was perhaps no longer meaningful to anybody. Only this image remained, an image to which any woman's name could be attached.

·

When the dead were believed to be in Purgatory, they received the charity of the living, and they cared for the living in return. The dead were close. But with the revision of The Book of Common Prayer in 1552, the dead were banished to an infinite distance. The burial service would now take place at the graveside, not in the church; in place of prayers of commendation and committal, there was to be just one reference to the deceased, who had been delivered, thanks be to God, from the "myseryes of this sinneful world." Now the dead were in a world that had no contact with our own; even prayers could not reach them.

·

Beatrice at the piano, playing a Chopin prelude for her husband.

The music is not dubbed—this is Imogen playing. Inaccuracies and hesitations have been left uncorrected; they impart authenticity. She played the same prelude for me, on the family's old Broadwood. "If she had studied harder," her mother confided, "she would have been better than me. Much better." Imogen persuaded her to play for us. I was to take it as a sign of her approval that she consented to be persuaded, Imogen told me. The little waltz that her mother played was by someone whose name I did not know—a trivial piece, she said, opening the score. No notes were fluffed; the tempo was perfectly even; the movement of her hands was economical, undemonstrative. It was almost as though playing the piano were an exercise in comportment. One would not have been inclined to dance to the waltz that Imogen's mother played, error-free though it was. "I am not truly musical," she said, as though admitting that the colour of her hair was not natural. Imogen, on the other hand, was "deeply musical." This was an opinion with which her daughter disagreed: she liked to play, but had reached the limit of her competence at the age of fourteen, she insisted. But there was a pulse in her playing, and there is a pulse in the music that Beatrice makes; it has spontaneity; life. I watch Beatrice at the piano: this is Imogen, as she was. She is lovely, and there is a terrible pathos in this lovely image. In adoration Julius Preston watches his wife. Candlelight glows on her face; it glows on her hands, which are raised in mid-bar, as Beatrice stops and scowls at the page of music.

Inevitably, the thought is present: the character will always be this age, but the actress is no longer young. Some might know that this actress, who is young in this film, is no longer living. Imogen could not watch any of her films with me. "It would be like reading my own obituary," she said.

•

William's mother has informed him that it is completely out of the question for her to attend the wedding without her husband, as William had suggested she might; therefore she will not be present. His father has sent his best wishes, by text; he hopes his son has "better luck" than he had. So I will be *in loco parentis* too. The speech is proving to be difficult—how to balance best-man jocularity and quasi-parental pride? Some explanation of how we had come to know each other might be expected, but the specifics of our case do not seem appropriate to the occasion. He was my lodger—that will suffice, with vague references to our prior acquaintance. As an anecdote: watching the trawlermen on TV. William heckling the clueless first-timer: "I could do better than that," he shouted. And he did do better: he managed more than one trip, and was even more seasick than the lad on TV. Pause for laughter, or mild amusement. Some might like the slapstick of William failing to take the wind direction into account before vomiting. Were I of William's age, I would be expected to provide at least one such item. Light embarrassment of the groom is conventional. The coda is the easy part—the joy of Tilly.

November

EIGHTEEN VISITORS; no prospect of any rescue.

•

Crossing the road, a young woman walked directly towards me, head down, swiping her phone, oblivious. At the last moment, without looking up, she swerved as I swerved, and we collided. She gave me a scowl and went on her way, still swiping. I watched her until she turned the corner; not once did she look away from the phone. Twenty people, more or less, mostly young, were walking down the street from that corner; ten of them, I'd say, were staring into their phones; several had ear-buds rammed in. Downcast eyes, like prisoners in the exercise yard. But had they looked up, what would they have seen? Advertisements on all sides. Perfect young women, bikini-clad in dazzling Caribbean water, or striding along the streets of immaculate cities, hand-in-hand with perfect young men. With their glorious faces, their resplendent hair, their magnificent dentition, their superlative limbs, the superhumans transform the sweatshop clothes into covetable items. On a billboard, a car gleams in white space, as if it were a masterpiece of sculpture. Gorgeous children laugh in a film-set of a bedroom, under the gaze of their strangely youthful mother. Everywhere, false images; generators of money. I recall a moment with Imogen, on Oxford Street. "All right, Jeremiah," she said, "we get the point."

•

On the occasion of her sixtieth birthday, Val has thoughts on the topic of getting older. Her body is not what it was. Of a morning, her joints seem to have rusted while she slept. Her eyesight requires ever stronger correction. Her sense of taste has become duller; she is aware that certain frequencies have become inaudible to her. Ageing is indeed no picnic. She has friends who have made use of hormone replacement therapy. It must be said, some of these proponents of medicinal enhancement do look marvellous. They have recovered something of the lustre of their earlier selves. But HRT, for all its benefits, was not the right way for Val. This had nothing to do with whatever risks such treatment might entail—though naturally one must be aware of these risks before making the choice that every woman is entitled to take. No, Val has preferred to let nature takes its course, unobstructed. Body and mind will remain in step, and the latter will be enriched, she believes, by learning to accommodate the changes to which the former is subject. Our culture's cult of youth is deplorable. To counter it, we should take a lesson from those societies that still maintain a reverence for the wisdom of older people. It is a sign of what we have lost that it is almost impossible to use the word *wisdom* without embarrassment. Val makes no apologies for using that word. "The wisdom of experience" may be a cliché, she concedes, but clichés become clichés because they are true, she reminds us. The road becomes harder as we grow older, "because we are climbing perpetually." And because we are climbing, "with every year we see farther."

•

Our society enforces an imperative to preserve oneself at all costs, while at the same time pretending that death is not the end, said Imogen, after the first operation. But death was simply nothing, she said. Just look at a butcher's counter; look at the insignificant little corpses flattened on the road. There's nothing to be afraid of, she said; there's no mystery—flesh is merely stuff, like everything else. And we can all, easily enough, come to terms with the death of anyone, with one exception, said Imogen. Though she had no fear of death, the sorrow of the thought of no longer being in the world was often too much for her, she admitted.

•

Fireworks had always thrilled her. I can see her face, the grin of wonderment at the geysers of silver light, the huge flowers of coloured fire that bloomed for an instant and vanished above us. We were watching from a road, at a distance from the bonfire. Shrapnel of firework casings—curved segments of thick grey cardboard—clattered on the ground around us. The detonations were as loud as thunder directly overhead. Francesca's boyfriend stood behind her, with his arms clamped around her waist; he produced a laugh sound, but seemed pained by the pointlessness, the profligacy of it all. "Frankie" was what he called Francesca, which nobody else ever has, to my knowledge. We felt sorry for him, because he knew his time was almost up. Fireworks were an art form, Imogen proposed to Francesca: the display had been crafted with great care, to give delight, and it had no meaning that could be put into words.

•

But the other year: the parade of pirates and sailors, eighteenth-century yeomen and American Indians, Mongol warriors, Vikings—every one of them with a torch of fire. Belligerent jollity. A bandolier of firecrackers, hanging around the neck of an effigy of Guy Fawkes, detonated with the noise of an ambush. Then we saw, at the top of a tall pole, the words *Lest We Forget* in letters of fire. Two grim-faced men held up a banner that proclaimed *Faithful Unto Death*. Another: *No Popery*. Their demeanour was adamant; the papist hordes might have been massing in the hills.

"I thought this was just an excuse to dress up and make a racket," said Imogen. She had to shout to be heard. "These guys don't seem to be pretending," she yelled, making frightened eyes.

•

Our species took its great leap forward when it stood up and looked around. No longer were we genital-sniffing hominids, scuttling around on all fours. We stood upright, and sight became our primary sense. Now the optic nerve of *Homo sapiens* has nearly twenty times as many nerve endings as the cochlear nerve, the second most sensitive organ of perception. Conversation at normal volume becomes incomprehensible at a range of less than one hundred feet, but the human eye, unaided, can discern the flame of a single candle at a range of a mile and a half. It can distinguish in the region of ten million different colours, by some calculations.

•

"It is time to abandon the world of the civilised and its light," wrote Georges Bataille in "The Sacred Conspiracy," published in 1936, in the first issue of *Acéphale*, a journal founded by Georges Bataille to publish writings from the secret society of the same name, also founded by Georges Bataille. "Secretly or not, it is necessary to become other, or else cease to be," he declared. "WE ARE FERO-CIOUSLY RELIGIOUS," he proclaimed, in capitals. "What we are undertaking is a war." The war was to involve a sacrificial ritual, a sacred game such as Nietzsche had proposed as a means by which humanity, having brought about the death of God, might find it possible to overcome the consequences of God's removal. The sac-rifice was to be conducted at the Egyptian obelisk in the centre of Place de la Concorde. It appears that an animal was to be slaugh-tered, but precisely what species of animal was to give its life in the cause of spiritual regeneration remains open to question. It might have been a goat, or a rabbit, or a gibbon. A female gibbon, of course. The members of Acéphale seem to have considered performing a human sacrifice, perhaps in the forest of Saint-Nom-la-Bretèche, where the group often gathered by a tree that had been riven by lightning. Writer and ethnographer Michel Leiris, with whom Bataille and Roger Caillois established the Collège de sociologie in 1937, pronounced this sacrificial project "puerile."

On January 21st, members of the Acéphale group, I have learned, gathered to commemorate the execution of Louis XVI, who on that date, in 1793, had been guillotined on Place de la Concorde.

•

When she was ten years old, Imogen had learned from a schoolfriend that during the French Revolution the men who worked the guillotines had worn chain-mail gloves, because the severed heads would try to bite their fingers when lifted out of the basket. Years later, she was still having nightmares in which the biting heads appeared. The heads would roll across the wooden platform, mouthing words that they could not make intelligible.

•

"Our desire to consume, to annihilate, to make a bonfire of our resources, and the joy we find in the burning, the fire and the ruin are what seem to us divine." So wrote Bataille—pornographer, anthropologist, numismatist, archivist at the Bibliothèque Nationale and, some (eg Antoine Vermeiren) would say, philosopher. "Our only real pleasure is to squander our resources to no purpose," he wrote.

He is buried in Vézelay, in Burgundy, where he died on July 8th, 1962, at his house in Rue Saint-Étienne, close to the basilica of Saint Mary Magdalene. As a young man, Bataille considered becoming a priest; for a short time he attended a seminary.

•

Coming out of a slump, Imogen joked: "Everybody, at some time, wants to be dead—but just for a week or two."

•

Franck Boudet waited at a distance until the family had left, then approached the grave again. He looked into it, frowning deeply, as if he had happened upon a murdered body in a field. His attire was uncompromising: black suit, black shirt, black tie, black shoes. But he had the appearance of a man who had just stepped off a long-haul flight: the clothes were creased and a shave was needed; it looked as if some sleep would be beneficial too. The hair and forehead put me in mind of images of Benjamin Franklin in his later years, though I doubt that Benjamin Franklin dyed his hair as Franck Boudet dyed his—an unnatural tone of charcoal predominated, with lanes of deep chestnut near the scalp. The belt of his trousers dug a groove into his belly, and the shirt buttons were under some strain. He could have been cast as a rock guitarist who hadn't yet quit, after four decades in the business. At the graveside he put his hands together and murmured inaudibly, for some time. That done, he looked up, into the branches of the trees, steadying himself with the sight of them. He looked at me, and nodded, as though we had been in attendance together by agreement. We had not yet spoken, but I had intended to speak to him. "You are David?" he said, putting out a hand. Through Imogen, there was a kinship. We walked to the cars. In everything Imogen did, he said, she was a very strong woman. In *Maintenant et à l'heure de notre mort* she was "sublime," he told me. He stopped and turned to look back, in the direction of the place where Imogen lay. She was "very true," he said, as if seeing her image in the air. "There are things that are more important than technique. Imogen was not a technical person. She served the truth," he said. He looked at me; the look announced that a moment of significance was imminent; a momentous parting. "We knew her," he said. "Lovers are easy to find, but not friends. For Imogen, we were friends. We know this," he said, and he shook my hand martially. "We remember her," he said, making the words sound like the oath of our two-man sect.

•

Benoît, I see, is now a professor at the university of Grenoble, specialising in environmental economics. The list of publications is impressive, as is the website photo: a strong-jawed man, with closely cropped dark hair and a trim grey-flecked beard. The eyewear—circular lenses, sturdy metallic frame—is distinctive; this boffin has a sense of style. It is not a casual snapshot—it's a portrait such as one might see in a publisher's catalogue. The gaze is percipient; here is a man who sees the big picture.

When he learned what had happened with Imogen, he came to Paris at the first opportunity. Benoît had followed her career with interest, he told her. They talked about *Maintenant et à l'heure de notre mort* but not about the films she had made with Vermeiren. Benoît looked well—a little heavier, and more expensively dressed. Politicians, journalists and company directors now consulted him for his opinion and analysis. He had achieved a certain position in life, a position of some eminence, influence and reward. As Imogen put it: he was not self-satisfied, exactly, but he struck her as a man who was comfortably clothed in success. He had married an Italian woman, a physicist, and they had two children, of whom a photo-graph was produced; the beautiful children sat in kayaks, on placid blue water, in front of snow-topped mountains. As soon as Imogen was feeling stronger, said Benoît, she would have to come and stay with them; they had an apartment on Lago d'Iseo. When she showed him the bag and the stoma, he was momentarily at a loss. "You will get better," he declared. She was to take this as praise for her strength of character. He was invited to the funeral, but was unable to attend. I study the face of Benoît; a different Imogen is remembered by this man; only in his mind does that Imogen exist.

•

After the first operation: I recall a walk along the river, with little conversation. It was not quite fearfulness that I saw in her gaze, as she looked across the water. It was more, I think, an almost desperate avidity. She stopped at a bridge, and seemed to take in the scene as if every object within it were over-charged with meaning. Elsewhere, she frowned as one would frown at something that might prove to be not as solid as it seems.

•

I stepped off the train into a crowd, but I saw her immediately, at the end of the platform. She looked weary, but no worse than weary. She put a hand on the knot of her scarf, at her throat; a gesture of self-protection, it seemed. And the way she stood back from the surge of departing passengers suggested a new fragility. Yet the embrace she gave me was strong. The first words she spoke were:

"Behold the cavalry." This was not to be a romantic reunion. I had not been summoned to take the place of the disappointing Loïc, and I had no desire to replace him. This had never been said, but it had been understood. We walked for a while, before taking the Métro. She took my arm; as we waited for the traffic to stop, she pressed her cheek to my shoulder. I was reading when she came in to say goodnight. She showed me where her body had been cut. When I touched the scar, she ruffled my hair and laughed, then whispered: "I am bound to thee forever."

•

Driving out to the *maison de maître*, what I had felt, above all, was dread—perhaps, intermittently, a dread akin to what I imagine might be felt before a first sky-dive, as the door opens onto the depths of air. A trial was imminent, from which I might emerge changed in some way. As we drove back into Paris, the city was awakening; we were returning to the familiar world. We had emerged from the underworld, into the light. I kissed, in courtly manner, the back of the hand that she held out. My position might have seemed to be one of servitude, but she had confessed everything to me, knowing that the one who receives the confession has power over the one who confesses. An irreducible intimacy had been established; an absolute friendship. I regarded her with something close to wonder; with an admiration in which there was also an element of fear.

•

Memory: the background noise of the sensory world, sometimes barely audible, but always there. Making sentences of it, we amplify the signal, introducing distortion.

•

A list of things seen in a single glance: chestnut trees; a slope of grass; other zones of grass, beyond the trees; several human bodies; starlings; a dog; thin formations of water vapour and crystals of ice, known as cirrus clouds; cars. More than this was seen, much more. I could list what is seen of those bodies, in that single glance: the form, the clothes, the movement. The tumult of things, the irresistible visual deluge, of which the brain makes a scene, in the instant of seeing. One seems to see a picture, an arrangement of objects with names attached: starlings; chestnuts; cirrus clouds. Stopping, I looked. I tried to make no sense of it, to give up, to lose myself in the torrent of the visible. Impossible, for me.

•

"To be full of things is to be empty of God. To be empty of things is to be full of God." Again, Meister Eckhart.

•

I turn into Green Street and almost collide with Bianca's owner. The dog, at the end of a lengthy lead, is urinating in the gutter. It's a likeable animal. Bianca gazes skyward, as if patiently waiting, like her owner, for this tiresome procedure to be concluded. "Excuse us," says the woman. Bianca steps out of the road and walks towards me.

I hold out a hand, and the dog raises its head to touch my fingers with its muzzle. One might be inclined to think that Bianca too has some recollection of our previous encounters; I find myself persuaded that this is the case. "This is unusual," her owner informs me. "A stand-offish little madam, as a rule." She is on a mission to buy a book for a grandson. It's not his birthday; she just has an urge to send him something, for his parents to read at bedtime. He is the same age as Francesca's Jack, more or less. I recommend *Each Peach Pear Plum*—my niece's son's favourite, I tell her. She thinks that little George already has *Each Peach Pear Plum*. "Let me make a call," she says, looking for a place out of the flow of shoppers. Ten yards from where we are standing there's a recessed doorway. In response to my offer, she hands Bianca's lead to me. The dog and I follow, at a discreet distance. Within half a minute George's mother has answered: they do indeed have *Each Peach Pear Plum*. The three of us walk together as far as the bookshop; I am going that way, I decide. Gorgeous Georgie and adorable Jack are the topics of conversation.

•

An email from my father: his friend Bill has won a prize at a photography exhibition. He thinks I'll like Bill's picture. A click on a link brings up the winning photo: the subject is a barn, in a very photogenic state of disintegration. Tyres and pallets and gas canisters are strewn outside, with lengths of pipe and engine parts and sheets of corrugated iron. The variegated tones of rust are nicely distributed.

One day in December, in the first year of unemployment, Bill took a diversion to the factory in which he and my father had worked. Nobody had taken over the premises. A chain-link fence surrounded the site, but a section of the fence had been uprooted; all he had to do was duck his head to get in. A skim of grit now covered the concrete floor of the workshop. In the offices, pens and cigarette packets were strewn on the desks; health and safety notices were pinned to the board; invoices and letters had curled into shapes like flowers. Everything was turning grey under dust. A week later he went back, with a camera. Belatedly, Bill had found his hobby, to the relief of his wife. He became a connoisseur of dereliction. Soon a filing cabinet had been filled with images of his discoveries: a saw mill, a flour mill, a half-built house that had been left to rot, a barracks, two schools, a pillbox, a field of gutted cars, an evacuated farm, dead factories. He tried to persuade my father to come along: the expeditions kept him in good shape, he pointed out, with all the fences to be breached and walls to be surmounted. Sites at which trespassers were threatened with prosecution had an additional attraction: having been discarded prematurely by the world of work, he was taking revenge in flouting the law.

•

When I think of Imogen, what presents itself to my mind is not a story. I think of her, not of a life. A story, a life, is something one makes; it is not what one remembers. She, the living Imogen, is what I remember. Each memory is a reliquary; each memory contains something of the substance of her. Not an account, but a constellation of moments, or of their remains.

•

The death of the Châtelaine—a beautiful scene. All we see of the young woman's body is the motionless hand, almost touching the floor, with one finger extended, pointing down—as if directing our attention—at the beads of blood on the flagstones, from which the camera then departs, to observe a basket of oranges and an ivory-handled knife in a pewter bowl, in sunlight, and particles of dust drifting across the window. Relishing every surface, the camera roams the room that had held the lovers. Sunlight rakes the walls, showing the grain of the stone; it soaks the flesh of a blood-red rose; it makes the rust glow on the blade of a sword. When the servant enters the chamber, we are at a remove from the tower, so the woman's cry comes to us quietly, more quietly than the birdsong in the garden and the footfalls on the gravel path.

•

Antoine Vermeiren, discussing *La Châtelaine*, tells us of his distaste for "American film sex." He hates "all that pounding, all that grasping." It is like the mating of cave people, he says. When we grasp something, we try to take possession of it. *La Châtelaine* is a "celebration of the caress," he would have us believe. When we caress a body, we do not attempt to conquer it, he states.

•

In today's paper, an interesting article: neuroscientists propose that the human brain is wired to administer doses of dopamine when we are in pursuit of a goal, rather than when we attain it. Discontent is rewarded, in other words. The evolutionary advantage is clear:

happy Ugg, loafing with the wife and kids around the fire in the family cave, loses out to the never satisfied Agg, who is out in the woods, working on a new and better spear. As my sister knows, the customer must never be allowed to feel that enough is enough. And what lessons for the lover?

•

Last night: sitting on the harbour wall, thinking of nothing. The rich perfume of the sea. A black sky of remarkable clarity; uncountable stars. Contentment; pleasure in the happiness of William and Jenna. Then a memory of walking with Imogen, to the farthest part of the garden, out of the light that came from the house. Her breathing was effortful. At the fence we stood arm in arm, facing the hills. I put my coat around her, but still she shivered. The sky was cloudless; we looked at the stars. I remember some of her words: "tiny cold points of light" that we saw were "unimaginable fires" in reality. With mock portentousness she pointed to the sky and proclaimed: "Our ancestors. Our destination." Entering the house, she said: "I really was having a Zen moment back there. If I had an Off switch, I would have happily used it."

•

The top table: Jenna and William; the bride's parents; Jenna's best friend, Katie; and myself. Most of the father's speech is devoted to Jenna's qualities as a daughter and as a mother; William is praised as an incomer who is putting down roots—a young man who went so far as to try his hand on the boats. Light-hearted and affectionate reference is made to William's ill-starred maritime career. "But that's commitment for you," the father-in-law pronounces. "Commitment" is the key motif.

The trawler anecdote has been used up; improvisation is therefore necessary. All jokes are jettisoned. Having known William for some time, I can vouch for his determination. But the idea of destiny is what I want to talk about: William's feeling, within days of arrival, that he had at last found the place where he was meant to be; and the powerful sense, on first sight of Jenna, that they would meet; and the certainty, on talking to her, that this was his soulmate. I quote from our conversations, embellishing only a little. And I talk about his love of Tilly. No laughs, but here and there a tissue is applied to an eye.

Jenna's mother wants me to know that she is happy that her daughter has found a replacement for Tilly's father. "That one was about as much use as a blind guide dog," she tells me. William is a level-headed and dependable chap, I assure her. "So he lived with you for how long?" she asks, with the suggestion that something does not quite add up. "Not for very long," I answer, unsure as to how much of William's back story she knows. "But you've known him for years," she reminds me. I explain that I had happened to get talking to him one day, and from that point on we had always stopped for a chat whenever our paths had crossed. "He has some funny ideas, doesn't he?" she says, when William and Jenna, clasped in a dance, have passed out of earshot. I feign curiosity as to what she might mean. William has introduced her to his research on black holes. He has a lively imagination, I agree. "One way of putting it," says her husband—his first contribution for many minutes. He is on his third or fourth pint. "So," he says, "you're not wearing the yoke yourself?" I am divorced, I tell him. Putting an arm around my shoulder, he promises me that it's better second time round. "First time, you don't know what the hell you're doing," he says.

Jenna points her phone at us, then shows me the result. I look like a melting candle. A slow song is playing; as with most of the evening's music, I don't recognise it. Jenna thinks I should dance with her; the parents too think I should dance with her; I am excusing myself when William intervenes, as if to protect a visiting dignitary from excessive attention. The parents are summoned to the other side of the room. A friend of Jenna's, an attractive and burly young woman in a short strapless dress, slaloms across the dancefloor, huge cocktail in hand, to tell me that her mum likes the look of me. She takes a deep drink, then points across the room at a woman who is making wiping motions with her hands, to disassociate herself from whatever it is that her daughter is saying to me. "Thank you," I answer, and Jenna's friend gives me a wink.

Time to go. I give a goodbye kiss to Jenna and another to Tilly, who is clinging to William's back while he dances. William puts his stepdaughter down, in order to execute a manly embrace. Promises are made.

•

Seneca reports that in the garden in which Epicurus taught his pupils the following words were carved: "Stranger, here you will do well to tarry; here our highest good is pleasure." (*Epistulae morales ad Lucilium*, Book I, Epistle XXI.) These words are well known, but are widely misunderstood, Francesca explained; Epicurus was no hedonist. Her favourite tutor was an authority on Epicurus, and was working on a translation of the letters. His keenest students were occasionally invited to join him and his wife, a professor of archaeology, at their riverside house. The garden of this house had a reputation, as did the wine cellar. In the sunset hour the chosen few would sip fine wines and admire the prospect. Though Epicurus is commonly taken to be an advocate of self-indulgence, he was nothing of the sort, her tutor impressed on her. What Epicurus meant by "pleasure" is not what we generally mean by the word. "I am more of a sybarite than Epicurus ever was," he told her as he replenished her glass; this man cultivated a roguish manner that was almost camp, but was turning out to be a camouflage for real roguishness. Epicurean pleasure, he explained, was rather the elimination of pain and suffering, both physical and mental; it was the achievement of a state of tranquillity—*ataraxia*—that was free from covetousness, desire and the fear of death. There should be a bust of Epicurus in the museum, by the front door, Francesca suggested; nothing should be believed, he had argued, except what has been tested by observation and analysis.

•

The people presented here are word-puppets, imperfectly controlled; the writer included.

•

"Bill's just like you," my father once remarked. "He likes looking at things," he said, as if looking at things were a small peculiarity, like a preference for overcast days.

December

MARCUS AURELIUS, *Meditations* iii 11: *Make for thyself a definition or description of the thing which is presented to thee, so as to see distinctly what kind of a thing it is in its substance, in its nudity, in its complete entirety, and tell thyself its proper name, and the names of the things of which it has been compounded, and into which it will be resolved. For nothing is so productive of elevation of the mind as to be able to examine methodically and truly every object which is presented to thee in life, and always to look at things so as to see at the same time what kind of universe this is, and what kind of use everything performs in it, and what value everything has with reference to the whole.*

•

Looking into a mirror, I see a face that is scrutinising the scrutinising face, and reacting to being scrutinised. Confronting oneself, one begins to play the part of the examiner, the judge.

•

To love truly, wrote Simone Weil, is to consent to the distance that separates us from the object of our love. Attention, as she uses the word, is a receptivity in which one's self is suspended; it is open and passive, not active and focused. What people mean by "love" is usually appropriation, sometimes camouflaged with tenderness, but sometimes barely camouflaged at all, as Imogen said. The life that I sometimes allowed myself to imagine, a life shared for many years with Imogen, was not a life that she could have lived.

•

Sight is the only sense that responds to the assertion of the will; we impose our will on what we see. But at the *maison de maître* it was necessary to suspend the will: I possessed Imogen only in so far as my eyes received the sight of her.

•

Val writes of a conversation with a woman—not a client, she is at pains to point out—whose "every waking moment" is consumed by her resentment of her ex-husband, a man from whom she separated more than ten years ago. This man treated her abominably. Of this there is no doubt, we are told. He was a philanderer. His business, unspecified, brought him into regular contact with alluring young women, a temptation to which he all too willingly surrendered. Since the divorce his career has taken a steeper upward trajectory. Every year there's a new car; his girlfriend is startling. It is all so unfair. Val's acquaintance, the wronged woman, revisits every day the crimes this man committed against her. She replenishes her grievances. The woman is in the right, but there can be no resolution if she continues this way. She must, says Val, "let it go," even if this means living with the acceptance that the wrongdoer has, in a sense, won. Anger is a "barrier against the present." Sometimes one must forget, if not forgive. George Santayana is quoted: "Those who cannot remember the past are condemned to repeat it." But Santayana was wrong, Val proposes. Recollection of past injustices rarely helps to bring about reconciliation. Our culture is obsessed with commemoration, with demands for apology for events that occurred many lifetimes ago. Perhaps it is best not to reopen old wounds. Forgetting is good for us; indeed, it is essential to our well-being, "just like sleep."

•

I pause *Le Grand Concert de la Nuit* at a sequence that always moves me: Agamédé and the twin maidservants, the deaf girls. It appears that she has instructed these children in a private language of gestures. She converses with them by means of flurrying fingers, complex arabesques of the hand, quick caresses of her own face and arms. Agamédé sweeps a finger around the palm of each of the girls, as though playing notes on a glass harmonica, and the girls smile at whatever favour it is that their mistress has promised. From this intimate choreography, we know that the unfathomable Agamédé, the cold and subtle Agamédé, loves these children as she loves no one else.

•

The Count, walking past the belvedere with Agamédé, makes an observation. We do not hear his words, but the expression is sardonic; we assume that the subject of the remark is the pensive young Guignon, who has just crossed the path on which the Count and

Agamédé are strolling. Agamédé laughs. At this moment, in the background, in the belvedere, the nervous-looking theorbo player, who is evidently a real musician and not an actor, directs a brief but longing look at the poised and pretty flautist, who seems to be aware of his attention, though her gaze does not stray from the score on the stand in front of her. This moment is accidental, I'm sure; but it has been allowed to remain because it could be seen to serve the purposes of the film. I find it touching, this glimpse of the truly real amid all the high artifice.

I freeze the scene at the instant in which the flautist, at the end of a long phrase, lifts her lips from the flute for a fraction of a second; a small smile appears, in response to the admiring gaze, I believe. In that frame, Agamédé's laugh is reaching fruition, but if one looks at that frame alone, her face is not laughing: if one were to see this image in isolation, the expression might be read as one of pain. Freeze the action a moment later, and one now sees weariness in Agamédé's face. But twenty-four frames flash onto the retina in each second of the film, and in watching this tiny episode one sees not a succession of photographic images but a single event—an outburst of gaiety. By means of the phi phenomenon and beta movement, our brain converts the sequence of unmoving images into a perfect illusion of motion. We see the movement of life. Agamédé glances to her left; touching the tip of her tongue to her teeth, she laughs, and in the same instant the theorbo player glances at the attractive young flautist. That sentence might be said to consist of thirty frames. In description, the scene becomes a bodiless tableau; there is no illusion of movement; no illusion of anything.

•

But does he who loves some one on account of beauty really love that person? No; for the smallpox, which will kill beauty without killing the person, will cause him to love her no more.

And if one loves me for my judgement or my memory, he does not love me, for I can lose these qualities without losing myself. Where then is this "I," if it be neither in the body nor in the soul? And how love the body or the soul, except for these qualities which do not constitute me, since they are perishable? For it is impossible and would be unjust to love the soul of a person in the abstract, and whatever qualities might be therein. We never then love a person, but only qualities.

Let us then jeer no more at those who are honoured on account of rank and office; for we love a person only on account of borrowed qualities.

Blaise Pascal

•

An announcement: the Sanderson-Perceval Museum will close to the public on March 31st next year. A hotel group has expressed an interest in acquiring the building. There are no immediate plans to auction any more items from the collection. I am authorised to put in place as many loan arrangements as possible; unloaned items are to be stored, for an indefinite period.

•

In the last hour of full sunlight we came upon a tiny bay. The tide had turned an hour ago: a thin curve of sea-smoothed sand, dark with water, was now exposed; small pools shone in the low-lying rocks. A narrow path descended steeply through the grass, bringing us to the back of the inlet. There we sat. The sun was in our faces, a disc of gorgeous tangerine, within a shallow bank of cloud that ran across the whole visible horizon, a wall of violet and mauve. The higher sky, above the mauve, was palest lemon. A windless evening. We heard only the rushing of the little waves; the sighing of the sea. "My God," Imogen whispered, staring across the water. The pleasure was inexpressible, but it compelled acknowledgement, an exclamation. And in the moment of that exclamation it waned a little, necessarily, having been acknowledged; by no act of will could the pleasure now be recovered completely. I recall her face before she spoke: the widened eyes, momentarily ingenuous; the slight parting of the lips; she combed her hair with her fingers. In one of the rock pools, a blenny swam among the beadlet anemones. She watched it, fascinated.

•

The plausible atmospherics of the little bay. Some of those words may have led me astray. Was the sky "violet and mauve"? Perhaps it was; it should have been. The colours seem right; the colour-names, rather. The scene cannot be seen; the mind's eye is not an eye. In bringing the past closer, into words, a distance is created. In writing, one steps outside of life.

•

We watched a pair of jays foraging in the oak trees. It would have been one of the last times we walked to within sight of the copse.

The birds delighted her—their agility, the gorgeous colouring. Everything delighted her that afternoon. Her thoughts were like the birds, she remarked. Perhaps, she said, what was happening in her mind could not be characterised as thought. Impressions and notions alighted weightlessly and quickly departed. Everything that she saw was of interest, but her interest was disinterested, she told me.

•

Interview not a success. By the time I arrived, I knew that I could not live in London again. At the Tube station, I found myself acting the part of the bewildered provincial; I actually flinched at the noise of the approaching train. My self-presentation lacked conviction.

Having a couple of hours to spare, I retreated to the National Gallery, and went directly to Tiepolo's melancholy Venus, as if expected there. Whenever Imogen was in the vicinity, she would pay her a visit, to see that lovely face and the otherworldly pink of the fabric that spills from her cloud-throne. She brought me to look at her, the first time I stayed at Imogen's flat. This Venus directs her gaze at Time. Other Venuses regard their own reflection, or Mars, or Adonis, or merely avert their eyes from their beholders. The multitudinous Virgins, however, live among us. Even here, in exile, among people for whom she is merely an image, the Virgin looks at us, or down on us, returning our gaze. Whereas Venus looks away, at the object of her passion, or at nobody at all.

An altercation in the Velázquez room: a guard steps in front of a dozen teenagers who have run into the room as if the place were a playground. "God, what's her problem?" shouts the queen bee, departing at the head of the gang. Later, I meet them again. The queen bee has paused to take a picture of herself, in front of a painting which she has been told is really famous. She grins as though the painted face were the face of a celebrity. Nearby, a teacher is talking to a school group. Half of her audience are looking at their phones.

•

"But every time you do something it's the last time you'll ever do it," Imogen remarked. We had walked to the village; it would not be the last time we walked that far—not quite. "This afternoon is never going to happen again, the same as every afternoon," she said, serenely. That evening, however, she was distraught.

•

I am drinking more than I used to, and more than I should. I read and I drink. I watch films and I drink. I drink as I try to write. Grammar and syntax help to keep me in order. Charles Perceval's laudanum is something I would like to try. It gave him wonderful visions: the garden became a lake of viscous liquid, emerald green; he roamed across glaciers that were the colour of amber and yielded to the pressure of his feet; impossible animals, monstrous yet benign, fed from his hand; voices spoke from the leaves of trees.

•

In a letter to Adeline, Charles Perceval quotes admiringly the writings of Thomas Sydenham (1624–89), the "English Hippocrates":

283

"The physician who earnestly studies—with his own eyes—and not through the medium of books—the natural phenomena of the different diseases, must naturally excel in the art of discovering what, in any given case, are the true indications as to the remedial measures that should be employed." Writing in his journal after Adeline's death, Charles Perceval cites Sydenham again: "Of all the remedies it has pleased almighty God to give man to relieve his suffering, none is so universal and so efficacious as opium." And, five years before Charles's death, another line from Sydenham: "The arrival of a good clown exercises a more beneficial influence upon the health of a town than of twenty asses laden with drugs."

•

I have found certain materials and instruments conducive to this ritual: ivory high-grade vellum paper, manufactured in France, unlined, of optimal smoothness, absorbency and opacity; my grand-father's pen; Italian ink, profoundly black. The words are produced more easily this way; perhaps too easily, sometimes. There is an element of fetishism at work here, one could say: the French paper; the antique pen; the Italian ink, in its elegantly functional bottle. That would be Emma's analysis: fetishism and a wilfully eccentric devotion to antiquated technologies, akin to our father's loyalty to vinyl records and his unreliable old watch. A mechanical watch is an absurdity nowadays, Emma insists, though she can appreciate that the elegant sweep of a mechanical second hand is more pleasing to the eye than the stuttering of a quartz-regulated item. Nonetheless, why squander money on something that tells the time less competently than a battery-powered watch that costs a fraction of the price? We discussed the subject in her kitchen, amid an array of high-end culinary equipment and appliances. The point, I tried to explain, was that the mechanism of the flatteringly costly watch had been manufactured and assembled with great care and precision, to impose a structure on the flux of reality. The divisions of the day are a human creation, and it is fitting that they should be measured by a hand-made mechanism, a compact and complex machine that functions by means of the precise interaction of extraordinarily delicate cogs and levers and springs, rather than relying on the mere quivering of a crystal. "But the fact is," Emma answered, "mine is more accurate than yours. And that's what a watch is for." But she was impressed by what the gift represented. "She really must think a lot of you," she remarked, on first seeing it; as I recall, there was some amazement in her voice.

•

The sense of sight—the insatiable philanderer of the senses.

•

Maston House, flagship hotel of the group that intends to create the Perceval House Hotel, offers "the perfect balance of authentic Georgian style and contemporary living." In each of its rooms and suites, "classic antique pieces and stunning period features" are found alongside examples of "superlative modern design." Discreet luxury is the keynote. In the Ridotto Bar of Maston House guests can relax with a bottle selected from the hotel's "world-class" cellar of French, Italian and New World vintages, or a glass from the vast menu of spirits. The Ridotto Bar offers whiskies such as the Springbank 30 Year Old 1965 and the John Walker, of which a mere 330 bottles have been produced. "Crafted from specially selected casks to create a whisky as close to the nineteenth-century style as possible," the John Walker represents "the epitome of exclusivity." The mirrored room will be rebranded as the Silver Lounge.

•

Today's attendance: thirty-seven. "Pricy for what you get, but a shame it's closing down," someone writes in the visitor's book. "Loved the gross stuff," writes another. A quick calculation: a single bottle of the John Walker costs four hundred times the admission charge for the Sanderson-Perceval Museum. Retail price, not bar price.

•

On the night before he was due to undergo the amputation of his cancerous leg, Peregrino Laziosi, the future Saint Peregrine, wonder-worker and patron saint of those afflicted with cancer, experienced a vision of the crucified Christ, who came down from the cross to touch the diseased limb. The following day, the surgeon could find no trace of any tumour. There have been many cases of apparently spontaneous recovery from cancer. In New York, in the 1880s, a man by the name of Fred Stein endured several operations to remove a sarcoma from his neck. The operations failed, but when Stein developed erysipelas, a bacterial skin infection that produces a severe fever, the tumour disappeared. Stein was interviewed by a doctor named William Bradley Coley, who reasoned that the sarcoma had been destroyed by the patient's over-stimulated immune system. Coley went on to treat successfully a number of tumours using a mixture of bacterial toxins. Recently, researchers have examined cases in which acute myeloid leukaemia has apparently regressed of its own accord, and have found that the great majority of the patients in question had suffered from pneumonia or some other serious illness prior to the regression. Diphtheria, syphilis, gonorrhoea, hepatitis, malaria, influenza, measles and smallpox have all been associated with the sudden disappearance of tumours.

A fever was recorded in the case of Dinah Morley, who was examined by Cornelius Perceval in the spring of 1818. She presented with a goitre, for which the doctor may well have prescribed "blue pill." Many of Perceval's contemporaries prescribed this toxic compound for a variety of illnesses and disorders, a practice decried as "quackery" by one Erasmus Schütz, to whom Dinah Morley took her goitre when it became apparent that it was not responding to Cornelius Perceval's treatment. Schütz was an acolyte of Samuel Hahnemann, the creator of homeopathy, and was thus, in the eyes of Perceval, an arrant charlatan. Mrs. Morley bought a phial of one of Schütz's fraudulent liquids. The growth of the goitre seemed to stop. She bought more, then fell ill with a fever. And the goitre vanished, for reasons that—as Erasmus Schütz gloated—were beyond the comprehension of the city's physicians. His triumph was temporary. A few months after Dinah Morley's recovery, Schütz was obliged to flee the city, having been discovered *in flagrante* with the wife of one of his patients.

This might make a good story; even a book.

•

Imogen's mother made mention of a woman who had lived in the village for five or six years, with her elderly sister, and who had only taken note of young Imogen, it appeared, on days when Imogen was on her bike or taking one of the dogs for an extended walk. On the basis of a few sightings, the lady had decided that this girl was a happy-go-lucky child, a description that she employed, without fail, every time she happened to encounter a member of Imogen's family. It was as if her happy-go-luckiness were as incontrovertible as the colour of her eyes. "Every single time," said her mother, who now found it more amusing than she had used to, though she still did not know, said Imogen, quite how inapposite the label was. "Who we are has so little to do with us," said Imogen, as if quoting, and her mother considered the remark, and smiled, seeming to find in the observation some pertinence to herself.

•

Francesca has work to do: editing of the Domus Aurea book has to be finished before the end of the month. On her laptop, she has the images that will accompany the text. We look at the mighty brick pillars that are thought to have been supports for the *coenatio rotunda*, the circular dining hall, of which Suetonius wrote that its ceiling "would turn constantly day and night like the Heavens." Archaeologists believe that it was in fact the floor that rotated, under a depiction of the night sky, and that the mechanism was powered by water. The book will include a diagram of how the revolving dining room might have functioned. Francesca shows me the diagram, and an animated film in which the viewer is taken on a flight over the lake and the vineyards of the Golden House, past the colossal statue of the emperor, before swooping into a courtyard, where our virtual tour of the interior begins.

Emma comes in. "Take a look at this," says Francesca, beckoning. The camera slows down, so that we can appreciate a spectacular painted wall—the frescoes of the Domus Aurea cover more than ten times the area of the Sistine Chapel frescoes, Francesca tells us. Pointing to the hole in the centre of the vault, she tells her mother about the boy who, one day in 1480 or thereabouts, fell into a hole in the Esquiline hill and found himself in what he took to be a painted cave, but which was in fact one of the three hundred rooms of Nero's Golden House. Within a mere forty years of the emperor's death the palace had been built over so thoroughly that no trace of it was visible above ground. After the discovery, holes were cut into the hill so that people could descend into the fabulous grotto. Raphael himself had explored the ruins. "Can you imagine what that must have been like?" wonders Francesca. "Raphael dangling on a rope, peering into the murk." I marvel with her. But water pouring in through the holes has caused great damage, as have the roots of the trees that were planted on the hill when the site became a park. When it rains, the weight of the soil and vegetation on top of the Domus Aurea increases by as much as thirty per cent. "It's a big problem," Francesca tells her mother. Emma takes her daughter's word for it, but she is not convinced that all this work on the wreckage of Nero's palace is the best use of however many millions of euros of public money are being lavished on the project. It might be better to just call it quits, she suggests. The old frescoes are pretty, but she'll take the Sistine Chapel any day, she apologises. She leaves us to enjoy the pictures of ancient brickwork and rubble-strewn corridors. We hunch over the laptop; the incorrigible ruin-buffs.

•

It's ridiculous how little Francesca is earning at the moment, Emma protests to me. It's insulting. "She'd be better off working in one of our shops," she says. Francesca shouldn't have to be working at Christmas. Nicholas has to do a few hours, of course, but that's to be expected: his company depends on him; he's well paid, as he should be. "It's a waste of her intelligence," she tells me.

"She enjoys what she does. Many people can't say that," I answer.

"She could enjoy what she does and get paid properly," Emma counters. The discussion follows its customary course, to resignation. "My daughter is an economic invalid, and it's your fault," says Emma, administering a whack with a towel. The course of Francesca's life, my sister pretends, was diverted into its present unlucrative channel by my influence. "All those afternoons with you in the British Museum," she says. "You and Mr. Martin," she curses, clamping her teeth on the name of the teacher who had escorted young Francesca around Pompeii, turning the girl's head, while her classmates improved their tans.

•

Emma and Nicholas at work in the kitchen all morning, preparing the two Christmas feasts: one for the meat-eating seniors, and one for Francesca and her husband and their child. Every now and then, Emma tells me, her daughter makes some sort of attempt to convert her to the cause of virtuous eating, but not with the zeal of earlier years. The turkey is no longer lamented as the "murdered bird." Today is a domestic carnival; all tribulations are set aside. Emma will make no mention of the current state of the retail environment, nor will her husband refer to the impact of recent political developments on his company's business; Francesca's dwindling income will not be a topic; likewise the closure of the museum. We are fortunate people. The food is sumptuous, and the wine is special—and, I am sure, unconscionably expensive.

We withdraw to the living room. A corner has been set aside as Jack's play area; assisted by his father, he assembles a wooden train track. Emma's gift from Francesca is a set of nature documentaries, her favourite genre. When she needs to unwind, she gives herself up to the spectacle of the natural world. In keeping with the season, she selects a winter-themed programme. We follow an Arctic fox on the hunt, then a polar bear. The camerawork is remarkable, as is the definition of the new TV set. Crystals of snow glint like diamonds on the fox's whiskers. After fifteen minutes we're off to the Southern Hemisphere, to observe a flotilla of penguins endeavouring to ride ashore on the waves. Geraint brings Jack over to watch the comical birds as they skid on the ice; they waddle through blizzards in their thousands. When things take a violent turn—seals ambushed by killer whales—Jack is carried back to his trains. The black water, the luminous ice, the spray of blood—the colours are sumptuous. State of the art, as the blurb on the box proclaims. Back in the Arctic, a polar bear waits at a breathing hole. It has been waiting for hours; sooner or later, a seal will put its head up. The tension is high. Emma, anxious for the seals, takes her husband's hand; they have been married for more than thirty years, and still they hold hands. Contentment and prosperity; there is a vein of envy in my affection.

When the programme is over, Emma takes Jack in her lap to read to him. With one hand she turns the pages, and with the other she holds her grandson; her fingers are spread on his chest, and he places his hands over them, as if to secure their protection. "Giraffe," says my sister, and Jack tilts forward to touch the page. "That's right," says Emma; she kisses the top of his head. "Gorilla," she says, and again Jack puts a finger on the book. "Very good," she says, and she angles her head so that he can see her smile of praise, which becomes a gaze of adoration, which is returned. At risk of embarrassing myself, I withdraw to the kitchen. Pans have to be scoured.

•

Geraint has brought a sample of the material with which he's working: a tangerine-coloured square of sponge, a quarter of an inch thick. Inserted into clothing, it will protect people whose occupations entail a risk of severe impacts—oil rigs, demolition, motorbike racing. Non-Newtonian fluids are the key to the technology, he tells us. On Francesca's laptop we watch a video of students messing around in a pool of cornstarch and water. Two of them run across the surface of the mixture again and again. Their footprints vanish within seconds. Then one of them stops running, halfway across, whereupon he slowly sinks. It's the same principle, Geraint explains. Emma inspects the fabric, turning it over three or four times, as if checking a magician's prop; she crushes the square in her palms. "Sweetheart, if you'd be so good," says Geraint, and Francesca passes the mallet to him, then places her hand on the table, forming a fist. He lays the square over the back of her hand. "Ready?" he says, and at Francesca's nod he brings the mallet down. It bounces off, as if it had struck wood. "Nothing," Francesca assures us. The demonstration is repeated. "Can I have a go?" asks Emma. She invites me to place my fist on the table. She puts some effort into her second blow, like a medieval agent of the law maiming the hand of a thief.

•

Scenes from *Devotion* have been put online. Beatrice's therapeutic orgasm, of course. *Would be a lot better if she wuz nekkid,* someone has remarked. *In those days did people do sex with all there clothes on?* someone else enquires. The death of Beatrice has also been excerpted. *Whats wrong with that fucken baby??? Looks like a squid or something.* The most frequently viewed scene, and the one that has attracted most comments, is the discovery of Beatrice's body, many years after her death. The corpse has the appearance of Beatrice alive, asleep. The flesh is pallid but pliant, as if death had occurred that very hour. The doctor draws the scalpel across the skin of the forearm, releasing a flow of clear and oily liquid, like glycerin—the embalming fluid concocted by Julius Preston, a compound of unknown composition. Some are not wholly impressed by the fakery:

So obvious it's a rubber arm.

Lame effects, lame movie—not horror, not anything. Ninety minutes of boredom and a pickled chick. YAWN. Dont waste your time.

Further comments:

Never heard of this movie before. Some mad shit. Cool.

Wow, this made me get very emotional. She was perfect for that roll.

If you like Frankenstein you will like this.

Frankenstien is classic. This is bollox.

Sooooooo slow. An hour and half of my life I wont get back.

Did they make up the story or is it real?

The movie is OK. Interesting and not to graphic.

What's the song??? Love it. So sad.

Victorians were sick. Show's how wrong we are in what we think about history. Darkness everywhere, in every one.

There is some place in italy with a girl who died 100 years ago and it looks like she is asleep. They have put her on the bed in the church and you can go and look at her. I think that is where they got the idea.

Does the dude take her out the box to bone her or what?

your a retard

She is cute I would do her dead or alive. I'm an animaaaaaal.

No tits

I like this movie there is beauty in death though but I'm defiantly not turned on by it in sexual ways.

•

Should the opportunity arise, I shall bid for a print: the picture of Sequah, the Native American medicine man, pulling teeth by lantern light, on a stage in Chester, in 1890. Purveyor of such "world renowned remedies" as Sequah's Oil and Sequah's Prairie Flower ("a boon to suffering females"), Sequah was so successful that there were as many as twenty-three Sequahs on the road at any one time. On the night of the Chester tooth-pulling, Sequah was simultaneously bringing succour to the people of Manchester, Norwich and Cork. The original Sequah, founder of the brand, was born in Yorkshire, c.1857; real name—William Henry Hartley.

•

At the end of Brock Street a sudden noise—a roaring rush of air— made me look up, and there was a huge white balloon, low enough for me to read the faces that were gazing down. It was overtaking me, drifting over the park. Everyone on the grass looked up; and ahead of me, at the railings, I saw the carmine coat and silver hair, and Bianca, also looking up. My approach was noticed and acknowledged with a raised hand; the woman turned her attention back to the balloon, which was rising with another blast from the burner. "Have you ever been in one of those things?" she asked, still watching. "I went up in one once," she went on. "Years ago. In Mexico.

The City of the Gods. Terrifying experience. Never again. How are you?" Now she looked at me. "Lovely day, isn't it?" It was a very lovely day, I agreed. Bianca had raised a paw. "She really does seem to like you," her owner remarked. "I'm flattered," I said. And I remembered Francesca, after a boyfriend had let her down, taking consolation from the fidelity of the family dog. Then I heard myself repeat the line that Francesca, in self-parody, had quoted: *Mentiri non didicere ferae.* "Animals have not learned to lie," I translated, regretting that I had not kept quiet. But the woman looked at me as though I had said something profound, and intriguing. "On the whole," she agreed. "Though this one isn't entirely straightforward," she added, directing a quizzical gaze into the eyes of her pet.

It was time for me to get back to work, I told her, not making it obvious, I hoped, that I was inclined to remain.

"The museum is closing, I hear," she said.

I explained the situation.

"Such a pity. As if we need another hotel." She would visit the museum again before it closed, she assured me. Then she said: "Alexandra." We shook hands.

•

Reading, I look across the room to the chair in which Imogen used to read. I can picture her, turned to the side, with her legs curled up and a book propped on the arm of the chair, angled into the light of the lamp. I would sit here and she there, on opposite sides of the room, each in a small zone of illumination, and the rest of the room in shadow. The pleasure of reading together—of being solitary together. It was like acting, in a way, she said: we become someone else when we read, and each book changes us, for a while, even if only for as long as we are reading it.

•

To describe Imogen, I could write: five feet eight inches tall; of slender build. Hair: dark and heavy, straight, usually shoulder-length. The eyes, essential to any description of the beloved, were also dark—brown, with a russet tinge. The fine arch of the eyebrows would have to be mentioned. The hands: delicate and long-fingered. I could write about the regularity of her features, the "openness" of her face. Still she cannot be seen. This character named Imogen speaks words that Imogen spoke, but Imogen's voice cannot be heard. "Imogen pauses; she looks down at her hands, arrested in the act of forming an awkward chord; frowning, she leans forward to scrutinise the notes on the page; she bites her lip; the candlelight glows on her throat." An ideal Imogen, in the perpetual present of the sentence, where nobody is alive and nobody dead.

J ONATHAN B UCKLEY is the author of the novels *Ghost MacIndoe, So He Takes the Dog, Nostalgia,* and several others. He was the 2015 winner of the BBC National Short Story Award. He lives in Hove, England.